PRAISE FOR THE N

Enticed

"Stupendous! Exceptionally written with interesting characters and clever dialogue . . . with sizzling-hot erotic love scenes and the touch of magic."
                                               —*Coffee Time Romance*

"Masterful . . . fabulous."
                                               —*Fallen Angel Reviews*

"[E]xpert crafting of setting and mood . . . The reader is drawn in to a world of magic, danger, and sensual heat . . . a feast for the senses."
                                               —*Paranormal Romance Reviews*

"The characters are complex, the romance and sex [are] hot, hot, hot."
                                               —*Romance Reviews Today*

Entangled

"I was absolutely blown away . . . Brava!"
                                               —*Fallen Angel Reviews*

"A triumph."
                                               —*Just Erotic Romance Reviews*

"Enticing . . . stupendous."
                                               —*Midwest Book Review*

"Sexy, smart, and touching . . . Prepare to be spellbound."
                                               —*Romance Reviews Today*

Berkley Heat titles by Kathleen Dante

ENTANGLED

ENTICED

DREAMWALKER

Dreamwalker

Kathleen Dante

HEAT
New York

THE BERKLEY PUBLISHING GROUP
Published by the Penguin Group
Penguin Group (USA) Inc.
375 Hudson Street, New York, New York 10014, USA
Penguin Group (Canada), 90 Eglinton Avenue East, Suite 700, Toronto, Ontario M4P 2Y3, Canada
(a division of Pearson Penguin Canada Inc.)
Penguin Books Ltd., 80 Strand, London WC2R 0RL, England
Penguin Group Ireland, 25 St. Stephen's Green, Dublin 2, Ireland (a division of Penguin Books Ltd.)
Penguin Group (Australia), 250 Camberwell Road, Camberwell, Victoria 3124, Australia
(a division of Pearson Australia Group Pty. Ltd.)
Penguin Books India Pvt. Ltd., 11 Community Centre, Panchsheel Park, New Delhi—110 017, India
Penguin Group (NZ), 67 Apollo Drive, Rosedale, North Shore 0632, New Zealand
(a division of Pearson New Zealand Ltd.)
Penguin Books (South Africa) (Pty.) Ltd., 24 Sturdee Avenue, Rosebank, Johannesburg 2196,
South Africa

Penguin Books Ltd., Registered Offices: 80 Strand, London WC2R 0RL, England

This is an original publication of The Berkley Publishing Group.

First edition: May 2008

Library of Congress Cataloging-in-Publication Data

Dante, Kathleen.
    Dreamwalker / Kathleen Dante.—1st ed.
        p. cm.
    ISBN 978-0-425-21963-8
    1. Intelligence officers—Fiction.   2. Parapsychology—Fiction.   I. Title.
    PS3604.A57D75   2008
    813'.6—dc22   2008002170

PRINTED IN THE UNITED STATES OF AMERICA

10 9 8 7 6 5 4 3 2 1

Thanks to Marc A. Almagro, who started me down my path;
Surajit F. Agarwal, for grounding me in reality;
and especially the P-1, for urging me to pursue my dreams.

CHAPTER ONE

He'd gotten it right. Damon forced down a surge of excitement at the realization, careful to keep the emotion off his face. Somewhere in the milling crowd was the elusive master thief who was his target. The focused anticipation stood out in sharp contrast amidst the bored humdrum buzz of daily life. As he'd suspected, the upcoming exhibit of Oriental art had drawn out his thief . . . who was a *woman*?!

He nearly missed a step in his surprise. The aura he sensed was unmistakable—a rich, changing spectrum of "colors" or "scents." Definitely, enticingly female. He took a few slow breaths to recover his equilibrium. Although he'd tried not to make any assumptions about his target, that discovery had taken him off guard.

Ignoring some boys skylarking around a group of stone

statues a few feet away, Damon parked his ass on a low brick planter and surveyed his surroundings casually, trying to identify the source of the potent emotion.

The park was crowded with ordinary people taking advantage of the rare sunny day. A pair of sweaty, red-faced joggers huffed along a trail winding among the trees. Some office workers were clustered around a taco stand at the corner. An artist sketching the marble fountain. Tourists posing and taking pictures. An old woman knitting on one of the park's cast-iron benches with a large bag at her feet. He made a note of the last item, knowing appearances could be deceptive.

None of the women in sight was doing anything remarkable, not that he expected to locate his target that easily. To date, his master thief had yet to slip up.

His scan led to a trio of nubile college students lying on the grass, sunning their next-to-naked bodies. He made the mistake of allowing eye contact, resulting in a blast of arousal from that direction and an eruption of giggles.

High-pitched titters drew Rory's attention from the sinuous curves of the fountain and the museum beyond it. The teenagers making the noise were posing in blatant invitation, their attention focused on a man lounging near the sidewalk.

Rory had to admit the recipient of their favors was a prime specimen. If she were truly the artist she was pretending to be, she'd be after him to model for her.

Still, she'd learned what she needed to know, so her time was now her own. There was no reason she couldn't indulge herself.

Since it would be in character, Rory flipped to a blank page and made a quick sketch of the Adonis. Slashing brows. A strong nose and jaw. Deep-set eyes. Dark, wavy hair rising from a sharp widow's peak and flowing down to brush broad shoulders. Definite pectorals. *Hard to miss that, given that muscle shirt.*

With his Mediterranean coloring, it was a good bet he was hirsute like her brothers. She added chest hair to her sketch, including a treasure trail down the abdominals.

Once she had, it was as if her hand took on a mind of its own. Lines bloomed beneath her pencil, presenting her with an anatomically correct nude sitting in that typical American male spread-legged stance.

When Rory looked up, the Adonis had left. Which was too bad; she'd have wanted to ask how well she'd done. As she made to close her sketch pad, a shadow fell across the page.

"I'm bigger than that." The lazy bass growl sent a shiver of awareness racing up her spine.

She looked up to see her erstwhile model standing over her, his expression indistinct against the bright sky. "Really?" She inspected his pelvis critically, the body part under discussion conveniently at her eye level, though shrouded by the loose fit of his slacks. "It's rather hard to tell."

He snorted at her response.

As Rory watched in fascination, his pants tented with an undeniable bulge that spanned several inches. *Oh, man!* Presented with temptation, she licked her suddenly dry lips and sallied forth, stretching her fingers along the ridge, the webs of her hand protesting the strain as she tried to span it.

He caught her wrist and pressed her palm against him, guiding it over his hard length and bulbous head before releasing her with a leisurely stroke on the back of her hand.

Rory quivered with sensual delight. Unable to resist, she palpated him and nearly groaned when he proved to be broad and firm beneath her fingers—all man. Her core clenched with hunger. Too bad she was here on business; she could think of several things she wanted to do with that hard-on.

"You're right. You are much bigger. Sorry about that." Feeling overly warm from her exploration, Rory turned back to her sketch and quickly corrected it. "Here. How's that?" She presented the final drawing to her critic.

"Better." He eyed her appreciatively, a thorough head-to-toe with a polite stopover at her average bust and a definite invitation in his chestnut brown gaze that sent a delicious shiver of desire through her. "But there's still room for improvement. With some help." He shifted his weight, moving a slim hip in her direction and drawing her eyes back to that tempting bulge. "How about we discuss it over drinks?" He extended a dark hand to help her up. The heated look he gave her said he wanted to drink her . . . or perhaps vice versa.

Rory grinned at his confident stance, the thought of taking that thick cock in her mouth making her nipples tingle. The way he stood over her, blocking the light, was pure male posturing, but it also made him look that much taller and his chest seem impossibly broad.

"Tempting, but you'd need more than that to satisfy me." It was a real pity she was here on business; she would have liked to spend a few days exploring that lean body. Unfortunately, she still had a lot to do before the day was over.

The Adonis grinned back. "I've also got a mouth, two good hands . . . and imagination," he added in a deep, tantalizing drawl that resonated in her core.

"I'll bet you think so." Deciding to cut the teasing banter short, Rory checked her watch, then made a show of needing to leave for class. "Too bad I'm out of time."

"Your loss. I have an extremely fertile imagination." Damon fought back a laugh as the pretty artist walked off with her chin in the air, her perky brown ponytail bobbing in time to her sensual stride. She had sass to spare. To think someone with her wholesome, girl-next-door looks had drawn him nude with a hard-on, albeit a puny one.

Shaking his head, he turned back to survey the busy park. Sometime while he'd been distracted by the sunbathers, his thief's focused anticipation had vanished, lost in the surrounding buzz. Then he'd been disarmed by the artist's unblushing, forthright manner and playful desire.

No problem. He'd felt his thief's aura. Even better for their purposes, it had none of the avarice one might expect from a thief. No anger or sense of injustice. Just objectivity and calm professionalism. She was doing something to the best of her abilities and she enjoyed it. Precisely what they needed.

He had her now. So long as she remained in the city, he'd find her when she slept.

Fighting back the temptation to follow the pretty artist, Damon took a deep breath, forcing his arousal to subside. Although her bawdy appraisal had heated him faster than a striptease, he really didn't have time to pursue her. Besides, despite her boldness, she didn't seem the type to welcome an assassin into her bed.

Damon waited until it was past midnight to reach out to his master thief. She had to be asleep for his attempt to be successful. Inexplicably, it occurred to him to wonder if she slept in the buff. Some of the heists she'd pulled off had required a high degree of athletics, so he imagined she was in good shape. Maybe with a compact gymnast's body?

He shook his head at the irrelevant thought. Just one more sign that he was better off with his regular missions. What did it matter how she slept? He wasn't going to seduce her. He was on Company time, not his own.

Stripping down to bare skin for comfort—this was just a fishing expedition, after all, not an assassination—he stretched out on his hotel bed, closed his eyes, and let his mind soar free. Probing the night with mental fingers for nuances of his master thief's aura, he homed in on her dormant thoughts and slipped into her dreams.

The darkness that confronted him was familiar ground. With proper manipulation, it would yield the answers he needed. He smiled, confident of success.

Then warmth surrounded him. Wrapped him in a spicy, sensual perfume he'd never encountered in the dreams of other women. It seeped into him, waking his body to carnal alertness with a siren song of desire. Exotic. Like something one might encounter in a harem.

At that thought, the darkness changed, took on shape. Suddenly he stood inside a fantasy harem straight out of the Arabian Nights, *complete with thick carpets and lounging pillows. Smoke wafted up from several places, solidifying into naked women smelling of that same spicy perfume. Blondes, brunettes, redheads, they surrounded him, pressed against him, caressed him with their nubile bodies, knowing hands, and lush lips. Lascivious laughter filled his ears as they brought him to rampant attention.*

Alarm stirred in Damon. He was losing control of the mental contact. In a dim corner of his mind, he realized his cock had swollen to aching proportions. He'd never responded so quickly to a dream, especially not on a mission. Was it some kind of psychological defense he'd never encountered before? To play it safe, he'd have to keep this short before he lost control.

Gathering his will, he banished the imagery, calling back the formless darkness. Then he framed his query and released it into his master thief's sleeping mind. Long moments passed, surrounded by that sensual perfume tempting his mind to return to the harem, rousing his body to crackling fire. His treacherous imagination teased him with flashes of bare thighs and breasts with long, tight nipples, and wet, creamy pussy in all colors, just waiting to be taken.

The results Damon eventually got were vague as dreams tended to be, but he didn't dare extend his contact to solicit clarification; his body was urging him to return to the harem and slake his lust. An urge he had to resist. He couldn't risk revealing his presence, not this early in the game.

The heavy throb of his loins greeted him at his return. His balls ached, close to bursting. Not at all his usual response to a fishing expedition, but nothing about the contact had been normal. Pure need shot through him, jolting his body to steel hardness.

Not a believer in mortification of the flesh, Damon took himself in hand, wishing he'd gone after that pretty artist. She seemed to know what to do with a man. He stroked his shaft, imagining her slender fingers doing the same. Her touch would be firm, the way it had been when she measured him. She'd try to wrap her hand around him—and fail.

His cock swelled even more at the thought of her touching him. He closed his eyes, blocking out the featureless ceiling, focusing on his fantasy.

She hadn't seemed the type to cavil at sex. If he'd tried, he probably could have talked her into a quick romp behind the bushes. The risk of exposure might even have been an added inducement, a dash of spice to the adventure.

He trailed callused fingers along his length, the rough sensation no comparison to soft, slender hands.

Maybe her brown eyes would darken, the interest he'd seen in them taking on heat. *Oh, yeah.* That clear skin blushing pink. He'd bet she was silky all over. He'd have loved to rub his cock between her breasts and over her smooth belly.

Damon groaned, imagining what it would have felt like to stroke her with the sensitive head of his cock. He pumped his shaft slowly, letting the pressure build. He should have gone after her. She'd been willing enough, wanting him to chase her. So what if all they could've had together was a one-night stand? It would have been infinitely better than this.

He cupped his balls with his free hand. She'd had talented fingers, light and sensitive, oh so feminine, and she'd known how to use them. The way she'd explored him . . .

Remembering how she'd sat at his feet, her lips glossy and red as her hand masturbated him, he growled, need coiling in his balls and drawing them tight. If they'd been alone, he probably would have unzipped himself right then and there. Learned if her lips were as soft as they looked, against his cock. Given her what she wanted before she could change her mind.

He sped his strokes, his hips lunging off the bed.

She'd have been hot and snug, so wet he'd be deep inside her in one quick thrust. He could almost feel her long legs around his hips, holding him close. She'd buck under him and he'd ride her hard and quick, storm her defenses until she could only scream her satisfaction.

Yes! Holding that image in his mind's eye, Damon let the tension erupt from his swollen balls, his release boiling up his cock in a wave of fiery pleasure.

A good night's sleep did little to clarify the results of Damon's fishing expedition. He knew he'd managed to enter his master thief's dreams last night, but the images he'd gotten still left him puzzled. He'd asked what she intended to steal. Her answer had been vivid; yet he couldn't see how it related to the Oriental art exhibit.

In her dream, she'd been a mermaid with a mermaid's traditional nudity, swimming among water lilies under a blue sky. Damon set his jaw against a flash of awareness. Just remembering that part made him hard. There'd been a bridge, then the pond had become the pool around a fountain—the same one in the park near the museum.

Strangely, he hadn't been able to bring her face into focus. Most women whose minds he'd touched retained their own features when they dreamed, perhaps somewhat idealized or overly critical, but still recognizable as theirs. He supposed it would have been too much to expect that the same would apply to his master thief; nothing about this mission had been simple or straightforward.

Pondering the images from his fishing expedition, he ran a search of the museum's inventory on its website. *Mermaid* pulled up several pages worth of art. *Lilies* had fewer. The description of one included a bridge. A quick click showed him water lilies that matched his thief's dream.

Damon grinned. *Eureka.* He called his FBI contact.

Reynard Suder, the special agent in charge handling extra

security for the Oriental exhibit's opening night, was in a better position to coordinate with museum security and catch Damon's thief. With all the senior diplomats expected to make an appearance, someone high up had twisted enough arms to garner an FBI presence.

The man scoffed at Damon's suspicions after Damon finished relating what he suspected. "Hit the museum with all the increased security? Why would anyone do that?"

Damon frowned at Suder's response. This wouldn't be the first time his master thief timed her heist to coincide with a big opening. Despite his explanation, the FBI special agent remained skeptical, although he did promise to brief his team on the situation.

"Then you won't mind if I stand watch over the east side?" Just because the other man didn't put stock in his suspicions didn't mean Damon could do nothing.

Suder snorted, making his opinion of Damon's intentions clear. "Be my guest. Just don't set off any alarms."

Dabbing her cheeks dry, Rory admired the wrinkles on her papery skin and the faded blue of her round eyes. The liver spots were the perfect finishing touch.

She had to admit she was getting slightly worn around the edges. If nothing else, meeting that Adonis in the park yesterday showed her it was high time to blow off some steam. After this job, maybe she should find some sand and surf somewhere and make like a beach bunny. She hadn't gone blond lately because it was so eye-catching, but it wouldn't be a problem on vacation.

The door finally closed behind the last matron, leaving the ladies' room to Rory. A beep from her watch told her the museum

security had just finished its hourly patrol. Satisfied that everything was going according to plan, she pressed a button beside
the dark dial, activating the program she'd inserted into the
server of the closed-circuit cameras. For the next half hour, the
guards would be blind in one wing. Not that they were likely to
be paying attention to it, what with the added security for the
opening of the new exhibit—exactly as she'd planned.

Reversing her shawl with its glittery threads for the dark underside, she Changed from her old lady persona to an Oriental
look chosen in honor of her diversion, then entered the empty
corridor. Navigating the serpentine halls took only a matter of
minutes. She removed a framed painting from a back room and
swapped it for one on display, the one she'd been commissioned
to steal. Returning to the back room, she freed her target from its
frame and rolled it up, reducing it to a narrow tube of rather stiff
fabric, with a small smile of satisfaction.

Slipping the canvas into her hollow cane, Rory debated
whether to sneak out into the darkness or return to the cocktail
party. Leaving now would be easier and she really wasn't in this
line of work for the adrenaline; she enjoyed the thrill but it was
the challenge more than anything else that kept her coming back.

She ghosted toward a fire escape, intent on a quick departure
and her bed. As she neared the glassed-in walkway that led to the
gray door, a passing car lit the grounds below to reveal a familiar
figure.

It was him!

Rory's core clenched in instinctive response.

She froze at the edge of the walkway, careful to stay out of
sight. It took a while for her night vision to adjust, but when it
did, she saw she hadn't been mistaken.

Broad shoulders. That long, wavy hair. His chest was hidden

by a dark jacket, but there was no way she could forget that confident stance.

It was the Adonis from the park. He of the delicious hard-on. He stood in the shadows, watchful and unmoving. He didn't appear to be waiting for someone. There was no fidgeting, no impatience, just bone-deep equanimity. He was on guard—not just cautious but a sentry.

Strange. She hadn't taken him for simple muscle.

Rory wasn't surprised the museum had taken extraordinary measures. She'd chosen this time to go after this particular commission specifically because of the distraction the grand opening of the Oriental art exhibit would provide through its high-level international connections. There were even Feds around the exhibit, trying their best to be inconspicuous. She just hadn't expected her Adonis to be one of them.

Her watch vibrated: five minutes left in her window. After that, the security cameras would be back online.

Rory hurried back to the wing of the Oriental art exhibit. Reversing her shawl and Changing back into the old lady persona she'd assumed for the festivities, she entered the ladies' room to freshen up, leaning on her cane for a touch of realism.

Her departure would have to wait until the communal egress.

Damon watched the museum patrons trickle out of the building, chattering in excited tones. Limousines lined up by the dozen to pick up their diplomatic charges, then drove off with a sedate flutter of tiny flags. As he stood in the shadows, the museum's interior lights went out, one after another, in slow progression. So far, nothing. Had he been wrong? He'd thought he'd sensed her presence earlier but hadn't seen anything suspicious. No one had sneaked in or out through the darkness.

Now, he didn't pick up anything unusual, just general relief at reaching the end of another workweek. He fought back his frustration with his current assignment. Normally, he was a weapon at the end of a long string; the Old Man aimed him at a target and loosed him. None of this chasing after chimeras with little to show for it at the end of the day.

Part of the FBI detail came to the parking lot, got into different cars, and drove off—all without seeing him. From the way they'd borne themselves, nothing out of the ordinary had happened at the opening. Had she changed her mind?

Damon was about to call it a night when his phone vibrated in his pocket. Caller ID showed it was Suder. "Yeah?"

"You were right. The Monet was the target." The FBI special agent's grudging admission did little to console Damon.

Damn, she'd slipped through his fingers!

CHAPTER TWO

Uniformed guards sat before the monitors, backs ramrod straight, obviously aware they'd failed in their duty. Suder and another agent stood by their shoulders; judging by their formal wear, they'd been on-site the whole time.

Damon ignored them, keeping his eyes on a particular screen. The video on fast-forward barely changed, save for the regular appearances of patrolling guards. "Well?"

"We can't even tell when it was taken," Suder admitted, his heavy features curdled with disgust.

The assistant curator wrung her hands, her tension an irritating ache like a dentist's drill in Damon's teeth. "All I know is when I went past it before six, to help with preparations, it was there. On my way back to my office, to get my things, another painting was in its place." She gave him a sidelong look, clearly uncertain as to why he'd been called in.

Meeting her gaze, Damon sent her a thin smile, tilting his head to emphasize his unconventionally long hair and rugged attire, playing up the differences between him and the other men in the room.

The woman's eyes widened, then darted away as a dull flush spread across her cheeks. At least her tension eased enough that Damon could ignore it.

Seemingly oblivious to the byplay, Suder had security show two segments of video: one with the curator approaching quickly, her brown pageboy setting off an abstracted face; the other of her back, her shoulders stooped with weariness. He tapped the monitors, indicating a rectangle hanging on the wall in each video. "That's the Monet and this is the place-holder." The replacement was the exact size and shape of the original—it even had an identical frame—which was partly why the swap had gone unnoticed by security. From the angle of the camera, the viewer couldn't tell much about the painting inside.

Damon shook his head in silent admiration. His master thief's attention to detail was astounding. She'd be perfect for their needs, if only they could acquire her. He shot a look of inquiry at Suder, who shook his head once, a brusque right-left movement redolent of frustration.

"Nothing was detected. Nobody reported anything suspicious. It'll take time to isolate when it was stolen, much less how it was done."

The blond agent beside Suder spoke up. "You didn't see anything?" He frowned at Damon, his close-set gray eyes narrowed, radiating suspicion and hostility.

Territorial one-fuckmanship Damon didn't have time or patience for. He did wonder what the man's insecurity said about his nightmares, as a matter of professional curiosity.

"Nothing." Damon didn't bother informing them he'd sensed her presence earlier. The fewer who knew about his abilities, the better. Besides, the knowledge wouldn't do them any good. He couldn't tell them if she'd been inside or outside the museum at the time—only that she'd been nearby. He could make an informed guess, but helping them catch his master thief at this point was contraindicated.

The ensuing conference failed to bring anything new to light. When it turned to plans for investigation, Damon took that as his cue to bow out. He'd seen the results of previous heists. There would be nothing to tie her to this job—she was that good—which meant there was nothing more for him here. In the weeks since he'd taken over this unusual assignment, he'd learned that much.

He took his leave, picking up a flyer that caught his eye on the way out. To catch his master thief, he'd have to go on the offensive. To do that he'd need suitable bait.

The silence of the nearly deserted museum descended around Damon, a pleasant balm after the contentious discussions and unbridled emotions he'd just left. It was broken all too soon by the rapid slap of leather soles on hard granite.

Suder had abandoned the hostile blond agent, catching up with Damon to scowl at him across his shoulder. "You're leaving, just like that?"

Damon fanned himself with the glossy leaflet; the museum was much warmer than outside, but he hadn't wanted to take his leather jacket off and flash his pistol. "Not my job."

"You're the one who knew someone was going for the Monet

tonight," Suder whispered in heated tones as they passed the front desk. "You telling me you won't help?"

"Recovering the painting isn't my concern." Acquiring his extremely competent thief was. He lengthened his stride, eager to get back to his hotel room and dive into his thief's dreams.

"You've got to give me something to work with, Venizélos." Suder's face and ears were turning red. He worried at his tie as though it was choking him, probably thinking about how this fiasco would look on his record.

Damon weighed the possibility that giving the FBI special agent a lead might bollix his own mission to acquire his master thief against the probability Damon would need his help in the future. As he saw it, the odds were against Suder's efforts interfering with his own. It also wouldn't hurt for the other man to owe him a favor; that was the way the system worked.

"Venizélos . . ." A strangled growl that sounded more like a plea than a threat.

Taking pity on the man, Damon shared the short list of heists executed during the opening nights of high-profile exhibits, confident that Suder wouldn't learn anything from them—except that Damon's master thief covered all her bases. He liked that in a woman, especially one he'd have to work with.

Despite his admiration for the flawless execution of the heist, Damon loathed reporting a setback, no matter how temporary. He had to force himself to make his next call once he was back in his hotel room.

As soon as the phone was answered on the other end, he reported the bad news: "She got away."

"She?" the deputy director of operations countered immediately. Past midnight in his time zone and the Old Man sounded like he'd just had a fresh pot of coffee.

"Our mysterious master thief," Damon gritted out.

"Is a woman?"

He paced to the picture window to stare down at the deserted, lamp-lit streets. His jaw ached from gritting his teeth. "No doubt about it. Waltzed into the museum, took what she wanted, and left without a trace."

"A woman, huh? That's more than we had before. Hell, boy, quit growling. That's progress."

Damon rolled his eyes at his superior's response. The Old Man had been his uncle's protégé at the agency and had known Damon most of his life. He made it a point to try to get Damon to "lighten up." If discovering his master thief's gender was progress, it'd take him a year to acquire her—a year they didn't have. Once that tactical nuke surfaced, they'd have to move fast to get it out of terrorist hands.

"We need to set a trap." Damon flipped open the glossy flyer from the museum and studied it with narrowed eyes. "I've got an idea." And this time, he'd be ready for her.

Rory left the twenty-four-hour Kinko's with a bounce in her step, assured that the cane with its hidden canvas was on the van that had just left. The painting should be in the hands of her client soon after her father received the package. Another commission accomplished without much of a problem. She headed back to her hotel, more than ready for a few hours of sleep. With the canvas out of her hands, she could now devote time to planning how she'd spend her vacation. Too bad she couldn't go hook up with the Adonis of the park; the fact he was a Fed made it too risky. As much as she enjoyed a challenge, seeking him out would be tempting the Fates.

She mourned the stillborn affair, wishing she'd had the benefit of carnal knowledge of her Adonis before she'd learned he was off-limits. Fondling that exceptional erection had whetted her appetite for more, had spawned explicit daydreams that almost distracted her from her commission. Despite the risk he posed, she couldn't forget the sketch she'd made of him naked. She'd bet he looked even better in the flesh.

Back at her room at the Residence Inn, Rory peeled the magnetic Do Not Disturb sign off the door and checked her keychain for a green light—no one lurking inside—before entering.

Her laptop lay on the desk where she'd placed it earlier that evening before she'd left for the museum. Her suitcase was propped open, revealing a messy spill of clothes. She cultivated the image deliberately, since the apparent naïveté made her appear less suspicious. Besides, any determined thief would be able to break the paltry locks of her suitcase and the room safe; more than anyone else, she should know. Why invite additional damage?

A quick glance told her everything was as it should be. Or else whoever had searched her things was even more paranoid than she was—and a lot more skilled. She didn't think she could duplicate the careless drape of the red blouse on top of everything. Since she didn't think anyone else could, she was probably fine.

Rory untied the dark shawl that had served as a skirt for her trip to Kinko's and dropped it in her suitcase. Rolling down the legs of her pantsuit, she undressed quickly, making sure to invert her jacket so that the red side was hidden once more, before she hung it in the closet.

She fell into bed, considering vacation spots. Maybe the Riviera or Australia's Gold Coast? Someplace where the sun was shining and she could sate the hunger that Adonis had awakened in her. She snuggled into her pillows, rubbing her tingling nipples against the crisp cotton.

It was definitely past time for some nookie. She'd spent so much time planning the execution of this commission that she'd let fun and games fall by the wayside; evidently her body believed enough was enough and was making its requirements known. She closed her eyes, ignoring her clamoring libido, too drowsy to consider soothing it.

Her sensual craving followed her into sleep, taking form in restless dreams.

It started with a gentle breeze that carried the enthralling scent of male musk to her nostrils. The zephyr whirled around her as she floated in the darkness, flowing over her bare skin like a soft caress.

Sultry darkness wrapped her in safety, cradled her in warmth, hid a phantom lover waiting just for her. His presence didn't frighten her, accustomed as she was to living in the shadows. She didn't question his choice to conceal his identity. It didn't even occur to her to ask.

Dream hands stroked her, played teasing games on her body, melted her tension with a masterful massage.

Turning over in her bed, Rory moaned, welcoming the sweet comfort. The pleasure built slowly, pulling her deeper into sleep. With a happy sigh, she surrendered to the dream, abandoning herself to its hedonistic delights.

Knowing fingers roamed her body, trailing sparks of desire in their wake, summoning a growing response. They whetted her carnal hunger, then fed her to the fire.

Pleasure splashed through her, sweet and easy. A gentle rapture banishing all her cares. So wonderful to relax with no thought for the next job.

Her lover stroked her through the gentle orgasm, stoking her desire with his hands and body, tempting her to greater heights. He teased her, toying with her sex, brushing his own against her body. Whispering that she could have even more.

She wanted more, her appetite hardly sated.

Taking her into his arms, he bore her deeper into the darkness, and gave her more.

Mobile mouths made free with her body, planting kisses on her breasts and thighs and belly, suckling her nipples to throbbing points, licking and teasing her erect clit. Large hands caressed her all over, fondling her breasts, squeezing and kneading her buttocks, plunging long fingers into her hot, dripping sheath.

Enthralled by the intoxicating pleasure sweeping through her, Rory gave herself over to the intimacies and invited more. Her phantom lover dazzled her with his attentions, kindling a blaze in her body. With stinging kisses, masterful touches, and probing tongues, he stoked her need hotter, driving her past her previous rapture, sending her toward a higher peak.

She sought it avidly, participating in her own seduction, mad for what awaited her and greedy for pleasure. Scintillating need coalesced in her core, razor sharp with hunger, golden with voluptuous promise.

He awarded her enthusiasm with greater zeal, showering her with honeyed delight, amplifying her desire until it burst in a thousand, thousand shards of crystal bliss. Yet even while she drifted, lost in the magnificence of her release, he tempted her with more.

Invisible hands caught her arms and legs, holding her spread-eagled as more hands and mouths lashed her with raw pleasure. Delight rocked her quivering core, sent flares of rapture shooting through her over and over. They fueled a wild hunger in her body that consumed all sense, whetting her desire with incendiary caresses. Branded carnal need into every aching cell of her being.

Rory writhed, desperate for release. Her phantom lover fed her scorching emptiness, using his large fingers to stroke her inner flesh with masterful skill. But this time it wasn't enough. She yearned for more, for something that would stuff her to stretching, piercing fullness.

She begged him to take her, then begged for relief when he wouldn't. At her words, the darkness eased as a pale green form glowed softly. A thick dildo carved with exotic figures.

Rory reached for it eagerly, desperate to fill the throbbing emptiness inside her. It was cool to the touch, a shocking contrast to her slick, heated flesh. She sank down on it, sheathing it in her body, impaling herself on its thick, unyielding shaft. Her flesh was like butter to its blade, melting before its advance. It stretched her channel, an ineffable pressure that soothed her intense craving. She rode it recklessly, taking it to the hilt.

As it slid home, ecstasy erupted inside her, a fiery explosion that blasted through her, overwhelming her with its power. She screamed as rapture enfolded her, transforming her into a being of pure sensation, radiant with carnal delight. It went on forever. An unending series of glorious orgasms, rolling one into another, with peremptory disregard for the frailty of her mortal body.

The scalding force of her release shocked Rory awake. Her womb spasmed in the violent aftermath of wicked pleasure, her legs quivering, her thighs wet with cream. Breathless, she lay for long moments, swathed by rumpled sheets and shuddering from her release, not knowing what to make of it. She hadn't responded that strongly to a wet dream in a long time.

And dreaming of a dildo? How weird was that? Even weirder was a niggling sense of déjà vu, a feeling that she'd seen that dildo before.

Rory groaned at the sunlight leaking past the heavy drapes, her heart pounding in her ears, her core fluttering once again. Her folds ached, hypersensitive from constant arousal. The dream had reclaimed her every time she'd gone back to sleep after another shocked awakening from more bone-melting orgasms. She hadn't had two straight hours of sleep all night as a result. Now, the haze of musk and need surrounding her was almost overpowering, every breath she took, every gasp and gulp, a potent reminder of the night's strange fascination.

To think she'd fixated on an object. After all her carnal plans for her vacation, she'd have expected to dream of a lover, perhaps even of that Adonis, being tall, dark, and hung—not a dildo of magical powers!

That sense of familiarity returned, pricking her dazed euphoria. Where could she have seen that dildo? It hadn't been part of the Oriental art exhibit—she was certain of that—but there was something distinctly Oriental about it.

Rory closed her eyes to better envision the dildo from her dreams, flexing her hands as she tried to remember how holding it had felt. Cool and smooth despite the ridges . . . solid jade and covered with elaborate carvings! Chinese work, perhaps.

Sunlight reflected off something on the nightstand, drawing her eye to the flyers she'd collected at the museum.

Freeing herself from her cocoon of blankets, Rory flipped through the glossy papers quickly. Her memory of the exhibit was impeccable; what had been on show were articles from daily life: clothes, weapons, and whatnot. Beautiful and worthy of display in themselves but nothing truly unusual.

The last pamphlet was something different. Another traveling exhibit, also of Oriental art, but at another museum. Here was the exotic: screen paintings and woodblock prints of erotica in the Ukiyo-e style, stone panels of amorous couples in high relief, and more artwork with the same motif. Rory turned the paper over and spotted the dildo that had haunted her dreams in a group of highly figured sex toys.

Her womb pulsed reflexively, a spurt of hot cream trickling between her clenched thighs.

She read the description with avid interest. What could have caught her imagination so thoroughly that it triggered such powerful dreams? A Ming dynasty jade embellished with flying dragons.

I want it.

Rory blinked at the atypical thought. Never in her entire career had she stolen anything for herself. *Aurora diScipio, that's crazy. Think of what Dad would say when he found out.* And Felix would find out since he kept tabs on developments in the art world.

Avoiding the limelight was one of the core tenets of the family; stealing that jade would probably bring all sorts of hell down on her stupid head, if only from her father. Absolutely out of the question!

It wouldn't hurt to look.

The thought made her pause. That was true enough. Maybe if she saw it for real, she could figure out why it had caught her imagination. As her father liked to say: know your enemy and know yourself. Particularly apt when you're your worst enemy.

Knowing she was trying to rationalize what she wanted to do, Rory shook her head in disgust. *At least it's in Florida.* That was a plus. It would get her closer to sun and surf.

Chapter Three

The dildo lay on its side, the position emphasizing the Chinese dragons winding up its length. It stood out even among the exotic sex toys on display. All were works of art with detailed carving that took the breath away, but something about this specific dildo drew her attention like a magnet.

Her nose practically pressed against the case, Rory stared hungrily at the exquisite jade, making sure her almond eyes were wide, in keeping with her guise of tourist. Maintaining the look of amazement wasn't difficult: the dildo was easily thicker than her wrist.

This was what she'd been dreaming about?

Her core heated in confirmation. The reminder of how she'd

dreamed of taking that smooth coolness into her yearning body for the past nights was enough to make her feel flushed.

Mindful of her purpose, Rory made sure the camera on her watch captured what she needed about the security details, both electronic and physical. She'd already obtained the original plans for the museum's security system, but it was never wise to depend solely on those. The museum could have upgraded it or requested customization that was yet undocumented. She hadn't gotten as far as she had by being careless.

Her spotty conscience nagged at her with her father's ruined tenor, berating her on the stupidity of what she planned: diScipios weren't reckless, didn't tempt the Fates by taking unnecessary chances. Didn't risk exposing the entire family to harsh scrutiny for selfish reasons.

She almost forgot herself enough to shake her head.

This wasn't unnecessary. That jade with its sinuous dragons flying through stylized clouds was haunting her. She had to exorcise it somehow. The only solution that presented itself was to take the dildo and use it for real; maybe then she'd have some peace.

Anyway, she didn't have to keep it. She could return it once the dream was banished. The risk really wasn't all that great, not when no one knew she intended to steal it.

Rory's belief in her anonymity was shaken the moment she left the museum, the unexpected sight before her stopping her in her tracks. This time her eyes widened automatically. *Him again?*

The Adonis of the park stood in profile at the foot of the steps, his back to a large terra-cotta pot with a small fishtail palm that towered over him. Dark sunglasses covered his eyes, but that luxuriant fall of hair and the body inside the polo shirt and chinos could belong to no other.

His appearance was an even greater shock to her system than the hot sun pouring down on her shoulders and the heavy humidity she could practically swallow. He made her frightfully aware of her body, of the sweat beading between her heavy breasts and trickling down her spine. Recognizing prime beefcake on the hoof, her unruly libido issued a clarion call to arms, sending blood rushing south to pool in her womb and wet her sex.

Clawing through her purse, she fumbled for her own sunglasses, unable to tear her gaze from that undeniable male form. What was he doing here?

He tilted his head in her direction, almost as if he'd known she was there all along, the widow's peak the new angle revealed confirming his identity. Hooking a finger on the bridge of his sunglasses, he studied her over their wire rims, his dark eyes intent and predatory as he stared up at her. Then his lips curled as though in recognition. A hunter spotting his prey.

Damon wanted to roar in triumph at the sight of the slender woman standing motionless like a particularly lifelike statue at the top of the steps. She was the one responding to him, the source of the emotion buffeting his mental antennae. Shock and desire, fear and excitement radiated from her, all out of proportion with the situation.

Obviously Asian with the pale complexion he associated with northern Chinese and Koreans, she had straight chin-length black hair, wide-set almond eyes, a small nose, and rosebud lips—an exotic figure against the Spanish fortress-inspired exterior of the museum. She wore a long-sleeved shirt over loose pants and low sandals. Definitely not a local.

She'd recognized him, hadn't expected to see him, wanted him. The wariness that followed those tangled emotions suggested the knowledge was unwelcome. And she'd just emerged from the museum where his bait was on display.

Was she his master thief?

Nothing about her precluded it. She looked to be in good health and wasn't in any pain. She was slim enough to fit into the narrow ventilation ducts, if she wanted to get in that way. On the other hand, she wouldn't stand out in the middle of a cocktail party, such as those given for certain exhibits' opening nights.

A definite possibility.

Damon committed her appearance to memory. After these past weeks of studying his target, he might finally be face-to-face with his master thief.

The woman slid on a fancy pair of shades, the smooth motion belying the defensive gesture. If he hadn't known better, he'd have dismissed her startlement as a reaction to the brightness of the afternoon sun, instead of a very personal response to his presence. Especially when she pretended to ignore him, throwing her big bag over her shoulder carelessly and strolling away without another look.

A cool customer. If her carnal awareness weren't lapping at his senses like an affectionate kitten, he might have bought it.

How did she know him?

Pondering that question, Damon allowed her to get to the end of the block before he set off in slow pursuit, using other pedestrians as a screen. She'd recognized him from somewhere. But where? His missions generally took him out of the country and overseas. Had she been involved in one of them?

———— ⚬⚬⚬ ————

Rory couldn't shake the feeling the Adonis was stalking her. Why else would he be here, of all places? Gut instinct told her he hadn't let her get away. He was behind her somewhere; she could feel him like an itch in the small of her back.

Try as she might, she couldn't spot him. His reflection didn't appear on the glass as she window-shopped. Random glances over her shoulder didn't catch him. A few times she thought she saw the top of his head above the crowd, but never more than that. Was she imagining things?

Just because you're paranoid doesn't mean they're not out to get you, her father's voice counseled her. Caution was a byword of Felix diScipio; it was how he'd lasted so long in their business despite his lack of her advantages.

Ducking into a busy restaurant, Rory hurried to its thankfully empty restroom, stripping off her top and stuffing it into her shoulder bag as soon as the door closed behind her. Changing to a bleached blonde with frizzy hair and dark roots, a broader build with bigger bones, and a dark tan took only a little thought. She finished off with a square jaw, round eyes, a wide mouth, and a long nose. Plumping her breasts in their respectable sports bra, she went up two cup sizes to an impressive cleavage. As a final touch, she clipped on to her sandals some sparkly gewgaws she normally used as hairclips. After remaking her shoulder bag into a knapsack, she slipped it on her back and tweaked her hair until the coarse tresses covered the top of the bag.

Checking the new woman in the mirror, Rory adjusted her bra strap slightly to bare a noticeable tan line, and twitched the waistband of the now-formfitting pants to a more comfortable position. She grinned. *Not bad.* The Change had taken less than five seconds. Aunt Stella might have done it faster, but unlike Rory, she had a lot of practice with quick Changes as an assistant in Uncle Justin's magic act in Las Vegas.

She left the restroom, keeping to a brash saunter. She got confirmation of the suitability of her transformation almost immediately: the rapid double takes and sudden slowing of men's motion, the stares at her bust, all assured her few of them would remember her face. It gave her the confidence to step into the crowded lobby full of waiting diners.

And there he was, by the wall, somehow blending into the woodwork: the Adonis of the park, unobtrusively studying the patrons in the entry. He saw her immediately, scrutinizing her as though he would peel off her disguise if he could just find a crack in its surface.

Her heart racing, Rory almost smiled, confident on that front. That was the advantage of being a lamia: he couldn't penetrate her disguise because it wasn't makeup and prosthetics. The Change went bone deep. Secure in her masquerade, she gave him a cheerful leer on her way out the door, noting as she passed that—*Damn it all!*—his buns were just as spectacular as his package.

Nearly beside herself with glee, she had to maintain an iron grip on her impulses so she wouldn't tempt the Fates by approaching the Adonis. No easy thing since she remembered how well he'd filled her hand. He was probably a good match for the jade dildo.

Rory shook her head at her train of thought, her frizzy hair tickling her shoulders. *Aurora diScipio, you have sex on the brain.*

Damon stared hard after the brassy blonde, doubting the proof of his senses. He'd trailed his slender target through the busy tourist-hungry downtown and the boardwalks of nearby beaches and marinas. The inordinate shock and arousal that had called his attention had long since dissipated, giving way to a more general buzz of caution and excitement. But he could have sworn that same buzz was now coming from the woman leaving the restaurant.

Except that's impossible. He glared at the broad, sun-broiled shoulders framed by the doorjambs. That was definitely muscle he saw flexing under that tanned skin; there was no way it could be padding. Even if current technology were capable of effecting such a radical transformation, it should have taken more than thirty seconds—which was how long she'd been out of his sight.

He turned back to the restaurant's interior, looking for anyone who vaguely resembled that Asian woman. All the while, his mental antennae screamed that his target was vanishing in the distance, disappearing into the background static of daily life.

Logic wrestled with instinct, a lethal combination that threatened to grind his teeth to dust and leave him with a permanent case of lockjaw. *It's impossible, damn it.*

The Adonis's presence had given Rory second thoughts about going for the jade dildo. Stealing it now would be undeniable folly. Except the dream returned with a vengeance, haunting her nights with torrid, impossibly transcendent orgasms until she couldn't bear the strangeness of it any longer.

Even now, breathing deeply from the climb to the museum's

roof, her body persisted in heating to the memory of the dream, leaving her nipples poking at her top to rub against it with every inhalation. She forced the dream from her mind. Now wasn't the time for distractions. She'd be able to unleash the fullness of her carnal craving soon enough.

Besides, it had been too hot to wear anything under the thin skin suit, and she couldn't afford to leave footprints wet with cream on the museum floor. That would be *so* unprofessional.

Ignoring the sweat beading around her nose under her black ski mask and the familiar weight of her tool belt, Rory disarmed the alarm on the door to the rooftop garden. It took her only seconds: a trifling obstacle to one of her training. Museums tended to scrimp on security to the roof, probably due to budgetary considerations. There wasn't even a single camera for the roof! The oversight made her grimace in professional disapproval, but she couldn't complain since it made this unsanctioned theft so much easier.

Finding her way through the darkened maze that was the museum at night was hardly a challenge. She'd walked it in her mind several times, and with her program duping the surveillance cameras, she only had to worry about wandering guards.

Under the narrow beam of her penlight, the display of sex toys appeared even more exotic. Like forbidden fruit, all the more desirable for being taboo. The pale jade glowed with almost sentient life, promising pleasure beyond her wildest fantasies.

Forcing herself to breathe, Rory flashed the light around the case, double-checking that its security matched the results of her research. Sensor leads were right where the design said they would be, ready to catch careless thieves. Everything looked precisely as it ought to.

The thought made her queasy.

Kneeling down to work on the lock, Rory froze in midreach, instincts that had seen her safely through hundreds of thefts shrieking in horror. It was a trap! Somehow, somewhere, she'd seen something that set off her gut.

Flowing to her feet in one continuous motion, she sped silently through the route she'd mapped, heading back to the roof. A quick descent down the rope and in a half hour she'd be resting in her hotel, shaking off her close call.

Except the rope wasn't where she'd emplaced it.

"Looking for this?" The deep growl sounded from the depths of shadow behind a tall bush, almost as if it were part of the night. A bodiless hand held out her grapnel, the same one she'd anchored on one of the crenels on the darkest side of the museum, preset for a quick getaway.

With the barest scuff of heel, the Adonis of the park emerged into the half-light, a slight quirk of his lips giving him a triumphant air. He was dressed in dark clothes, his long hair tied back in a low, loose ponytail.

Rory's nipples beaded in welcome as sensual awareness zinged her core. Even as she berated herself silently, she couldn't deny he looked wonderful. If he weren't a Fed out to get her—which was the only possible reason for his presence—she wouldn't hesitate to take him as a lover.

He coiled her rope along the shank of the grapnel and tied it off neatly, guaranteeing that even if she managed to take it from him, she couldn't deploy it with any speed—certainly not quickly enough to escape.

"Maybe." Rory searched the shadows of the rooftop garden, looking for museum security and finding none. He was alone and wasn't making any moves to call for support. Why was that?

Dismissing the question as irrelevant, she darted back, heading for the door to draw him away from her egress point. She didn't plan on going back inside, but he couldn't know that. If he wanted to capture her himself, he'd have to stop her.

He took the bait, chasing her in silence, the slight thuds of his boots the only sounds he made. She hadn't been far off the mark when she'd labeled him a predator.

Her traitorous body thrilled to his pursuit, a definite wetness creeping down her thighs. Rory could feel her labia swelling, her strides rubbing the damp lips together in sensual friction. Her unruly imagination titillated her with a scene of caveman sex: the Adonis throwing her down and claiming her. She shivered in reaction. *Damn it, now isn't the time for that!*

A glance stolen over her shoulder found him catching up with every step, his long legs eating up the distance between them. The determination squaring his jaw had desire pooling in her belly, hot and heavy, throwing off her stride.

He shot past her, blocking the path to the door.

Changing direction, Rory swerved around a large ceramic pot, her feet feeling leaden, as though she were running through molasses. The humidity in the air didn't help; it felt like a sauna.

He blocked her again, forcing her to round a pungent hedge. He was toying with her, herding her to where he wanted. Well, two could play that game.

She veered into a stand of palms, hoping her agility would offset his greater speed. For a moment she thought it would work, but the low, leafy trees ended too soon, leaving her racing over a well-kept lawn.

He slammed into her like a runaway locomotive, sending her flying through the air. Then the night spun and she landed on hard, unyielding muscle. Before she could catch her breath, he twisted around, planting her facedown on the grass and under his big body.

His weight drove her breath out again.

Rory's mind raced as she panted, the smell of dry soil and hot grass heavy in her mouth. She had to get free; pinned down, her options were limited and dwindling rapidly.

She twisted her body, trying to push him off, but she barely moved him. That didn't stop her from trying, furious at how easily he'd caught her. If her family ever learned of this, she'd never live it down.

"Calm down. I just want to talk."

Yeah, right. Like that ridge rubbing between her cheeks wasn't an erection.

It felt marvelous—long and wide—more than enough to fill her the way she'd been craving in her dreams. Chagrined by her reaction, Rory renewed her efforts to get him off, stopping only when she felt herself in danger of overheating. Passing out wouldn't help.

Through it all, he didn't budge. His hands remained on either side of her head. His chest with its hard pectorals pressed on her shoulder blades. His legs controlled hers. His cock rode her buttocks.

Come on, Rory. Be smart about this. Use your head . . . or his. He was bigger than she was. She couldn't do anything about that. She couldn't lever him off unless she Changed right under him—and she couldn't do that on top of the foolhardy risks she'd already taken.

She had to make him drop his guard, enough to get on her feet with enough of a head start to let her Change in secret and escape. Easy to say, but how to do it?

His scent surrounded her, clean and musky, overwhelmingly

male. It shot a thrill straight to her loins, prompting another spurt of cream.

After the past week of sex-soaked dreams, she really couldn't blame her body for responding, not when she had a living, breathing Adonis right on top of her, grinding her into the grass and—

What was he *doing*?!

He had a hand between her aching breasts, fondling—no, he was groping, in search of something. The buzz of her zipper told her what. He pulled the tab down to her waist, leaving a gap for the grass to poke through.

What's he up to?

"Damn, you're a wildcat," he rumbled. "I guess we'll have to do this the hard way." In one quick motion, he grabbed her lapels and tugged her skin suit open and off her shoulders, trapping her arms against her body.

Understanding dawned. *Oh, that's just perfect!* She exploded in another furious effort to throw him off, stabbing a hard nipple into his palm to make sure he got the message.

He hissed in surprise. "You're not wearing any—" His hand slashed downward, sliding under her skin suit, finding and cupping her wet sex with what appeared to be typical efficiency.

Rory bucked again, impaling herself on his long, large fingers, driving them into her empty sheath. She closed her eyes, mewling with delight as rough pads stroked her sensitive inner flesh. This was so much better than any dream.

"That's the way of it, is it?" His deep growl surrounded her, vibrating against her back and sinking into her bones.

Her Adonis was no slacker. He immediately picked up on what she wanted and plied his hands with great skill. Keeping her trapped, he tweaked her nipples, rolling and pulling them mercilessly, sending darts of pleasure sparking to her womb.

Oh, God. Somehow he knew exactly what turned her into a melting puddle, called hot cream from her core.

His other hand delved deep in her dripping sex, his thumb circling her swollen clit, lighting a bonfire in her blood.

"Oh, yes!" Rory ground her pelvis on his palm, undulating against the hard ridge pressed to her buttocks. She clenched her muscles around his fingers, relishing their presence inside her. Just because she was trying to distract him didn't mean she couldn't enjoy herself.

Stiff grass rasped against her breasts, the hairs on his arm adding to the sensory delight. His shirt was rough against her bare back, emphasizing the difference in their positions. This was no dream that would leave her waking to solitary emptiness. This was real and she craved every bit of it.

Wanting to touch him, she wriggled her arms in their sleeves, trying to roll the bunched fabric off.

Her Adonis kept her imprisoned while his hands worked magic on her body, drawing out her cream to anoint her clit, teasing the sensitive nub, kneading her aching breasts. He encouraged her pursuit of rapture in a growled stream of commentary about her hotness and things he wanted to do to her, ways he intended to pleasure her. His deep croon alone was almost enough to send her over the brink.

She came apart in his arms, shuddering as his fingers detonated a string of delicious orgasms inside her. He continued to stroke her, drawing out the ecstasy until she lay beneath him, panting, her release leaving her boneless.

Now all she had to do was reduce him to the same condition.

Rory had managed to free her arms by the time he turned her over and folded up her ski mask, exposing her sweaty face to the warm night air.

"What the—?" Her Adonis stared down at her, short strands of his wavy hair dangling down between them.

Ignoring his exclamation, she worked at his fly, totally uninterested in any conversation. He'd flaunted that enormous cock at her from their first meeting. She'd fantasized about it, staring at her sketch for long minutes while her imagination ran wild. She wanted it inside her, stretching her to overflowing, and she wanted it *now*.

She growled in triumph when he finally spilled into her questing hands, thicker than a baseball bat and hard as steel, his cock's plum head already wet. Perfect and more than a match for cold, lifeless jade. "No talk. I want you, *now*."

"What?" He loomed over her, kneeling between her thighs, his shoulders blocking out the light. His cock bobbed between them, taunting her with possibilities. "Say that again."

Lying back, Rory splayed her legs in unequivocal invitation, pushing her zipper past her tool belt to bare her hungry sex. "Take me. Please."

Yanking her skin suit to her ankles, he aimed his cock at her portal, its blunt head nudging her labia, spreading them for his entry. He worked his thick length inside her in short, powerful thrusts, giving her exactly what she wanted, relentless in his possession.

Rory threw her head back, moaning breathlessly at the sensation. She could feel every inch of him catching on her inner membranes, hard and hot, so vigorously male. She wrapped her legs around his hips, pulling him close, drawing him deeper until she couldn't take any more. She was stuffed full of cock and he still had a couple of delicious inches left.

He pumped her slowly, holding back, his restraint blatant in the steel tension of his body.

She couldn't have that. Her plan depended on her screwing his brains out. That wouldn't happen if he stayed in control. Arching her back, she grabbed his tight buns, trying to take more of him inside her. "Harder," she insisted. "Faster."

Her Adonis gave her what she asked for, his thrusts pounding her into the grass, forcing soft cries of pleasure from her throat. The green scent of bruised leaves wafted around them, mingling with the smell of sweat and raw sex.

Rory clamped her muscles around him, squeezing him, and fluttered her sheath over his massive cock.

He cursed prayerfully, adjusting the angle of his thrusts. His renewed attack drove his cock head over her G-spot and tweaked her clit, sending starbursts up her spine.

Damn, he was still thinking! "More!"

"More?" He leaned back, his eyes wide in his shadowed face.

She took advantage of his surprise to push him off balance, rolling with him until he lay on the grass and she straddled his hips. When she sat down, the position drove him deeper until he was sheathed to the hilt.

"Holy shit," her Adonis whispered. His eyes glazed over; his skin stretched tight over his cheekbones.

"Oh, yes." Rory groaned at the thoroughness of his possession. She could feel him snug against her core, filling her completely. This was what she needed. It'd been too long since she'd had a man this deep inside her.

"You're so damned tight." His hands clamped down on her hips, holding her in place as he pumped her, his body pistoning beneath her in smooth motion, tireless in his efforts.

Digging her fingers into his shirt, Rory hooked her heels under his thighs, hanging on as he drove into her, hammering her in a brutal, breath-stealing ride to the stars.

He lunged up, lifting her off her knees, and rolled his hips, swirling his cock around her sheath.

She lost her breath on a low moan, the glorious sensation like a live wire skipping across her nerves. How could he know how wonderful that felt?

Countering his efforts with her own hip rolls and flutters, she milked him with her body. If she wasn't careful, she'd be the one screwed brainless.

She could feel his tension increasing, his chest working under her fists, his thighs like stone against her feet. If she didn't do anything, he'd come soon—too soon for her purposes.

"Not yet." Rory reached inside his pants for his balls, pulling down gently as he arched beneath her, the tendons of his neck in stark relief. She wasn't ready for this to end just yet. Besides, he was still very much in control of himself.

He held his pose for a few heartbeats, his face caught in a rictus of pleasure, his cock twitching inside her. But he remained hard.

She grinned at her success. As he relaxed, lying back on the grass, she rose to her knees, allowing him to withdraw until only his head was in her sheath. Then she reversed direction, taking his thick cock all the way back inside in a glorious friction that nearly had her eyes rolling back in her head. He reached deep into her, massive against her swollen membranes yet still growing impossibly larger.

"What the fuck did you do?" He stared up at her, his gaze hot and demanding, a dark flush visible on his cheeks even in the poor lighting.

Rory shook her head, riding him, coaxing him back on the breathless trail to the heights of ecstasy. He responded to her overtures, his eyes shuttering, turning inward, focused now on his own pleasure. Exactly the way she wanted him.

Need coiled inside her, rising with every stroke and caress she bestowed upon her Adonis, drawing her onward with memories of orgasmic wonder. Even the sounds of their wet flesh slapping together magnified her desire. Rapture lurked just over the horizon, a gathering storm, its approach inevitable, unstoppable, and much longed for.

His thighs tensed under her, his muscles vibrating with need. "Now, damn it!" He slammed into her, claiming her, the violence of his possession tipping her over the brink.

"Oh!" Rapture broke over her, poured into her, roared through her, bright with lightning and wild as the open seas. It flooded her veins with endless pleasure, raining decadent delight over every inch of her body.

As another surge of ecstasy stormed her senses, her Adonis choked on a curse, his cock jerking and pulsing, his body rigid. His eyes went blind, his fingers digging into her buttocks as he came and came and came.

Rory collapsed on his chest, riding out the waves. The aftershocks of her release thundered through her, threatening to sweep her away until she forgot she was supposed to escape.

Her hard lover groaned as his cock gave another spasm, bathing her womb with heat. His heart drummed under her ear, the rise and fall of his broad chest creating a pleasant friction with her nipples.

Her core fluttered weakly, almost as if in reminder. She couldn't wait much longer.

"Well, that was fun." His thief had a husky contralto that sent shivers running up and down Damon's spine and made his cock twitch with impossible renewed interest. "Too bad I can't stay."

She pushed off him, her wet pussy clasping his semierect shaft in a slick embrace as he slid out of her body. While he struggled to clear the dense fog of pleasure clouding his brain, she pressed a kiss on his neck and purred: "You were marvelous."

What?

As she stood up, she dragged her jumpsuit to her waist in one efficient, graceful motion. Still half-naked, she ran into the trees, her top flopping around her hips, her dusky skin blending with the shadows.

Jerking his pants up his hips, Damon struggled to his feet to give chase. Not that he thought she'd get far. Try as she might, there was no way she could escape him now. He still had her rappelling gear.

His thief headed for the far corner of the roof, her determination strong in his mind. Then, with a sudden thrill of excitement, she was beyond the roof and rapidly opening the gap between them.

What the hell? He put on a burst of speed, sprinting after her on shaky legs. He reached the battlement with no thief in sight. Leaning through a crenel, he checked the grounds around the foot of the museum, his heart clenching with surprising dread despite the impossibility. She couldn't have killed herself—he was certain of that much—since he hadn't felt any pain from a sudden impact. She was somewhere beyond.

A flash of movement on a high-rise apartment across the street and a few stories down caught his attention. His thief was quickly making her descent via fire escape, calmly pulling her jumpsuit back to rights, her lack of underwear now obvious in the absence of a panty line. Somehow, she'd bridged the wide gap between the two buildings in the short time she was out of his sight. Lowering herself from the last metal rung, she dropped to the pavement, landing as easily as a cat. At the corner, she turned back and looked up, gave him a jaunty wave, then disappeared around the building.

Fuck. There was no way Damon could get to the street in time to pick up her trail, even with so little to hide it this late at night, and he knew it. The fastest way down would have been to use her rope, but he'd been too efficient in tying it off.

Shaking his head in disbelief at how his thief had given him the slip, he couldn't deny a glow of admiration at how well she thought on her feet. Or her back, if he wanted to be accurate. *By all means, let's be accurate.*

She'd found a weakness in his defenses and exploited it ruthlessly—and how!

He closed his eyes against a surge of breathless memory. Despite the spike of adrenaline her escape had given him, his body was still humming from his release, wanting nothing more than another bout of sexual acrobatics.

Even though it wasn't possible.

Not if the mission pushed through.

Which was a damned shame, since he'd have welcomed a few nights of horizontal tango with her.

Turning from the battlement, Damon made his way back to his hotel. This was just a setback. His lovely thief hadn't escaped him yet. After all, she had to sleep sometime.

Chapter Four

That was close!

The potent cocktail of adrenaline and endorphins flooding Rory's veins urged her to run, to flee while she could, but she managed to keep her pace to a brisk walk. Running would only draw unnecessary, undesirable attention—not that gliding between buildings was less attention-grabbing. However, most people had a convenient habit of not looking up, and she'd done her best to fly in the shadows, so she was probably safe . . . or at least safer than remaining in that Fed's arms.

Now she had to focus on getting away.

Rory had to stifle a pang of regret at fleeing, but she was sure her female relatives wouldn't blame her for the sentiment. Damn, that Adonis had been so thick and hard. And he'd known how to use his inches. Just thinking of how well he'd wielded them inside her made her shiver. He'd certainly lived up to his claims. Too bad his interest in her was work related.

She ran her hands over her skin suit, making sure everything was in place and trying to ignore the memories the sensation invoked. Now wasn't the time for that. Later, she could relive the pleasure to her heart's content. But now she had to keep her mind focused on escape.

Her heart continued to pound from her reckless flight between the buildings. She'd had to Change twice in nearly as many seconds and almost hadn't completed the first before she'd jumped off the museum's parapet. She stretched her arms cautiously, her muscles twinging from the unaccustomed exercise. Making like a flying squirrel had been more difficult than she'd expected. It was a good thing she'd already been nearly naked; otherwise, she wouldn't have been able to pull it off in the little time she'd had. But she'd managed.

Rory grinned, remembering the way that Adonis had stood on the roof, not even making an effort to chase her. He'd known he didn't stand a chance at catching up with her. She sent a mental raspberry winging back to the Fed. *Close, but no cigar!*

A few short blocks from the museum, the darkened apartment buildings gave way to neon signs that lit up the streets, advertising bars and restaurants, private clubs and personal services. Despite the lateness of the hour, people still lingered on the sidewalks, making their presence heard with alcohol-fueled laughter.

Paying scant attention to the eclectic mix of Spanish-inspired, Art Deco, and modern architecture, Rory wove through the merrymakers, taking an indirect route back to her hotel in belated caution. But if anyone was on her tail, she didn't spot him. Her gut assured her she was in the clear.

Yet how had that Adonis, Mr. Tall-Dark-and-Hard-Bodied, found her—in an entirely different city she hadn't planned on visiting? As if he'd known what she was going to do before she'd even decided to do it.

With the euphoria from her escape fading, Rory couldn't suppress a thrill of dread. As a member of a clan of lamia—female shapeshifters slandered in myth as bloodsucking demons—she knew that reality was sometimes stranger than people wanted to believe.

She shoved her reaction to the back of her mind to consider the corollary: having predicted her movements once, could he do so again?

The latter question was cause for worry. While the Fed hadn't exactly done his utmost to arrest her, that could always change. And if he could anticipate her movements once, he might be able to again—which would be problematic. As Felix had taken pains to teach her, predictability was a bane in her profession.

Bravado made Rory toss her head. She'd just have to make sure her Adonis didn't succeed if he tried.

Brooding over his unaccustomed failure—the second in a row and therefore even more difficult to swallow—Damon stared out his hotel window and ran his fingers through his damp hair. The fact that he was alive was testament to his success rate with all the danger inherent in his missions. It galled him that one unarmed woman had managed to foil him.

And to use sex to turn the tables on him!

As an incubus, Damon rarely indulged himself with carnal relations—and only when the need for skin on skin proved overwhelming. Sex was an intimacy he doled out sparingly, usually as one-night stands. It would've been nice to think he did so to avoid endangering innocents or because the Company kept him too busy. But he knew better. His uncle Dion had shown him that work and family weren't necessarily oil and water.

His aversion to relationships was self-protective: it minimized his exposure to the excesses of ragged emotion that people broadcast. The distance he maintained was a necessity; it wasn't as if he could simply shut off his mental sense, not when he relied on what he picked up to succeed in his missions and for survival. Which was why he preferred his sexual encounters casual . . . and mainly a meeting of minds—in dreamland.

But his libido was still healthy, and his master thief had leveraged that need into a potent distraction. She'd gotten him by the short hairs and taken shameless advantage, manipulating him like a puppet on strings.

Disgusted by the comparison, Damon spun away from the window and threw himself on the bed, to bounce on inadequate softness. He'd been so close, yet she'd still gotten away! She'd kept her head while he'd lost his. Flipping over onto his back, he stared up at the blank ceiling. The score was two–oh in her favor. He supposed it boded well for the mission that she could give him the slip, but he didn't have to like it. And the longer it took him to acquire her, the less time they'd have to fulfill the objective.

That could spell disaster.

The breakup of the Soviet Union had created a number of potential nuclear states, but Russia had managed to retain most of that capacity for itself. However, the rise of the Mafia had brought to light a certain porousness in Russia's security—and guns, drugs, and people were being moved through the holes.

It was unfortunate that a suitcase nuke had been one of the things that had slipped through.

Heads had probably rolled for that fuckup, but Damon wasn't concerned with the fate of some hapless Russian muckety-mucks. What worried him was the potential cost in human lives. While a tactical nuclear bomb with a design yield of a few kilotons wouldn't destroy a major metropolis like New York or Los Angeles—nothing on the scale of Hiroshima—properly placed, it could still kill thousands of people.

Put in those terms, failure was unacceptable.

His cell phone rang in his pocket, the unexpected trill filling him with foreboding. No one was supposed to call him. Not unless there was a change of plans or . . .

Refusing to complete the thought, he answered the phone. "Status?"

Damon allowed himself a quiet sigh of relief at hearing the Old Man's voice. Yet this call and the tight rein it represented were out of character for his superior.

"I've made contact," he replied, nudging his concern to the back of his mind where it wouldn't distract him.

"We don't have much time." A rare fatigue hollowed out the Old Man's voice. He must be putting in incredibly long hours for that hint of weakness to show. "It's surfaced in Kosovo with Karadzic. Word is, he'll put it up for bidding within the month."

Damon closed his eyes as a chill ran down his spine. *Fuck!* Under UN control, Kosovo had become a haven for criminal gangs that used drugs and the sex trade to fund their operations. That made it the perfect place to auction off a stolen nuke, and was probably one reason the nuke had ended up with Alexei Karadzic, a KLA warlord turned gang lord and noted illegal arms merchant.

The Old Man had expected something like this, which was why they'd set out to recruit a master thief as soon as they'd gotten word a tactical nuke had gone missing. But *within the month* meant they had less than four weeks left to recover the bomb. And once sold, the odds of their finding it before it went into play dwindled dramatically.

On the other hand, the auction would likely draw terrorists out of the woodwork like ants to Kool-Aid. He could think of several groups that were probably salivating at the chance to acquire a nuke and had the funding to back their aspirations. "A target-rich environment."

"Exactly. Whether or not you get our thief, count on going to Kosovo."

His shoulders tensed at the suggestion of failure. "Give me a few more days to work on her."

"Three days. Then we'll have to consider alternatives." The Old Man hung up with his customary abruptness.

Returning the cell phone to his pocket, Damon swore at his superior's literal-mindedness. He should have asked for a week. Three days didn't give him much time to corner his master thief, who'd probably be twice as wary, now that she knew he was after her. To have to convince her to take on the job as well, within that time frame?

He had to think of something. Fast.

Without the need to escape to drive her, Rory's energy quickly ebbed, sapped by her carnal activities. Her body just wanted to lie down and relive her recent pleasure. She showered off the grass and sweat and other sticky evidence, then fell into bed.

Unsurprisingly, her subconscious started to replay the dream that started the whole fiasco. She thrust away the image of the jade dildo impatiently. She didn't want it. She wanted him—that dangerous man who'd nearly caught her.

Just like that, his image took form in her dream. The deep-set eyes and slashing brows. The widow's peak and wavy hair. Hard chest with its fan of dark hair. Muscular arms, narrow hips, strong legs. Exactly as she'd drawn him at the park. Exactly as he should have been earlier. At the thought, they were surrounded by greenery.

She wanted him, precisely like that—naked and totally accessible, in a Garden of Eden all their own.

"Me?" Her dream man's dark eyes widened in disbelief.

Rory ignored the strangeness of his response. It was a dream, and dream logic didn't necessarily make sense.

"You," she agreed, caressing that powerful chest.

After a heartbeat of hesitation, he stroked her arms with a tentativeness that was inconsistent with her impression of her Adonis. "Okay."

But it was her dream. Was that what she actually wanted?

She explored his body the way she'd imagined doing countless times while staring at her sketch of him. The broad shoulders that tapered to a lean waist. That flat belly and tight butt. If there were a male version of Pygmalion's Galatea, it'd be him.

Her sex moistened as her pat-down revealed only firm muscle.

And then there was the thick cock that her hand had stretched to measure, standing tall and proud, so utterly nonclassical in its dimensions.

"I'm much bigger than that."

Rory had to laugh at the familiar disgruntlement in his voice. Then his statement registered. Why did her own dream insist on arguing with her? She frowned and the details of the dream started to fray, the greenery fading to formless gray as she stepped away from sleep. Shouldn't he just reciprocate her attentions? So why wasn't he doing so?

Alarm stirred faintly. Something wasn't right.

When Rory tried to back away, he stopped her, wrapping his arms around her in a tight embrace.

Pushing against his chest, she arched back to glare at him. "What are you doing?" Being overpowered in real life was one thing; she wasn't about to tolerate a repeat of it in her dreams.

She tried to break his hold, but he held her close, no matter what she did.

"Meet me."

"What?" Rory twisted around, struggling to escape. This was her dream, damn it. Why couldn't she control it?

"It's no use fighting." Golden strands formed out of nothing to bind her to stillness, holding her in place before him, apparently in obedience to his instructions.

About to Change to escape her bonds, a sudden realization chilled Rory, made her wary. This was no ordinary dream. "You're the one behind those dreams about the dildo."

Stepping back, he frowned, the slashing brows meeting above his nose. "Something like that."

She recoiled, outraged by his tacit admission. He'd invaded her sleep! "Why?"

"I have to talk to you."

"You've got to be kidding me!"

"No, we need to talk."

"We're talking now." She wanted to wave her arms, but her bonds prevented even that.

"Seriously, we have to meet, discuss things."

"And why should I?" Rory braced herself to wake up. Surely she could do that. He couldn't keep her asleep.

He shifted to one side and shot her a calculating glance across his shoulder. "For a challenge like you've never faced before." With that cryptic statement, he stepped behind her.

The golden strands restraining her vanished.

She twisted—

And found herself awake, crouching on her bed in the hotel, grappling with a blameless pillow, the blanket twined around her body.

It had all been a dream.

Rory exhaled sharply, dropping to her knees as the absence of a particular, infuriating male registered. Another dream. Yet unlike the ones that had haunted her lately, not one that left her aching for a lifeless dildo. Just for a living, breathing Adonis. That had to be an improvement.

Of sorts.

She flung herself on her back in disgust. As the mattress quaked from the assault, she tried to explain away the haunting as the result of an overactive imagination.

Only she couldn't.

That dream had been too consistent. It had been the only reason she'd come to this particular city in Florida—where he'd found her. And now she knew he could enter her dreams. It didn't take a flight of fancy to wonder if he could do more . . . like manipulate her fantasies.

Could he have been responsible for the one about the dildo? Was that why he'd known she'd hit that specific museum when even her father didn't know?

Which reminded her that she still hadn't called in, to apprise Felix of her plans.

She reached into her purse for her cell phone, then paused as her hand closed around the quiet device.

What were her plans?

Vacation first. Right. Maybe she was just too wound up and needed to relax, time off to make like a beach bunny, like she'd originally intended.

Steeling her nerve, Rory pressed the buttons that would put her in contact with her father, starting her down the road to dealing with her dream stalker.

"Do you know what time it is?"

"Hey," she responded, the irascible rasp of Felix's ruined tenor bringing an automatic smile to her lips. He'd have greeted her with the same words even if she'd caught him at noon; anything else would have meant it wasn't safe to talk freely. "I'm going off for a bit."

"You okay?"

Rory blinked at the abrupt question. "Of course. Why'd you ask?" She wanted to smack herself as soon as the words were out of her mouth. *Way to go, Rory! Raise his suspicions, why don't you?* She didn't need him worrying about her.

"Paternal instincts. I know when my favorite daughter is up to some mischief."

"I'm your only daughter." Despite the familiar refrain, she glanced around guiltily. Suspecting her Adonis could manipulate her dreams made her wonder if there was more to her father's claims than she'd believed.

"Even better. Only one target. That's why they're infallible," he insisted incorrigibly.

She shook her head, her smile widening on a surge of filial affection. "I'm just going to have some fun."

A loud harrumph came through the phone, his doubt loud and clear. "That's the same thing you said when Lucas started you roof-walking."

Rory rolled her eyes. Felix had never forgiven her eldest brother for being the one to introduce her to that; he'd wanted to do it himself. "It was fun. Anyway, I just called to let you know I might be out of cell phone range."

"Don't do anything I wouldn't do."

"Too late." She shut off the phone on his sputters. Her father would only worry more if he knew the lascivious thoughts she was entertaining about a Fed.

Without her verbal sparring with Felix to occupy her, Rory's mind returned to her dream conversation with her Adonis. Had it even been real? Couldn't it merely be due to a driving need to explain her near capture that followed her into sleep? But how did that explain his foreknowledge when her decision to fly to Florida had been on the spur of the moment?

A challenge like you've never faced before.

How could someone she'd hardly exchanged ten words with know her so intimately—and not just in the carnal sense? Knew what kept her in her line of work despite having enough stashed in various numbered accounts to walk away from it all? Knew just what would intrigue her damnable curiosity?

Rory's heart picked up speed at all the questions—questions she had no answers for. She felt exposed, her skin scraped raw and prickling from a whirling dust devil, at the thought of someone studying her like a bug under a microscope. Probing her secrets with clinical detachment.

Hopefully, he hadn't gotten that far yet. Otherwise, he'd have penetrated her disguise when he'd followed her into the restaurant that afternoon.

The sound of the waves crashing into the shore gradually impinged on her consciousness, soothing in its repetitive beat the longer she listened to it. An assurance that life went on, no matter the strange curve she'd been thrown.

Her equanimity recovered, Rory considered her next step. He'd said he wanted to meet her to discuss something, a challenge. Should she agree?

On the face of it, there wasn't much of a risk. He couldn't have anything to link her to her jobs, nothing that would stand up in court, not even fingerprints—she altered even those when she Changed.

Besides, there was the fact that he'd nearly caught her once. He'd been at the park even before she'd first dreamed of the jade dildo. His presence there couldn't have been a coincidence. How had he found her? She'd have to find out before she could risk accepting another commission. If some habit of hers made her predictable, she'd need to fix it before someone else figured it out and nabbed her. Or used her to get Felix or some other diScipio.

That decided Rory.

She knew herself well enough to know she'd never give up burglary while she could still do the work. Nothing else gave her the same charge as pitting herself against a tough system. To continue as she'd been doing, she'd have to face the Fed and learn how he'd predicted that she would hit the museum when it hadn't been on her job list.

Too, she was cursed with the curiosity of a cat, and it would nag her until it was satisfied. Why hadn't he called to the museum guards for backup to catch her? She had to know, which meant agreeing to meet him. But that didn't mean she was about to abandon all her vacation plans. She'd wanted sand and surf, and intended to get some.

Rory fluffed her pillows into the configuration she preferred, then snuggled in, her body hyperaware of the smooth cotton sheets thanks to that sexy Fed's visitation. If her experience with the jade dildo's haunting was anything to go by, he'd be waiting in her dreams.

Might as well give him his answer.

With a leisurely stretch, she went to sleep, a smile of anticipation curving on her lips.

Time to get some of her own back.

CHAPTER FIVE

Damon paused before the doors leading out to the hotel's terrace to give his eyes time to adjust to the sudden brightness. The manicured tropical paradise with its lagoonlike pool was replete with bikinied women on towels and loungers soaking up the sun. At any other time, he might have lingered; he was a healthy, red-blooded male after all. But today the lure of eye candy did nothing for him. He had more important things to do.

Beyond a low retaining wall, the sea called to him, speaking of endless possibilities, its crashing waves punctuated by the shrill cries of hovering seagulls. The sun hung high in a clear blue sky unbroken by even a single cloud. A strong wind blew, lifting his hair off his shoulders, the salt air heavy with heat and humidity and nothing else. Altogether, it was an auspicious morning. Perhaps today he'd finally pin down his mysterious master thief.

He could only hope he would. Time was running out.

Ignoring the looks of invitation and darts of heated interest aimed in his direction, Damon crossed the sheltered pool area and made his way to the beach behind his hotel, a white towel slung over his shoulder. He felt almost as underdressed as he could be in the snug, dark blue racing trunks—not his idea of suitable attire for meeting an elusive and internationally renowned cat burglar— but it was one of the conditions she'd set for this meeting. He'd had to buy a pair, since he hadn't brought one with him.

So much for thinking he was prepared for anything. *I wonder how the Old Man will take* that *entry in the expense accounts.* Guns and ammo were one thing; overpriced fashionable swimwear was something else altogether.

The stray thought didn't distract him from his discomfiture for long. He was supposed to take a swim and get his trunks wet . . . to prove he was unarmed? That doing so would also short any electronics he might have planted on him was probably an added benefit.

It was funny how he wouldn't have noticed his lack of clothing if this had been one of his seduction dreams, though his forays into his master thief's dreams had had predictably frustrating results for his libido. As it was, he didn't like the feeling that the situation was out of his control.

Problem was, she had him over a barrel. If he wanted to meet her, he had to follow the very specific instructions she'd conveyed in her dream. He could only hope he'd interpreted them correctly. Dreams weren't exactly verbal communication, and he'd never had anyone try to pass a message to him through one before.

The pristine expanse of pale sand stretched out on either side of him, almost blinding in the high noon sun and radiating a tangible wave of heat. Despite the parade of hotels up and down the shoreline, the festive umbrellas dotting the beach were nearly deserted. The crashing surf was loud enough to make casual conversation—and recording any discussion—difficult. Which was probably what she wanted.

Damon dropped his towel under the first unoccupied umbrella he got to, checking his surroundings with cautious eyes.

His nearest neighbor, several feet away, was a voluptuous platinum blonde in a skimpy red bikini that hid none of her charms. She was slathering suntan lotion over her gold-touched skin, obviously intent on catching some rays. As he watched, she lay facedown on her arms, exposing exceptional curves to the sun, her mind projecting only simple satisfaction.

If he weren't here on business, Damon wouldn't have minded joining her; maybe he'd even offer to oil her back. As it was, he had to calculate whether her presence might discourage his master thief, and he briefly considered transferring to another umbrella—except instinct told him he was right where he was supposed to be. Hopefully, she was far enough away not to pose a hindrance to his meeting. He couldn't exactly ask her to move without a good explanation.

There was no one else in the immediate vicinity. No hint of dark skin—hereditary or otherwise—anywhere on the beach. If his master thief was around, she was keeping a low profile.

The blonde's unabashed enjoyment of the sun and the heat pulled at Damon's attention, a definite distraction but one he couldn't resist. What red-blooded heterosexual male could? To even try would blow his cover sky-high.

After indulging himself with a few appreciative glances,

Damon reminded himself he was on duty, dragging his mind back to what he was supposed to be doing. *Oh, yeah. The swim.* There'd been something about getting his skin wet.

As he stood up, he scanned the beach, searching for his dusky master thief or anyone else who might be acting as a lookout. The sand dunes leading to his hotel were devoid of anything larger than a seagull.

Best get this over with.

The water was blood warm, gently slipping up his legs with a salty caress. Its near-tropical clarity revealed rippling sand at his feet, marked by tide and countless swimmers. Further out, he dove beneath the waves and struck out for deeper waters. The seabed fell away gradually.

Taking advantage of necessity, he swam for several minutes, working out the tension in his body by staying underwater for long stretches to study the marine life around him. The exercise was exactly what he needed. By the time he returned to the beach, he'd regained his equanimity and was once more focused on his objective.

Everything was a means to an end, even this swim. Nothing could be allowed to stand in the way of the mission.

A half hour later, Damon was less confident. Enough time had passed without contact that doubt began to niggle at him. Had his master thief changed her mind? Or had he misunderstood her message? This was the first time anyone had deliberately communicated with him through a dream. Who knew what she'd actually meant to tell him?

At the next umbrella, the blonde got to her feet with sensuous fluidity and entered the water. Feminine grace incarnate in one sexy package.

Despite his concerns of a no-show, Damon was hard-pressed

to ignore the way the sun gilded her body. Even when her hair got soaked and darkened to pale gold, it didn't diminish her distracting appeal. He fought to remain unmoved, not wanting to embarrass himself with a very visible hard-on barely restrained by the abbreviated trunks that had been all that was available at the hotel's gift shop. But not looking didn't mean oblivious.

She remained in the shallows, splashing with childlike delight, the sounds of her enjoyment unconscionably loud to his pricked ears. Her gurgles of laughter were like velvet caresses across his skin. Did she take the same pleasure in bed, equally sensual in lovemaking as in her play?

He practiced deep breathing to quell his swelling cock, tried to derail the stirrings of desire by reviewing the project that had been interrupted by this assignment. When that didn't work, he was forced to resort to draping his towel across his lap to hide the visible evidence of his defeat.

And not a moment too soon.

Unable to help himself, he stole a glance at the sea just as the blonde walked out of the surf, a living Venus rising from the waves, her wet bikini clinging to her skin and leaving little to the imagination. The sunlight sparkling on the water didn't help, highlighting as it did her damp curves.

Heat scorched him at the sight, an unexpectedly strong response after his stroll through the pool area. He forced himself to swallow against the sudden tightness of his throat. *Damn it, Venizélos, get your mind out of your pants!* The problem was, it wasn't his mind that was coming out of his trunks. It seemed that all the seduction dreams he'd sent his master thief, and last night's explosive sex on the museum's rooftop, had only whetted his appetite.

Torn between duty and salacity, Damon cursed beneath his

breath, silently, prayerfully, unsure whether he hoped she would walk in his direction or not. This was one of the most fucked-up assignments he'd ever been given!

He was so focused on the shapely spectacle before him that he nearly didn't notice the footsteps crunching on the sand behind him.

A uniformed waiter came up, bearing a plate in one hand and napkins in the other. "Your order, sir." He presented the dish and two dessert forks with a flourish, set them on the napkins, then took his leave with the discretion of excellent training.

Upon seeing the decorative strips of snowy white fruit, Damon bit back his protest. Now that he thought about it, the dream had had something about coconut. Was this finally the prelude to contact?

He cast his mental sense out, fishing for a hint of what to expect. The nearest emissions he picked up were the blonde's in front of him and the waiter's vanishing into the incoherent buzz around the poolside. There was no one else.

But, still, the dessert had been in the dream.

Damon eyed the plate and forks dubiously. Now what was he supposed to do?

Just then, the blonde walked up to him. Her breasts bounced jauntily, the full slopes tanned a golden pink, the minimal cover of her wet bikini top stretched taut over perky nipples aimed right at him.

He swore in an undertone. Normally, he'd have been more appreciative of the bountiful display of female flesh before him, but right now he couldn't afford the distraction.

"You look lonely." Her husky delivery was pure bedroom voice—making him extremely grateful for the towel over his groin.

"I'm waiting for someone," Damon forced out through the tightness of his throat.

"Not anymore." She dimpled at him, looking entirely too certain of her welcome as she settled on the sand beside him. "Mmm . . . coconut custard. Exactly what I ordered." She picked up a fork and sliced a corner off. Meeting his gaze with unnerving directness, she offered him the morsel balanced on silver tines. "Have a bite."

Shock had him accepting the tidbit and chewing, not tasting what he ate. This was it, he realized. She was his contact. He stared at her creamy skin, which, despite its sun-kissed flush, was hardly the dusky complexion of the slippery master thief who'd screwed him senseless. The shape of her eyes and the length of her nose were also different; not even plastic surgery could account for the situation.

Damon swallowed absently, his mind going into overdrive as he tried to make sense of the disparity. A thieving ring? That was the only possibility except . . .

She'd ordered the coconut custard? But his master thief had been the one who'd sent him that message. He knew her touch. She'd recognized him in the dream!

He stared at her, this time deliberately probing with his mental sense. Now that she was focused on him, he recognized the cool determination he'd picked up when his master thief had climbed the museum's wall. Her aura was one and the same— there was no mistaking it.

"You?"

Despite appearances to the contrary, she had to be the master thief who'd eluded him. He continued to stare, stunned by his discovery. The difference was as jarring as . . . that Asian woman and the bleached blonde who'd replaced her. How had she pulled it off? She'd actually made him doubt his mental sense.

She took a bite of custard. "This is really good. You should have some more."

He ignored the meaningless remark, still grappling with her disguises. "You're the one?"

"You tell me." She sucked on the tines of her fork, her full lips puckered suggestively. "You've been entering my dreams. Traipsing around in my head. Manipulating me." Despite the blunt accusation, her delivery was calm and unemotional, her aura only tinged with wariness and curiosity. "What are you?" Her level stare demanded equal candor.

"An incubus, of course," Damon heard himself answer flippantly, with enough amusement in his voice to make a joke out of honesty. He could only hope she'd find it too ridiculous to give credence.

"An incubus?" Her brows winged up before knitting over her nose as her gaze sharpened, the jade hue of her irises darkening to bottle green with flecks of blue along the outer edges—no way that color came from tinted contact lenses. "Of course," she added, her voice soft with apperception.

Fuck, she'd taken him seriously. He shifted the discussion to safer waters. "So, how did you get to the other building so quickly?"

Still playing with her fork, she smiled, sphinxlike in her self-possession. "If I did, it's a secret."

Fair enough. He was here to acquire her services, nothing else. So long as they didn't impact the mission, she could keep her professional secrets.

"Have some more," she insisted, gesturing at the plate.

Wondering if she'd had the custard drugged—with truth

serum, maybe; how else to explain his inadvertent honesty?—
Damon took a bite, this time paying attention to what he ate.
Sweet and creamy, but nothing out of the ordinary—unlike his
companion. His incorrigible libido leaped at the unfortunate
description, his cock twitching in response beneath its plush
terry-cloth camouflage. "It is good, but that's not the point."

She shrugged, the movement flexing her bountiful assets ad-
mirably. "You're the one who asked for this meeting. To discuss
something, you said." Her excitement and attraction lapped at
his senses, belying the cool smile she gave him. Though she hid
it well, she was intrigued. "Well, what is it?"

He set his fork down, determined to get down to business.
"It's come to our attention that you excel in . . . clandestine acquisitions."

"Whose attention? You're a Fed."

Nodding, Damon cautiously fished out his official ID from
his trunks—to keep from flashing her—and handed it over.
"You probably haven't heard of us. Leastwise you shouldn't
have."

Holding the plastic card by the edges, she studied his picture
and data, then flipped the ID over to read the back. "Could be a
fake. Though Venizélos is a mouthful, so that part might be real
enough."

But that wasn't the mouthful he wanted to give her.

Damon's belly clenched as desire flared against his will, hot
and urgent, so strong he felt it deep in his bones. Damn it, he refused to let her get the upper hand in this. Sex was how she'd
escaped him last time. He couldn't let himself be distracted by
his libido again.

Not on a mission this important.

"That's as real as it gets," he snapped out, his jaw aching from the effort to keep the conversation professional. He extended his hand, silently demanding the return of his ID.

"Which doesn't tell me much. Like why you wanted to meet." She gave the card back, still holding it by the edges. Her care meant she didn't leave any fingerprints, but it also spoke well of her competence. "Well?"

He turned his gaze to the gentle surf, hoping to scale back his innate aggression, so his next statement would be less confrontational. The outcome of this negotiation was too important for ego. "We need you to steal something."

She gave a soft grunt of skepticism. "Why should I even listen to you?"

Damon considered what his mental sense was telling him before answering. "Because you're bored."

Rory blinked at his perceptive retort, further proof of his inexplicable knowledge. Wondering if he really thought she'd be that easy to catch, she arched a brow and widened her eyes, putting on what she considered to be an award-winning show of disbelief. Too bad he continued to watch the waves and didn't get the benefit of her acting. "Assuming I'm actually in the acquisitions business, you mind telling me what you're after?"

Her Adonis kept his eyes trained at the horizon, his clean profile almost heroic. "A nuke."

To give herself time to think, Rory laughed. Had she been mistaken and he wasn't a Fed after all? "You're kidding me!"

"I'm dead serious."

"You want me to stroll into some military base, load one of those big suckers on a truck, and drive off with it?" The mere thought was ridiculous.

He turned his head to give her a warm smile that made her insides jitter in a most unfair manner. "It's a baby nuke, just about the size of carry-on luggage"—his expression blanked so completely it was as though he'd been born grim—"in the hands of terrorists."

Conscious of the gritty sand heating up her backside, Rory sat there, her lips stretched wide, waiting for the punch line to his joke. Surely he didn't think she had anything to do with that violent lot.

"We need you to liberate it."

She stared at him in horrified fascination, losing her smile as he continued to meet her eyes with a level gaze that brooked no nonsense. He was *serious*. Cold dread swept up her spine. "And how did terrorists get their hands on a nuke?"

"The Russians lost it. While its payload can be measured in kilotons, it can still mean hundreds—if not thousands—of lives." His gorgeous features hardened into a mask of bleak anger. "New York, Chicago, Washington." He named the cities deliberately, as though knowing she'd spent time in all three, his deep voice like a death knell. "The consequences don't bear thinking of."

The Fed's unswerving gaze made it difficult to maintain her incredulity. He told his story quite well—so well that she had to suppress an instinctive shiver of horror. Still, she wasn't born yesterday.

"And you want me to steal it for you." She raised a brow that wanted to tremble, forcing it to arch steadily. "From terrorists."

He shook his head curtly. "From an arms dealer who's auctioning it off to terrorists."

That was scarcely an improvement. "Where?"

"Kosovo."

Rory heard his answer through a roaring in her ears, a sense of unreality enfolding her. Of course Kosovo. If he'd said China or Korea or one of the Stans, she could have protested that her grasp of the local dialects wasn't good enough to pass. But it hadn't been that long since her jaunt to Peć, a town in the UN protectorate. Language wouldn't be a problem.

"Yes," he continued, as if she'd spoken aloud, "the Ipek Crucifix. It's why we chose you—someone who can operate in the Balkans without drawing attention." An admiring smile lifted the corners of his chiseled mouth. "The theft was flawless. Not a trace left behind. No one had a clue who could've done it."

"Except you."

Her Adonis shook his head. "This isn't my usual gig. I was brought in much later. But from what I'd heard, the team was chasing ghosts, building a file full of negative results."

With his talent for tripping through a person's dreams, Rory had to wonder what his "usual gig" was, but that was irrelevant to the discussion. Needing to shield her thoughts from his scrutiny, she broke eye contact, dropping her gaze to the pale dessert between them. One thing was for certain: it didn't sound boring. "Okay, from an arms dealer in Kosovo. Why should I?"

"I'm authorized to offer you three million dollars, half up front, for your services." The Fed's abs tightened into a mouthwatering display of washboard ripples in her peripheral vision, momentarily distracting her from their conversation.

"Really now? In exchange for risking life and limb?" Smirking, she used her fork to doodle on the custard's surface, while her mind raced. Swipe a nuke from under the noses of terrorists? The challenge made her heart leap and gave her the shivers. "That's a paltry figure. Isn't the going rate rather higher?"

"You won't be working alone."

Rory looked up in surprise, her gaze immediately caught by his dark stare. "Oh?"

"I'll be with you."

"And that's supposed to be better . . . how?" She fed herself some custard, deliberately making a show of sucking the fork's tines clean. By the flicker of his eyes, it hadn't gone unnoticed. Good. She needed every advantage she could get.

He snorted, his nostrils flaring attractively. And, man, was she in trouble if she noticed that! "How much?"

The waves lapped against the beach while she debated how safe it would be to answer. Her Adonis hadn't asked her any incriminating questions, hadn't even fished for details after that one reference to the Peć job. "Seven and a half, U.S., five up front, and I'll consider it."

"I'll have to get authorization."

"You do that." Setting her fork on the plate with a gentle clink, Rory stood up, wanting to be the one who ended the discussion. She suspected the Fed could gain the upper hand, if she wasn't careful.

Her womb clenched, her folds growing moist at the memory of having him above her last night, thick and hard and desperate, grinding her into the grass as he pumped her. She steeled her spine against the temptation to make an exception in his case. Just because there were exceptions to every rule didn't mean he had to be one of them.

Surprisingly, he let her walk away without protest, not even trying to trail her. Or maybe not so surprising, if he could enter her dreams any time he wanted.

It did prick Rory's feminine pride that he hadn't tried to convince her to stay longer, after she'd gone to the effort of Changing into a voluptuous beach bunny. After last night on the rooftop, she'd half expected to spend the rest of the afternoon performing acts of indecency on the beach.

———— ∝∝o ————

Returning to her hotel room, Rory channel surfed until she found a show that she could stand hearing in the background, more as a habit than some vague suspicion that her room was bugged. Medical dramas were her show of choice, catering to her taste for the forbidden and the unknown. As a lamia, normal human physiology fascinated her.

Keeping a low profile meant diScipios never went to hospitals or consulted a medical professional who wasn't family, which made them a point of acute interest. The risk of discovery, however, was too much to allow, so she fed her prurience through TV whenever she could; though she did wonder if the shows reflected reality more accurately than the episodes of *Mission Impossible*.

With medical jargon as comfort noise, she went online and sent out electronic feelers, researching her Adonis and his challenge the same way she would any other commission.

"Damon. Damon Venizélos." Rory rolled his name in her mouth, letting it flow over her tongue like fine wine. A strong name—dark, full-bodied, and exotic—certainly more flavorful than James Bond or Matt Helm. An intriguing man with an even more intriguing commission. But was he serious? Could it be a trap?

If it was a scam, it was an elaborate setup—one specifically tailored to appeal to her.

And if it was a trap, her Adonis's easy admission of being something other than normal was an unorthodox approach. *An incubus.* Granted, he hadn't really taken physical form when he'd seduced her mind, but who better than a lamia to know that myth didn't always get things right?

Too, the target itself was irregular. They couldn't frame her for stealing a nuke, not when she'd have five thousand grand to prove they'd hired her to do the job.

And who would devise such a convoluted plot to acquire a bomb? If he was a front for a terrorist organization, surely there were easier—and cheaper—ways to guarantee they ended up winning the auction?

Rory couldn't imagine why anyone would go to the lengths his agency had apparently taken simply to trap or scam her. Which made the Fed's story more credible.

Knowing what was at stake, she could excuse his invasion of her sleep and his manipulation. But she wasn't ready to forgive him just yet. It still stung that he'd used her dreams against her . . . and that she'd fallen into his trap so readily. Granted, she hadn't even considered the possibility of an incubus screwing with her head—she'd never met one before, as far as she knew—but that didn't mean she shouldn't have questioned why she'd been driven to find that dildo.

In retrospect, she'd been a pushover taking the easy way out. The realization was galling. If Felix ever heard of how she'd almost been caught, he'd never tap her for another job. She made a face. Not one of her relatives would blame him. Heck, in his shoes, she'd do the same.

The responses that trickled in were ambiguous enough to feel legit. But almost before her inquiries produced results, Rory knew that her Adonis had her. Unless something obviously pointed to a setup, she intended to accept the commission.

She might be a thief, but even she had principles. Some

things were worth standing up for. She didn't do drugs. She didn't con people out of their life savings. She didn't kill.

Money was money, but murder got the cops hot for your tail. Any diScipio worth his name knew better than to draw that kind of attention.

Terrorists, in her estimation, were the muck at the bottom of the barrel, since they were out to destroy the world and life as she knew it. If they won, what would be left to steal?

And if terrorists got their hands on the bomb . . .

The thought of a nuke blowing up New York or Las Vegas or even Paris, in fact any major city her family might be in—and there were many since diScipios preferred to be moving targets and sought concealment among large populations—was unacceptable; Rory couldn't imagine that any terrorist would target Nowheresville, U.S.A. That meant she had to do something. The consequences of inaction were too dire for her to do otherwise.

To get the ball rolling, she started a checklist for what she might need for the job. Just to be on the safe side, she also dropped a note to Lucas to see if he'd heard anything. Unlike Felix, Big Brother would give her room to play, and he wouldn't tell the rest of the family what she was up to unless she pushed too many of his buttons.

And if something went wrong?

Rory shrugged to herself. Lucas would have a clue where to start looking for her body. She'd long accepted that her line of work had its risks, but so did ordinary office work. The one time she'd tried that, she'd nearly been bored to death despite the excitement of having to dodge the beat-the-clock messengers hurtling through their delivery routes, and, on one occasion, a disgruntled former employee shooting up the shipping warehouse next door. In many ways, being a cat burglar was safer.

It also gave her more control, better pay, and challenges worthy of her ability.

And, damn it, this job *was* a challenge. One she couldn't resist as—she suspected—the Fed well knew.

But that didn't mean her Adonis would have everything his way. Just because she'd decided to accept the commission, it didn't automatically follow that she couldn't have her vacation fling. Her mouth stretched in a reckless grin as she pondered her prospects.

Oh, yes. She intended to have her beefcake and eat it.

Or him, as the case may be.

CHAPTER SIX

He'd let her walk away without a firm commitment. After all, she was right. She would be risking life and limb; only a fool would sign up for that on the spot. Since they'd be partners, he was glad she'd shown a measure of self-preservation, despite her precarious line of work.

Nevertheless, it bothered Damon to be so passive, to have to wait for someone else to render her decision based on factors he knew nothing about. Unlike with the Old Man, he had no idea which way his master thief would jump. It made him twitchy, as if a set of crosshairs were centered on the back of his head. Mustering patience was one thing on a hunt; this current operation was entirely different.

Once he'd gotten the Old Man's approval for the payoff,

there was nothing left for him to do except wait . . . and kill some time.

Untying and studying the rope she'd used at the museum didn't take long. About two hundred feet of smooth, red-purple-black braided nylon attached to a three-prong grapnel, and not a single knot to make climbing easier, the rope had the earmarks of a familiar implement that she'd want back. Smiling, he recoiled it and carefully tied it off, making sure his tiny addition wasn't visible. Given how quickly she could turn the tables on him, he needed every advantage he could beg, borrow, or steal.

Damon had to resist the temptation to relive that hot encounter on the museum rooftop. It wouldn't do to fixate on it, especially now that there was a chance they'd be partners. The intimacy of a working relationship alone would be enough of a strain; there was no point in adding an affair on top of it.

To distract himself, he took out his cell phone and clicked through his files, returning to the project that had been interrupted by his assignment to this unexpected and highly irregular recruitment effort. If he couldn't control his master thief's decision, he might as well work on something he could control. He plugged earbuds into the small unit and played back sound clips of his target talking, acquainting himself with the man's speech patterns.

He immersed himself in his review, blocking the importance of one woman's agreement from the forefront of his mind. Impatience was rarely productive.

Over the long hours of waiting, he refreshed his memory of potential targets, running video and audio files over and over until he was familiar with them forward and back, examining their histories and failures, searching for vulnerability. Whatever her decision was, he'd still have his other mission to accomplish.

That auction presented too good an opportunity to throw the enemy into disarray to pass up.

"Ahem."

The discreet throat clearing from the balcony's shadows caught Damon by surprise. Leaping off the bed, he spun to face the intruder, his .45 appearing in his hand by reflex.

"If you use that, I won't be able to fulfill your commission," a jaunty soprano pointed out, its owner remaining out of sight.

His sudden exhilaration at the sound of that voice was another surprise. "You're in?" He lowered his gun.

"If you meet my terms, maybe." His master thief stepped into the light, dressed all in black, her blond hair tucked under a knit cap. Crossing the room on silent feet, she walked up to him, the bland walls of the hotel room throwing her dark curves into high contrast.

Despite the enigmatic smile on her face, relief flooded Damon at her answer, leeching the tension from his shoulders. The emotions he picked up didn't suggest overweening triumph or self-satisfaction at being able to dictate terms. She was in. Whatever addendum she wanted to attach, he was sure it would be reasonable. "You'll get your seven point five." He slid the semiautomatic back into its holster, making sure it was snugged down safely.

She tilted her head to one side, studying him with speculative dark green eyes. Excitement radiated from her in tantalizing waves that lapped at his mental sense like a hungry kitten. "One more condition."

Damon raised a brow in inquiry. The Old Man had readily agreed to her price and seemed to consider it a bargain. So long as she didn't double her price, they would soon have an agreement. "Name it."

Her full mouth quirked, deviltry sparkling in her eyes. She

laid her hands on his chest, a light contact that sizzled. "You in bed."

What?! His heart stuttered in confusion.

She stroked him slowly—possessively—her touch certain, leaving fire in its wake. Despite himself, his cock stirred in response. Her meaning couldn't be clearer. Especially when one hand slid down to outline that traitorous, twitching member and coax it to aching erection. Her attentions threatened to short-circuit what functional brain cells he had left.

"You want me as a lover?" Damon gasped out, around the exquisite torture of her knowledgeable fingers.

"Um-hmm," she murmured agreeably. "Put all that imagination to good use."

He recognized the reference to his conversation with that pretty artist. Had his master thief overheard them or was the artist an accomplice?

Irrelevant. How she'd found out had no impact on their negotiations. But her condition was the last thing he'd have predicted.

Damon had accepted the necessity of working with someone to recover the nuke and had resigned himself to an alliance with a thief. However, the prolonged and greater intimacy she proposed took him unawares. Weeks as her lover when he normally limited himself to one-night stands? Could he let her that close?

She smiled up at him, clearly aware of his quandary. Her fingers continued their dexterous encouragement, fanning the flames of arousal she'd kindled in his balls. There was no hiding his response. And given what had happened the other night, she knew he wasn't immune to her attractions. Yet while she reciprocated his desire, he could sense cool control at the heart of her, directing her actions.

This was a power play. More proof that she was the right person for the job. He gritted his teeth, fighting to maintain a calm demeanor in the face of her extreme provocation. But when her fingers danced over his hard-on, he could only widen his stance and let her fondle him to even greater firmness.

"How many women are we talking about?" Damon barely got the question past his tight throat, wanting full contact, aching to have her hands on him, caressing him, with nothing in between.

A triumphant grin flashed across her face at his question. "Just one. Me." The husky murmur played havoc with his libido.

Her and him. Alone. Naked.

Damon fought to rein in his randy imagination and clear his head. Two could play that game. His master thief wasn't going to get the upper hand without a fight.

Looking straight into her jade green eyes, he unbuttoned his shirt. "I'm game." Let the chips fall where they would; this mission was more important than his self-protective concerns.

She took him up on his challenge, her nimble fingers quickly unbuckling his belt. Her hands slid under his pants, pushing them off his hips, along with his briefs, in one impatient motion.

Leaving him clad only in his shirt . . . and even that didn't stay on long. She tugged it off his shoulders and flung it away, rendering him naked before her.

Her arousal flared as she stared at him, mirroring the hot flush that swept her high cheekbones. At least she wasn't unmoved. He'd have hated it if she were doing all this merely as a power play.

"Like what you see?" Damon puffed out his chest, getting into the spirit of her game. Just because he had to didn't mean he couldn't enjoy himself.

She licked her glossy pink lips before answering. "Oh, definitely."

"How about some equality, here?" He slid his fingers along her jumpsuit's lapels consideringly. He'd have sworn it was the same one from the night on the museum rooftop. Except she wasn't. He dismissed the puzzle for the time being, more concerned with clinching her agreement. "I'd hate to have to tear this off."

"Maybe next time?" she suggested eagerly with a playful glint in her eyes.

His master thief's rejoinder startled a laugh out of him. Maybe this enforced intimacy wouldn't be so bad, after all. The zipper hummed on its slow descent, building his anticipation as the black fabric parted to reveal pale skin, not dusky or sun kissed—totally unmarked by tan lines.

For an instant, doubt stirred.

It was one thing to go from pale to tanned. Damon knew there were all sorts of lotions and cosmetics that made it possible. But he'd seen for himself the golden tan she'd had on the beach. That hadn't been the product of a bottle. Yet here she was, all peaches and cream.

But his mental sense said she was the same woman. No matter what he saw on the outside, she was his master thief. He'd doubted himself once, but with his mental antennae and her claiming the same thing, he had to accept that she was the same woman. To do otherwise meant doubting the inner sense that had saved him on more occasions than he could count.

He pushed the jumpsuit off her shoulders, needing to see more of her. Wondering how far her disguise went.

Not that she made exploring her easy. She played her hands over him, doing some exploration of her own.

Her movements were distracting, to say the least. Especially when she ran her blunt nails over and around his nipples, provoking a shiver of delight. He'd never been particularly sensitive there before.

But Damon persevered.

Pulling her closer, he bent down to nuzzle her neck, getting a whiff of nothing more than light sweat and pure woman. No perfume. No lotion. No powder. No chemicals. No explanation for the fairness of her complexion.

A quick lick of her shoulder only reinforced his findings. Slightly salty, but no artificial enhancements. She was exactly as she appeared to be. For some reason, that only made his cock thicken even more.

His master thief shivered in his arms. "I hope you don't bite."

"Not usually." Though now that she mentioned it, he was tempted . . . and more than tempted, once he managed to uncover her breasts. Duty'd never looked so good.

Her areolas were large, puffy, and brownish pink, tipped with hard candy ready for sucking and quickly growing tighter. Certainly worth a nibble or two.

He took one in his mouth, drawing on the toffee nubbin, and plucked the other with his fingers. Surprise and delight dealt him double body blows as she squealed and writhed in his arms; clearly, his master thief was an unusually sensitive woman.

Despite the onslaught, Damon grinned to himself, gratified by her passionate response. While she might have gotten him into her bed, she wouldn't be calling all the shots—not if he had anything to say about it.

"Oh, you're good." She wrapped her arms around him, anchoring herself as she pressed her breast to his mouth. "And you feel even better."

She swept her hands up his back, across his shoulders, then down to his ass, her palms maintaining constant, steady contact as though she were surveying him for purchase or memorizing every inch of skin.

The sensual fire of her touch made Damon hiss, so aware was he of it. Never before had he felt so claimed.

"I want you," she whispered as she pressed her body against his, her jade eyes darkening to the green of holly leaves.

"Good." At least this treacherous desire wasn't one-sided. It was time to show her she wouldn't have everything her way. Pushing her jumpsuit off her hips, he dragged her minuscule bikini down her legs and pulled the black cap off her head, spilling wavy, white-gold locks across her shoulders.

She'd challenged his imagination? Well, then, he'd give her exactly what she'd asked for.

Burying his hands in her hair, he pressed kisses along her neck and collarbone, once more noting the fairness of the fine, silky skin beneath his lips. How was it possible?

"Mmm . . . that's nice." Despite the way her body shivered against his, the hint of doubt in her voice suggested that his lovemaking technique was on trial, stirring memories of the night at the museum.

"I'm just getting started." Damon pivoted around her, catching her elbow to hold her in place while he moved behind her. Then he resumed his kisses, tracing the firm muscles of her back with his mouth, then down along the curve of her spine.

"What are you up to?"

"You said you wanted me to use my imagination, right?" Kneeling, he paused to nip the upper slope of her high, round ass, noting its muscular firmness and promising himself a more thorough exploration of her body in the future.

She squealed in surprise. "Yes . . ."

"There's something I've always wanted to try." With her flexibility and physical strength, she would probably have no problem with the position he had in mind.

Already stiff and throbbing from the sensual byplay, his cock jerked with excitement at the prospect. The dominance of it held a dark appeal.

Her fingers tangled in his hair, pulling back until he met her gaze over her hip. "You mean there's something you haven't done before?"

Damon wasn't worried he'd scare her off. To his mental sense, she glittered with golden curiosity, not the muddier "hues" of caution. "Yes."

"I'm game," she informed him, running her hand through his hair, then releasing him in a gesture of permission.

"Kneel down."

She obeyed with a curious smile, going to her knees beside the bed, keeping her back toward him. Then she bent forward at the waist and arched her back, lifting her ass saucily. Her wide stance presented him with an irresistible image: her dark pink pussy lips spread wide in welcome and gleaming with cream.

The minx!

He took her up on that invitation. Easing closer behind her, he set his cock head against her slit and carefully worked it in, mindful of his size and her level of arousal.

Oh, God, she was so damned tight!

Panting softly, she pushed back, meeting his thrust, trying to take more of him, but she just wasn't ready enough, even though he wasn't as large as he would be later. She persisted, though, groaning and gasping while her pussy milked and squeezed his sensitive head.

Just the sound of her struggling made him feel enormous.

Damon paused to give both of them time to adjust to the delicious contact, while he figured out the mechanics for what he wanted to do next. As he'd said, he'd never tried that particular position before.

After a while, her breathing slowed and her inner muscles relaxed a bit, letting him press deeper, working more of his length into her body. Then still more, until finally his belly brushed her backside.

He held her in place, savoring her yielding flesh and the slick heat surrounding him. Damn, she felt good, and this was only the first step.

"Hmmm." Propping her elbows on the mattress, she looked over her shoulder at him and arched a brow in an expression of gentle tolerance, obviously having recovered her composure. "This is hardly—"

Hooking his hands under her thighs, Damon got to his feet and raised her up along with him, off her knees and into the air, and into his thrust. Her legs clamped around his hips spasmodically—an unexpected blast of raw sensation that nearly shattered his control.

They gasped in chorus, her grabbing the bed, him rocking on his heels while he fought to regain his equilibrium. The motion only drove him deeper, setting his cock jerking and twitching in her velvet wetness. Her heels clapped on his back, pulling him into even tighter contact.

Damon gritted his teeth against the urge to let loose. How the fuck could he overwhelm her with his imagination, if he shot his load at the first flash of pleasure?

It didn't help his self-control to see the round cheeks of her gorgeous ass clenched before him, the contrast of the pale curves with his dark arms emphasizing their differences. He wanted to fondle the mounds, to knead and caress and feel for himself if they were as tender as they looked.

And below them, her pink pussy lips stretched wide around his cock, straining to take him. He'd never felt more of a man than right then. A sudden, rapacious hunger made his heart leap. His cock hardened further, swelling as more blood rushed south.

His thief gave a low, breathless moan, her fingers digging into the sky blue coverlet, her hair a fall of pale gold against all the color. She tottered unsteadily.

"Um . . ." Finally, a note of uncertainty from the woman who'd thrown him off his stride from the first time they'd met.

He found that he had no taste for being the cause of it. He preferred her brash self-confidence and unashamed sensuality. "Put your weight on your forearms."

She did, her shifting balance swirling delight around his cock. "Oh! Oh, my." Her strong legs tightened their grip around his waist, securing her balance and squeezing him with her inner muscles.

The rippling caress flowed up his length, a nerve-searing sweetness that threatened to melt his knees. It was too much to take standing still.

Hitching her higher, Damon began to move. Since her stance kept him from withdrawing, he tilted his pelvis experimentally, first one way, then another, trying to find the most pleasurable angles. His reward came immediately: the motions amplified the carnal friction, eliciting more of that fluttering response. Sparkles of delight frothed through his cock to burst like champagne bubbles in his balls.

When his simple efforts were met with low, feminine growls of unqualified approval, he decided to attempt a faster beat. It would take more than that to win her over, and if her acceptance of the mission depended on his performance, he had to prove to her he was worth it.

A wave of pure delight rose from her at the shift in his motions. Adjusting quickly, she danced with him, her body twisting and swaying to his direction.

Damon smiled to himself, elated by the success of his maneuver. With her legs locked around him, he didn't have to use his hands to support her . . . and his master thief was vulnerable to his exploration, unable to release him without falling. It was an opportunity not to be missed.

With growing confidence, he let his hands wander, sliding them down to her hips, then up, discovering the silken skin around her groin, the taut rippling of her belly, the plush softness of her breasts. All tender flesh and vigorous muscle waiting to be claimed, flowing in a primal rhythm that couldn't be denied.

The gasps that met his caresses spurred him on, incited a need to hear more—lower and louder.

She quivered beneath his palms and stiffened when he captured her breasts, a whimper of need escaping her as she squirmed in his grasp. Long, hard nubs ground against his palms; if his mental sense hadn't been already awash with her delight, her distended nipples would still be incontrovertible proof of her arousal.

It soothed something inside him. The memory of her easy desertion of his lovemaking at the museum had stung.

This time, Damon had every intention of pushing her beyond anything she could imagine. He rocked his hips, hissing as his sensitive cock head ground over the hard mass of her G-spot, the contact like a match to gasoline, sending him up in flames.

She cried out in surprise, her lush pleasure a scarlet tenderness like velvet across his mental sense—unexpected and completely seductive. Arching her back, she answered his thrusts with her own, her legs locked tight.

He could sense her excitement increasing with each bump and grind, each rock and roll of their bodies. He wasn't immune to it himself, hard-pressed not to lose himself to the siren song of burning ecstasy. But not just yet.

Damon attacked her G-spot, bringing all his carnal attention to bear on that responsive flesh.

A throaty moan of desire filled the sultry night, low and needy, passionate and honest. No hiding her hunger. Her raw excitement fed his own, fanning the flames into a roaring wildfire that demanded his submission.

"Oh, God!" Her legs spasmed around his hips, her heels digging into his back.

Just a little more. She was right at the edge.

Hanging on to the shreds of his control by his clenched teeth, he stepped up his motions, fighting the aching pressure in his cock with everything he had.

Need coiled in Damon's balls, tightening around them until it was all he could do to restrain his fast-rising orgasm. Not yet! He wasn't done yet.

The carnal storm broke with sudden, breathtaking violence.

Brilliant color slashed across his mental sense as she convulsed around him, a low moan escaping her in the throes of her release. She gushed over him, as exuberant in her delight as in her lovemaking.

He fought to resist the call of ecstasy as she gave in to hers, straining to hang on to his vanishing control as she battered his mental sense with wave after volcanic wave of pure rapture. The glorious, incendiary moment stretched out forever, tantalizing him with sweet relief—if only he would give in.

"Oh, jeez," she panted, her soprano throaty with bliss. Her arms collapsed under her. "Wow." The haze of pleasure about her suggested it was an honest expression of her sentiments.

Damon couldn't have phrased it better. *Wow.* He'd barely managed to stop himself from taking his pleasure. His thighs shook with the effort, his balls throbbing thick and heavy. But he couldn't take his release yet. He had more planned for his master thief.

Reluctantly withdrawing his cock from her fluttering pussy, he lowered her to the bed and turned her over, onto her back, encountering no resistance—she was that limp. He must have really gotten to her, he realized, gratified by his success. But he wasn't done yet.

She just lay there, gasping softly, her pulse fluttering at her throat, her rapid breathing drawing his gaze to her flushed, full breasts. Pliant and contented. Ripe for taking. She smiled at him lazily, supremely female in her boneless lassitude.

But not for long.

He had a mission to fulfill.

Damon caught his breath and shored up his control, preparing for stage two. She had challenged his imagination, made sex a requirement for her acceptance of the job. He couldn't stop until he was certain of her complete satisfaction.

Kneeling on the bed between her legs, he dragged her onto his lap. Ruffling the pale curls at the junction of her thighs, he parted the dark pink folds of her pussy and slid in, biting back a groan as she surrounded his length with sensual heat. Slick, creamy female flesh clasping him firmly, squeezing him with powerful muscles. Fluttering over him.

"What—?" She gaped at him, wide-eyed, her aura hazing over with confusion.

"Shhh." Gripping her ass, he kneaded her cheeks as he drove deeper into the tight sheath of her body.

"Oh, God. You're not done?"

Damon grinned down at her startled face, confidence surging at her reaction. "Not by far."

He trapped her that way, her legs splayed wide, her back arched extravagantly over his knees, her breasts lifted in offering. She might be a master thief, but there was only so much she could do while flat on her back—and he didn't intend to let her get away until he was through.

With his throbbing cock buried inside her wet flesh, he bent forward, spreading her thighs further, to brush light kisses across her taut belly. Her abs rippled under his lips. She was in damn good shape, which was only to be expected, given the physical requirements of her chosen profession. But that didn't mean he couldn't appreciate the results.

"Ooooh." Her pussy spasmed around him in quicksilver quivers of excitement as her head thrashed from side to side, the motion setting her breasts bobbing.

He rolled his hips, swirling her heated, creamy welcome around his length. The sensual woman couldn't deny she liked that, and everything else he was doing to her.

Leading with his mouth, Damon mapped her torso from her concave belly to her full breasts with their brownish pink tips all tight and suckable. Hard candy waiting just for him.

Despite the enforced intimacy, being her lover promised not to be that much of a hardship. He nuzzled the soft slopes of her breasts, then caught her long nipples with his fingers and between his teeth, the sharp gasp that greeted his actions sweet music to his ears. Certainly there were compensations.

He took his leisure this time, determined to hold out until she begged. Now that he was in a better position to contain her movements, he could make the game last longer.

Lying on top of her, Damon could feel each and every response she betrayed. A gulp for breath. A shudder of pleasure. The goose bumps that greeted his suckling on her breast. The heating of her skin that accompanied the deepening of her flush of arousal. The soft exhalation barely heard that magnified her flagrant delight.

Just the knowledge was heady in itself.

Then there was her flavor.

Salt and sweetness. The scent of her musk rising between them, driving home the reality of sex. Something he rarely got in dreams.

Damon withdrew slowly, just enough for friction. To savor the sensation of skin on skin, her tight pussy clinging to his cock as he inched out. Not so far that he slid out of the clasp of her body.

Then he reversed his motion, gliding back in.

Sobbing, she undulated in his arms, trying to twist higher, demanding more. "I need to move, damn it!"

"Nah, you don't have to."

"Are you saying you know better?"

"My scene, my imagination. How do you know you won't like it, if you don't try it?" Nibbling on her soft breast, Damon rocked his hips, eliciting more of that tingling delight. "Unless you're scared?"

"Fat chance." A strangled scoff that ended in a mewl of excitement when he reached between them to strum her clit.

"I'm not hurting you, am I?" His eyes threatened to roll back in his head as she milked his length in a series of lightning-quick spasms. He buried his face in her cleavage and practiced deep breathing before he lost it, reminding himself of the many virtues of patience—which unfortunately meant more clit work was a no-go.

She tangled her fingers in his hair, pulling his head back to accuse him huskily: "You're enjoying this." Her green eyes shot sparks at him, her aura just as colorful with its flashes of lust and temper.

"Yeah? How can you tell?" Damon laughed softly, enjoying having the whip hand for once. The thrum of desire in his balls had backed down to a low flame, allowing him the pleasure of delicacy. The gentle thrills of delight, not just the frenzied kick of passion.

His master thief cursed him, low and fervently, as he continued his slow buildup, playing his cock inside her and swirling his length along her creamy sheath. If he had to be her lover, he might as well get the most out of it.

Ecstasy beckoned irresistibly, urging him to move faster. But not just yet. Now that he had the advantage on her, he wanted to hold on to it a little longer.

Damon strung out the moment. Holding them both balanced on the edge of climax. Slowing down when the pleasure threatened to overwhelm his control. Resuming his pace after he'd backed off from the point of no return.

Fireworks sparked the length of his cock, forerunners of the rapture he staved off by dint of willpower. He rolled his hips, savoring the friction engendered. *Sweet, absolutely sweet.*

She writhed in response, moaning her hunger. She was almost there, he could tell.

Now to see how long he could last.

Still bent over her, Damon slowed his movement even further until he was barely rubbing her G-spot, practically floating in place as he circled that one point. Bright sparkles of delight flowed up his spine like champagne bubbles frothing up, but short of spilling over.

Deep red exploded against his mental sense in a sudden burst of intense need.

Her legs jerked around his hips, her heels digging into his calves. "Oh, my God." She squirmed frantically, obviously fighting for the last bit of pressure that would bring release.

"No. Damon." Stopping all motion, he held her down easily, keeping them both short of the point of no return. Suddenly it seemed of towering importance to establish some guidelines between them.

"*What?!*"

"The name's Damon, not God," he insisted, holding still though his body screamed at him to move, carnal hunger coiling into a tight Gordian knot around his balls.

"I don't care if you're the Devil himself. Finish me!" She ground her pelvis against him in demand, impatience edging her aura with orange.

"Say my name." Damon prayed she'd give in, since he didn't think he could hold out much longer. His balls ached for relief, so swollen they felt like they would erupt at the slightest pressure. He needed her acknowledgment, needed to establish he wouldn't be merely a human vibrator in this transaction.

"Bastard." Scrambling for purchase, she clawed the bedding, struggling to raise herself and get his cock to where she wanted it, but her position prevented her from getting the leverage she needed—exactly as he'd planned.

"Say it."

Her mouth worked, opening and shutting wordlessly, as she fought not to give in, clearly suspecting more was going on than she understood. But her body vibrated with carnal tension, still balanced on the cusp of climax. "Damon. Now finish me, damn it!"

On a surge of triumph, he moved, driving hard and fast, answering the siren song of ecstasy with a pounding rhythm that shook the bed.

His master thief responded with a cry of welcome. "Finally." Her inner muscles jerked tight around him as he rode over her G-spot. She let out a thready sigh, her breath hitching when he ground over her G-spot again. No acting there, the bright delight flaring from her assured him on that front.

For his part, Damon almost forgot the point he'd been trying to make. Pressure had built up in his balls, a geyser of scalding hunger ready to blow.

But he had to satisfy her first. Convincingly.

Focusing his attack on her G-spot, Damon drove her to the edge, intent on reaching completion. This time, there would be no holding back.

"Yes. Oh, God, yes!" She arched, trying to meet his wild thrusts, her hips churning against his. Her climax ripped across his mental antennae, a wallop of pure sensation that struck almost before the spasms around his cock began.

Carnal fire licked his flesh, as explosive as gunpowder. Like spontaneous combustion, burning through his ragged discipline with breathtaking speed. He pumped faster, desperation fueling his pace.

Nearly there.

Her breath hitched as she convulsed around him once more,

a look of astonished delight flashing across her face. Her savage ecstasy continued to sear him, shredding his control to a meager thread.

His restraint snapped.

Unable to stop himself, Damon bore down on his master thief, lunging into her, immersing himself in the fury of passion she'd ignited. He pounded her with short, brutal strokes, deaf to her cries of transport. Then a firestorm of exquisite pleasure roared through his cock and he forgot everything else.

Rapture and power swept him away, his heart thundering in his ears. A transcendent bliss taking him beyond himself, free of the bounds of his mortal body and from all cares.

Panting, Damon slumped down, his face buried in his thief's ample cleavage. Though stunned by the magnitude of his release, he couldn't resist a sense of smug satisfaction at her purr of pleasure. *Looks like we both won that one.* If her current condition was any basis for judgment, he'd passed her test. The glow of happiness his conclusion evoked would have shocked him—if he had any working brain cells left to be shocked.

All too soon, he felt her stir beneath him, uncommonly energetic for one who'd come as strongly and as frequently as she had. She pulled away, leaving his limp cock with a final flutter of her inner muscles.

Damon found a dram of energy to grab her ass before she got too far. "Where do you think you're going?"

She chuckled. "Right now? Nowhere. I just need to breathe."

"Sorry if I'm too heavy." He reluctantly let her out from under him, kneading the firm flesh under his palm reflexively. Then the warm come on his cock registered.

Damon jerked away, levering himself onto an elbow. "Fuck, we didn't use any protection. I'm clean but—" He left the rest unsaid. His master thief was a smart woman; he didn't have to spell out the dangers of unprotected sex.

But there was no change to her blissful expression. "No worries. I'm clean, too, and my shots are up-to-date, so there's no chance I'll get pregnant. We can have our fun."

Relief neutralized the spike of adrenaline the shock had given him. Once more enervated, he settled back down beside her. "Oh! That's good."

His hand wandered over to her delta, ruffling the pale, wet strands he found there still dripping with their juices. He fingered her idly, absently noting her different textures: smooth skin, feathery curls, slick cream. *All woman.* The uncharacteristic thought jarred.

Her indolent purr shivered with remanent pleasure. "You do that very well."

"I learn fast."

Wariness met his idle remark. "That's good." She drew back, raising herself up on one elbow to look at him across the space she'd managed to put between them, quickly regaining her poise. "You never know when you might need a fast study."

"That isn't all I learned," Damon countered, to regain the upper hand. "There's one other thing."

A thin, golden brow arched in silent inquiry, light from the nightstand lamp glinting off individual hairs. The wariness he picked up from her belied the small, condescending smile on her full, pink lips.

"You're a natural blonde."

"Oh, really?" Despite her nudity, cool amusement glittered in her green eyes. She wasn't just maintaining an excellent facade; he couldn't sense any misgivings from her, not shock, not even mild chagrin at his pronouncement.

Her unwavering confidence gave Damon a sinking sensation in his stomach, an uncanny certainty that he was mistaken. But how could that be? Even her pubes were pale blond to the roots; he'd seen them up close. Surely that couldn't have been dyed?

"You know, you're right."

He frowned at her statement. *She really is blond?*

"You do have a great imagination." She stole a kiss, then pushed off the bed. "I'm in."

Savoring his success, Damon lay back upon the pillows, closing his eyes against the enervating wave of relief he felt at her pronouncement. He'd done it.

He opened his eyes at the hum of a zipper, to find her adjusting the fit of her jumpsuit. "What are you doing?"

"I'd think that's obvious. I'm getting ready to leave." She wrapped her tool belt around her waist and secured it, her hands moving to check its hang with the automaticity of long habit.

"But we still have things to discuss."

"Like what?"

"Like, what should I call you?"

Tilting her head to one side, she nibbled her bottom lip thoughtfully, studying him with unreadable green eyes. "Rory."

Damon raised a skeptical brow, trying to imagine a parent who could give a beautiful blonde like her a boy's name. "Somehow, I doubt that's your real name."

His master thief smiled, catlike and secretive. "You don't need to know that."

"What do we put on the passports?"

A careless wave of her hand interrupted him. "Put whatever you like. I'm sure you'll think of something."

"No, really."

"Yes, really." She shook her head at him. "I'm not about to tell you my usual aliases."

Standoff.

With a mental shrug, Damon dropped the subject. Pushing was more likely to change her mind than get him an answer. Besides, he wasn't up to an argument; he felt too good, his body still floating from his release.

He sat up, but that was as far as he could push himself without any imperative reason to move. She was in, so he didn't have to chase her anywhere. "We still have other arrangements to make."

"Here, send the money to this account." She pulled a small, plastic case from her belt and passed him a card with the logo of a Zurich bank. "I'll be back, once it clears."

The smooth paper with its long string of numbers and instructions for currency transfers was otherwise uninformative: mass-produced, lacking handwriting or any other useful distinguishing marks, undifferentiated from the others in the pack that he suspected had been issued by the bank. He turned the card over to confirm his suspicions. Absolutely homogeneous. Probably nothing of it tied her to the card, not even fingerprints, given the care she'd taken in passing it to him.

In exchange, Damon reached into the nightstand to proffer her coiled rope and grapnel. "I believe this is yours."

"I believe it is." She took the rig with an appreciative smile, hefting it with easy strength, clearly accustomed to its weight.

With bated breath, he watched her attach the rope to her belt, apparently considering it unnecessary for her decampment.

"Oh, by the way"—her dark form turned from the balcony door; a gloved hand with pale fingers extended to him—"this isn't mine." Flicking the miniature electronic tracker he'd planted on her rope toward him, she disappeared into the darkness.

Damn, she didn't miss a trick.

Ignoring the device on the carpet, Damon stared at the balcony, straining for some sound of her departure. Her aura moved away, that seductive, single-minded focus growing fainter until it disappeared into the background hum of less-disciplined minds; yet nothing reached his ears. Finally, he overcame the sensual lassitude that weighed down his limbs, and went outside.

The only thing that awaited him in the shadowed space was balmy night air that wrapped his naked body in a thin film of sweat. Just like that, she was gone. His master thief might as well have vanished in a puff of smoke for all he had to show for her visit. Almost as if she'd been one of his dreams. His hand drifted to his cock, still slick with her cream. Well, maybe not quite that visionary.

Rory.

He shook his head in rueful appreciation of her stealth. She was precisely what they needed for this mission . . . and they had her!

Triumph at acquiring her when others had failed finally broke through his carnal lethargy, setting his pulse racing. With a light step, he returned inside to inform the Old Man of his success. There were plans to be made and precious little time to make them.

Directing his attention to the next phase of his mission, Damon dismissed the unexpected wistfulness Rory's departure had evoked. He would see her again soon enough.

CHAPTER SEVEN

Rory studied the busy Maiquetía Airport, allowing the babel of conversations in Spanish and Portuguese, English, German, and Italian to flow over her unheeded. It was a cosmopolitan crowd, mainly composed of businessmen. They were taking a roundabout route to Europe and the Balkans with frequent identity changes intended to muddy the waters. Such precautions seemed excessive to Rory, but since she wasn't the one making the travel arrangements, she didn't protest.

Things had moved quickly once she'd accepted the commission. In a matter of days, Damon had provided her with fake passports for different nationalities that sported pictures matching her specifications, complete with requisite visas and stamped for past travel.

Close scrutiny of the passports in preparation for her Changes didn't reveal any difference from previous fakes she'd used. Either they were the real McCoy or Damon used the same supplier as her father. The thought of Felix diScipio having access to the same resources as the Feds was rather daunting. Rory wasn't sure which option she preferred.

They'd flown out of Miami, traveling separately, she as a different flavor of blond, Damon as a tourist. She had to admit that in bright resort attire, with his hair loose around his shoulders and sporting two-day stubble, he'd looked more like a beach bum than a typical Fed.

For the rest of their trip, they were supposed to travel together. Rory had already switched passports and Changed. All she needed now was her companion. So she sat in the lounge, watching the men around her and wondering how Damon would disguise himself. This time, her Adonis had the advantage. He knew what she was supposed to look like, while she didn't know how he would disguise himself, only the name he would be using.

The crowd parted around a man with sleek, short hair and a stubborn jaw heading in her direction, prowling in that way of Italian men who believed they were God's gift to women. His sleek charcoal gray suit hugged a powerful body that did nothing to contradict that notion of superiority.

Rory wasn't the only one who'd noticed him. The heads of several women and not a few men turned to watch his progress across the airport lounge.

Her hackles wanted to bristle at his arrogant approach. Then he gave her a warm smile and recognition clicked: it was Damon. But he looked so different, she hadn't recognized him. For a moment, she thought he'd cut his gorgeous hair; then she realized he'd merely clubbed it back, his wavy locks slicked to straightness, and done something to hide his distinctive widow's peak.

The effect was startling.

With only an adjustment in hairstyle, clothes, and posture, her Adonis was suddenly European. Gone was the easygoing, scruffy beach bum extraordinaire who'd flown on the same plane from Miami. In his place stood Marco Vasile, suave businessman and her Fed's current identity.

Was that how her Changes struck him?

Rory returned his greeting absently, still wrestling with her response to his disguise. She'd known he was good, since he'd managed to track her down, but his transformation was more telling—especially since he'd accomplished it without her advantages. It forced her to adjust her estimation of him, raised her respect for him a few notches higher.

Her gut spasmed in warning. Sex was one thing, but liking . . . She wasn't sure it was a good idea for a thief to like a Fed quite that much.

Unwilling to examine that dangerous line of thought, Rory forced her mind elsewhere, toward ways to occupy the empty hours of travel. The overnight flight to Rome would take more than ten hours, and that wasn't even their final destination.

Unlike on previous commissions, she couldn't spend the flights reviewing her notes; she didn't have much data to go on at the moment. She'd refrained from contacting Lucas again, wanting to wait until she was out of the country, so her brother wouldn't be tempted to talk her out of accepting Damon's commission, once he realized what it entailed.

Ignoring the fact that two-thirds of her agreed-upon fee was already in her Swiss account, this was something she had to do. The need to hide from public scrutiny had forged bonds of rock-solid affection among the wide-ranging diScipio clan. She couldn't countenance doing nothing when it could threaten her loved ones.

Once again she recognized her isolation. Most of her friends were relatives; she didn't have many outside of family. This admiration for Damon felt dangerously like friendship, maybe even affection—which wasn't wise since theirs was only a temporary business relationship.

Preoccupied with her thoughts, Rory accompanied her Adonis through the crowded concourse in silence, nibbling her lip in unease. Despite the long flight and the lateness of the hour, the savory aromas of roasting beef and pork coming from the restaurants failed to tempt her appetite. With her gut in knots, she was in no mood for food.

Damon's phone vibrated in his pocket in that special rhythm he reserved for communications from the Old Man, its unscheduled, inaudible summons heralding a change of plans. With a wave to Rory for her to go on ahead to the departure lounge, he turned aside to take the call, leaving the flow of traffic for a measure of privacy. "Yes?" The back of his neck prickled in wary anticipation of complications.

"Got another one for you." The code phrase for an assassination. His hunt was starting early.

Calmness washed over him, hyperawareness giving his perceptions a familiar, knife-edged quality. In response to his heightened combat readiness, his senses stretched out, seeking the threat—and registered Rory behind him, a bonfire of curiosity against a quick-moving mental stream of blandness and boredom.

No danger.

Damon checked the display of his cell phone and found the attachments he'd been sent. He clicked through them, studying the images of his quarry carefully.

He acknowledged the order with an innocuous "So I see" that wouldn't draw suspicion, even if an eavesdropper overheard him.

"Talk to you tomorrow morning?" After they arrived in Rome. That meant his target would be on their flight. Small wonder he was given the mission.

"Of course." Damon cut the connection, then spent a few minutes refreshing his memory. His target was a familiar figure, someone he'd researched and studied in the past, in preparation for this day. The files he'd received were merely an update. He'd seen most of them before.

He shut the phone to find Rory by his elbow, the bored pout on her bee-stung lips entirely in keeping with her persona, watching travelers trundling past, the wheels of their hand luggage droning a monotonous harmony. No doubt she hadn't wanted to leave him alone. Saying nothing, he continued to the departure lounge, confident that her professionalism would prevent her from asking the questions hovering on the tip of her tongue—at least until a more opportune moment.

One advantage of the wide stretch of floor-to-ceiling windows overlooking the runways was the reflections that allowed him to study the people around him without them being any the wiser. Which was why his back was turned when his target stepped out of the executive lounge.

A closer scrutiny as the black-haired man with an aquiline nose passed behind them confirmed his identity. It definitely was

---

Dreamwalker

al-Hazzezi—the Hashshash, as he was know in certain circles, for his involvement in the drug trade.

Damon recognized the ragged shape of his target's left ear, the result of a bombing gone awry. Al-Hazzezi hadn't even bothered with prosthetics to change its appearance, wearing it like a badge of honor, though it ran counter to the image he projected of a successful businessman.

But that wasn't what convinced Damon of his identification; it was the deep, abiding hate at the core of the man, the same hate Damon had sensed when he'd first encountered al-Hazzezi years ago: black, bitter cold, and spikier than a porcupine. There was no way the man could be anyone but al-Hazzezi.

He scanned the people around his target for bodyguards, but saw none. If there were any, they were keeping their distance. He smiled to himself. The odds of his success just went up—possibly into the eightieth percentile.

"Problems?" The curly haired redhead who plucked his sleeve looked like the perfect fluffhead mistress masquerading as a personal assistant. Only the sharp light in her round, aquamarine eyes belied the impression—and only if one were close enough to see it.

Rory had borne his silence well, and far longer than he'd expected, waiting until they stood in a modest pool of solitude to ask her question.

Damon shook his head. "No, just an update."

He tilted her chin up with a light finger to better study her disguise. It was flawless, down to milk white skin with a hint of blue veins at her temples and on her eyelids. She fit the picture in her passport so precisely—high cheekbones, mole by the left corner of her lips, and all—she might have sat for it herself.

But she hadn't. The photos in her passports had been

103

Company-supplied to match the specifications she'd given him.

How the hell did she do it? Up close, he couldn't see anything artificial to account for the vivid color of her eyes. She wasn't using contact lenses, yet he'd have sworn she'd had violet eyes on the flight down from Miami, and jade green earlier. There wasn't even a hint of peaches in her milk-and-roses complexion.

It was uncanny.

Damon still remembered that she'd somehow been Asian the first time he'd seen her, then quickly become a stocky Caucasian. It irritated him to no end that he couldn't explain how she'd managed it.

He must have been staring for some time, since the expression on Rory's face turned quizzical, her glossy, cherry red lips curving upward slightly in question.

"Just looking."

Blushing furiously—and how the fuck did she pull that off if her fairness was due to makeup?—she gave him an indulgent smile, then a quick kiss. "Don't worry about it."

Not worry when he'd just discovered that the redness of her lips owed nothing to cosmetics? No way in hell. He hated mysteries, and all those pesky details promised to bug him at a time when he couldn't afford distractions.

Damon was still puzzling over how Rory managed her disguise when boarding for first class and business class was announced. His target slid into the line, pulling a small, navy blue bag the Old Man would probably want to get his hands on for intelligence purposes.

That wasn't his mission, but perhaps someone was waiting in Rome to scoop it up when they arrived. He put it out of his mind. Not his problem.

After helping Rory to her feet, Damon picked up his own hand carry and followed her to the short line, keeping al-Hazzezi in sight.

His target was making himself comfortable in first class when they passed through. A few other seats were taken, none of whose claimants looked like bodyguards. The situation was good but not ideal since the flight attendants in that section were more attentive to passengers' needs. However, a staircase to the side suggested a sleeping deck; since al-Hazzezi liked his comfort, there was a chance he'd opt for privacy—and give Damon a better chance of success.

They had the business-class cabin mostly to themselves. Knowing he'd need privacy for the assassination, Damon took the seat by the window. An untimely awakening could spell failure for tonight's hunt.

The flight took off without delay.

Beside him, Rory was mostly silent, strangely withdrawn. Did she suspect what he was about? Or was there something else that might complicate the mission?

Complex emotions simmered behind the fluffhead demeanor she currently presented to the world, held in check by remarkable control. Discomfort was the least of them and the most understandable; after all, she was a thief and he did work for the government, albeit with a clandestine agency. He wasn't immune to the feeling himself.

But she radiated other, less definable emotions. Disturbing to one whose survival could depend on correct interpretation of such emissions.

Whatever it was would have to wait until after his hunt. He didn't have the luxury of choosing a different time to take out al-Hazzezi; he had only that night.

Damon sat patiently through the usual flight-safety announcements and the dinner service, accustomed to the wait. Eventually his target would sleep and then he could strike.

Hours later, the lights were dimmed and curtains drawn for privacy between cabins. Beyond the divider, the spiky aura stirred, its cold focus dissipated by drowsiness.

The time was approaching.

Al-Hazzezi retreated up the stairs to the sleeping cabins reserved for first-class passengers. No one followed him up. Even better. Fewer chances of someone waking Damon's target and saving him from a well-deserved death.

Mustering more patience, Damon scanned the cabin for danger and possible interruptions. The flight attendants had withdrawn, leaving passengers to sleep or otherwise entertain themselves. Rory had opted for the former, tilting her seat to nearly horizontal and spreading a blanket over her body.

He copied her, lying back and stretching his legs out for comfort. His target had yet to fall asleep, and even then, it would take about an hour for him to relax enough not to waken when Damon entered his dreams.

If he had his way, the Hashshash would never wake up.

The minutes ticked by, counting down the moments till death, spinning out into the small hours. The wait was an old acquaintance, made tolerable by the intended outcome. These days, he didn't mind it too much.

Closing his eyes, Damon sent his consciousness spiraling down to that half-drowsing state he needed, then extended his mental fingers, seeking out al-Hazzezi's dreams.

The familiar darkness resolved into a desert, one devoid of life. Searing heat and blowing sand that assaulted the lungs and scraped the skin dry under the rich blue sky. His target was a powerful dreamer, to see color and experience such exquisite sensation—possibly a latent incubus. Dangerous prey. Still, he had to die.

Seeking al-Hazzezi, Damon found his target standing thigh deep in a sea of pink-and-white flowers swaying in the hot wind. Opium poppies, some with fat seedpods dotted with brown lumps of drying sap awaiting harvest, an oasis of green in the middle of beige sands. Here, the Hashshash still saw himself as whole, undamaged by the bomb that had nearly claimed his life. His left ear was intact and shaped as it had been in earlier records.

That would be a problem.

Death held no horror for this man. With his cold hate and overweening pride, failure was what he feared most. The knowledge gave Damon an advantage, but only just. It was easier to scare a person to death.

The poppy field spread out into the horizon, the scene so distinct it could have been memory. This scenario wouldn't do. On his home ground, al-Hazzezi held all the aces, drawing strength from familiarity.

Damon suggested the man's final destination in Europe into his target's sleeping mind.

The sand and heat vanished, to be replaced by cold and rain, the hazy outlines of buildings, hard stones underfoot, and a raging river a short distance away. Al-Hazzezi stood at the embankment, looking about in triumph.

A small suitcase appeared at the man's side, one that matched the description of the nuke. Clearly, his target, too, was headed to Kosovo for the auction, and anticipating success. The nuke's presence in the dream told Damon something of the importance al-Hazzezi attached to this mission—and decided Damon's course. He sprang at his target, grabbing the bomb.

Mouthing imprecations, al-Hazzezi lunged for the suitcase. They spun on the embankment, punching and kicking, wrestling for a better grip on the slick, hard plastic. Caught in a deadly dance.

Damon's knuckles stung from his blows, the pain of battle a sure sign of the depth of the dream. A fist got past his guard, landing on his shoulder with a heavy thump he felt in his teeth.

The slippery stones worked in his favor. They fell into the river, still fighting for sole possession of the nuke.

Freezing water engulfed them, driving a spike of fear into Damon's heart. The verisimilitude of the dream could kill him, not just his target. Dying here could mean death forever. The power of al-Hazzezi's sleeping mind made the possibility more likely. Yet he had to accept it or his target would get away with only a nightmare that was soon forgotten.

Large rocks battered their bodies, then lost form. His target had remembered this was a dream and was trying to shift the scene. Damon couldn't allow that. He countered the move with a redirect to the river.

Al-Hazzezi struggled against him, resisting his compulsion. The river blurred, its roar fading, its cold waters losing strength. Before it could vanish completely, Damon wrested the nuke free and dove away, swimming with the current. Flailing in turbulent water, his target splashed after him, forgetting his attempt to escape the dream.

Now, Damon had him.

The river surged, its wildness redoubled, carrying al-Hazzezi in pursuit. Furious claws caught Damon's back, scrambling for purchase.

Water broke over their heads, filling their ears with its gurgling rush, trying to force its way into their noses. Even as they fought over the nuke, the river dashed them against unseen rocks, tumbled them end over end in suffocating chaos.

Damon fought to stay under, betting he could outlast the Hashshash in the water. His lungs screamed for air, urged him to open his mouth and breathe.

But he was still underwater.

Al-Hazzezi's struggles weakened. Damon grabbed him, letting the nuke's weight drag them deeper.

The river pounded his head, his chest. Driving into his throat. Strangling him.

He threw the choking sensations, the imminence of failure, the determination into his target's sleeping mind. Projected, too, chaos and loss, humiliation . . .

Until darkness overwhelmed him.

CHAPTER EIGHT

Damon snapped awake, the pounding of his heart like thunder in his ears. He gulped, sucking sweet, cold air into his lungs. He was alive! Relief swept through him at the realization. He stretched out his mental antennae and confirmed his assumption. Al-Hazzezi had put up a stronger fight than most, but Damon had succeeded in his mission and survived. He took another breath, savoring the recycled air of the shadowy cabin, relishing the very physical way it seared his starved lungs.

In his missions, there was always the possibility his target would turn the tables on him. He'd known that from the very start—back when another incubus had tried to assassinate his uncle Dion, and Damon had foiled the attempt and killed the assassin. He'd just turned thirteen at the time, but he'd had several missions since then.

The adrenaline flooding his veins slowly ebbed, leaving him shaky. This was the closest he'd come to dying. The knowledge sent a shudder through him. If al-Hazzezi had had any training to speak of, he might have turned the tables on Damon. The need to celebrate his survival transformed the fight-or-flight instinct into something equally basic—and just as urgent. Seeking release, he channeled it the only other way he knew.

The sand was hot and powdery soft beneath her bare feet, the sea a glorious mélange of color reflecting the sunset she hadn't seen. A sultry breeze swirled around her shoulders, blowing her hair around her head in playful abandon.

Rory laughed, feeling strangely lighthearted. But, of course, she was on vacation. Why shouldn't she be enjoying herself?

As twilight fell across the empty beach, the wind became warmer, stronger, but no less playful. It toyed with the strings of her bikini, swinging them gently to graze her sensitive skin, tugging suggestively on the ends.

Why not? She had the beach all to herself. There was no one around to witness her indecorum. The thought of skinny-dipping, of that warm sea flowing over her naked body with the full moon overhead, was too much to resist.

She flung off her swimsuit with reckless haste, laughing when the wind whirled around her to steal impudent caresses and carry the minuscule bits of fabric out of sight.

The water felt even more wonderful than she'd imagined, welcoming her with gentle splashes. It bore her, weightless, into the starlit night.

Rory floated on her back, her bare breasts above the water, delighting in the risk. Anyone could come by and see her . . .

Or perhaps a certain someone?

As quickly as the thought occurred, the dream swept her up in desire, sudden as a spring thunderstorm and just as violent. A man watched her from the shore, his muscular figure clear in the moonshine.

And he wanted her.

The distance between them made her overbold. Spurred by his presence, she played in the surf, letting it wash over her, deliberately hiding and revealing her body to her anonymous spectator in a thrilling game.

Taunting him.

Tempting him.

Inviting him.

Then he was in the water beside her, reaching for her. The shadows hid his features, but the hard chest that met her breasts was familiar, and the treasure trail rippling over sculpted abdominals even more so.

Her heart leaped in welcome, knowing the pleasures to come.

He was . . .

Rory snapped her eyes open as arousal spiked, knowing who the man of her dreams was. Irritation mingled with desire. Though she'd played a similar game with him in real life, that was of no import. It was unacceptable for him to enter her dreams again merely to seduce her. She'd already accepted his commission, hadn't she?

"D—Marco?" In the first stirrings of anger, she nearly forgot to use Damon's alias.

A harsh gasp from beside her told Rory something was wrong. When she glanced over, the Fed was gulping for breath, as though in a race instead of merely sneaking into her sleeping mind. She touched the back of his hand; he was hot, even feverish, the taut tendons beneath her fingertips almost searing to the touch. "Are you okay?" She forgot her irritation in the face of his apparent distress.

Opening his eyes, he gave her a fierce grin, the gleam in them unmistakably carnal. "Never better." He turned his hand over and captured hers, his heat sizzling up her arm.

Her pulse quickened in response to his overture, excitement thundering in her ears and drowning out her anger. *Here? Now?*

Rory glanced around, ingrained wariness prompting her to check for danger. The seats across the aisle were empty, as were the next rows. There were two passengers up front, but they were apparently asleep, their screens and reading lights off. The only illumination came from the exit and no-smoking signs.

And not one flight attendant in sight.

The steady shrilling of the jet's engines pervaded the darkness, weaving a wall of sound around them. A whistle of encouragement hinting at privacy.

But still . . .

"We'll just have to be very quiet," Damon murmured, his brown gaze dark and burning with sensual promise.

The implicit challenge decided her.

Rory leaned over and breathed into his ear, "I'm game if you are." She took his lobe between her lips and sucked on it, playing the tip of her tongue over the tender flesh. It was one of the few parts of him that was soft, and the unique texture intrigued her, tempted her to nibble on it.

Damon hissed, his grip tightening convulsively around her fingers.

She grinned to herself. He hadn't expected her to take the initiative, had he?

Catching his short ponytail with her free hand, she held his head in place while she explored his ear. She licked the intricate whorls and curving rim, blew on it, then giggled when he shuddered under her hands. Score one for her!

Naturally, he didn't let her have her way for long.

Damon released her but immediately wrapped his arm around her waist. Gentle tugs told her he was pulling her blouse free of her skirt, but that didn't distract her from her own reconnaissance. She found that the skin behind his ear was just as soft and—he jerked in startlement when she tongued it—even more sensitive. Perfect for her purposes.

"Tease." He twisted in her arms and reared back, capturing her lips in an openmouthed kiss that shook her senses. His tongue brushed hers, rough velvet delving deep. He kissed her as if she was his one hope of heaven, stealing her breath and returning it in the next heartbeat. Impatient in his insistence. Exigent in his exploration. Rapacious in his hunger.

Caught up in his desire, Rory hummed her approval, relishing his desperation.

Then it was her turn to hiss when his hard palm glided under her blouse, along her back, handling her with decided possessiveness. His hand moved upward to release the clasp of her bra, then pulled it down until her breasts were free of its constriction.

She bit her lip, suppressing a gasp of delight, when he cupped a swelling mound, fondling it to aching awareness. Then he rolled her nipple between his fingers, and she had to bury her face against his neck, unable to hold back a moan as tingles of excitement spun through her. He'd remembered how much she enjoyed his rough handling.

Alternating between her breasts, he tweaked the sensitive nubs, drawing them to tighter peaks with deliberate pressure. The simple motions were like live wires grazing her womb, a spark of electricity jolting her with raw pleasure.

Good God, he knew all the right buttons to press!

He urged her closer but the wide console between their seats got in the way.

"Get over here." In a casual show of strength, Damon lifted her into his arms and over the barrier, seemingly oblivious to her weight. He pulled the hem of her skirt up, then set her astride his lap. "That's more like it," he growled, grappling with the front panel of her panty and pulling it aside, baring her hot sex to the chill cabin air and sending a quick thrill of delight tripping up her spine. His knuckles dug into her mound and rubbed against her hard clit, the rough contact setting off small explosions in her belly.

Rory nearly swallowed her tongue at the nerve-jangling sensations. He was in a rush! "What's your hurry?"

"I want you," Damon growled, reaching between them to free himself. "Right here." His cock sprang up, thick and hard, to nudge her with its broad head. "Right now."

Boy, he *was* impatient! He was also scorching hot. In stark contrast to the cool air, the velvety tip of his hard-on was like a burning brand against her wet folds.

Rory swallowed against the dryness in her throat, the knowledge that only her legs and skirt prevented his public exposure sending a shiver of pure excitement streaking up her spine. She licked her lips reflexively. Someone could walk by at any moment, catching them in the act. Heat suffused her, the very risk seductive as hell.

"No waiting," he gritted between clenched teeth, his fingers digging into her hip. "I have to have you right now."

The strength of his desire was a complete turn-on she couldn't resist. Cream flooded her sex. The novelty of the situation and the chance of discovery only added piquancy to their lovemaking, fanning the flames of her own desire.

He thrust into her, working his way into her welcoming body with short, brutal strokes that stretched her wide, almost to the point of pain. "Oh, yeah."

Thrown off balance, Rory grabbed his lapels, startled by the barely restrained power trembling beneath her. It was so unlike him. Why now? What had brought on this driving urgency?

Just then Damon moved again and she forgot her questions in the wake of burning pleasure. He drove into her with a passion, as though trying to prove something, bucking under her like a wild stallion. His thrusts lifted her off her knees and drove the air from her lungs.

His cock inside her, stuffing her to overflowing, rubbing her inner membranes, was almost more than she could bear—and yet not enough. Panting, she tried to take more of him, to relax her sheath and let him in deeper.

He kneaded her butt, the pressure spreading her cheeks and pulling on her labia in a delicious motion that had cream spurting from her womb.

Suddenly, Rory slid lower, completely impaled on thick male flesh. "Ooooh!" She couldn't prevent the moan that escaped her, too startled by the abrupt plunge, her senses electrified by the contact. The fullness of her loins only emphasized the extent of his possession.

Damon caught her eyes with a fierce stare, his expression so predatory she couldn't look away. He continued to hold her gaze as he pumped into her, holding her captive as surely as he held her body.

He reached between them to trace a rough finger along the junction of their union, feathering over the straining edges of her folds and drawing back the hood of her clit to stroke that swollen bead.

The intimate friction on top of her earlier arousal quickly had her at the tipping point. She clung to his jacket, biting her lip to stifle the moans that begged for release. How could he command her body so completely?

With little regard for stealth, Damon manipulated her clit ruthlessly, circling it and rubbing its length, allowing her no respite from his carnal assault. Like an impatient safecracker cutting through with plastique, he set off explosions of delight in her quivering core. Then he tweaked the nub, driving her straight into climax.

Rory kissed him desperately, muffling her gasp against his lips as a wave of potent rapture spilled through her veins. Her Adonis jerked inside her, warmth flooding her core.

Breathless from his sensual ambush, she panted in his arms, surrendering to the lassitude spreading through her body, her nerves still jittering from the strength of her release. Her thoughts scattered in all directions. His lovemaking had come on too suddenly to take in.

Warmth settled across Rory's shoulders, cutting off the blast of cold air. She shifted lazily, rubbing her nose against rough bone—Damon's sandpapery jaw.

This close she couldn't miss the light scent of sweaty male or the thundering of his pulse. Proof that she hadn't been alone in the violence of her desire.

What had that been all about? She couldn't imagine his seduction had merely been a whim on his part; there had to be a compelling reason behind his sudden desire.

His arms tightened around her, his hands squeezing her butt as he rolled his hips under her. The movement drove him deeper, reminding her of the intimate mesh of their bodies and banishing all irrelevant thought.

She wanted him again. Slowly this time.

Rory pressed her mouth to the fluttering pulse on his neck, licking it and delighting in the vivid tremor against the tip of her tongue. "Again, again, again," she purred, stretching just to feel that hard body against her own. "That was over so quickly it barely had time to register. I want it to last."

Damon leaned back to look into her eyes. "You're insatiable." A wolfish grin accompanied his murmured observation.

"Complaining?" she whispered against his lips.

"What do you think?" He twitched inside her, lengthening and thickening, caressing her wet, inner membranes with each delicious extension.

Just that much was almost more than Rory could bear. Hypersensitive from his lovemaking, her swollen sheath heightened the effect of his erection, making him feel huge.

She swallowed a moan of delight at the intimate friction, shivering in excitement as cool air brushed her exposed skin. The contrast with his intense heat was a turn-on all its own. "I think you're all talk."

"Ah, a challenge. I'll make you eat those words." He kissed her thoroughly, a heated promise of carnal retribution. "You want 'again, again, again,' you'll get it." He nibbled her lower lip, then sucked on it gently, intently. "Now that I've gotten the edge off, I can last a long time." He drawled out *long*, making it sound almost like a threat with his deep rumble. "You'll register this. I guarantee it."

Rory's heart leaped, anticipation a roaring in her ears.

Aurora diScipio, you might have bitten off more than you can chew. But right or wrong, it was bound to be an experience.

This time Damon went slowly, lingering over each slick thrust, pulling out with excruciating slowness, then working back inside her with a deliberate focus on maximizing friction. Taking forever to return until he was back and snug against her womb. Doing it over and over.

Relentless.

His single-minded focus had need stretching her nerves to singing tension, until everything impinged on her senses. Her panting breath. The roughness of the seat under her knees. Damon's hard hands clamped on her hips. Her loose bra flapping at her waist. Her tight nipples rubbing against her silk blouse. The cold air searing her lungs and legs. His scalding heat.

With him raising and lowering her with unswerving resolve, Rory's attention spiraled down to that one point of intimate contact. She could feel the ridge of his cock head dragging against her sheath, in and out, as slow and steady as the tides. Building the flames in her core as surely as friction.

He led her on, up the dizzying heights of desire. Doling out pleasure in measured portions. Feeding the carnal bonfire raging in her loins.

Damon rocked under her, lifting her off her knees.

She tightened her legs against his thighs reflexively, the motion catching her clit between them in a sharp burst of pleasure. Gasping, she clung to his shoulders, fighting not to moan. Sweet heaven, it was even stronger than before!

The breathtaking sensation escalated as he continued to roll his hips, swirling his length inside her. It fanned the flames of her desire, a buoyant pressure that woke a need to moan and vent the hunger burgeoning inside.

But she couldn't! If she opened her mouth, she might scream instead, giving voice to her increasing desperation.

Damon watched her from half-shuttered eyes, a lazy smile ghosting his lips. The bastard was enjoying her dilemma. He'd meant it when he said he'd taken the edge off his hunger.

Rory cursed him silently, limited to urging him on with her body, lap dancing in the hopes of enticing him faster. Words were out of the question.

Obstinate man that he was, her Adonis persisted in his torturous pace, holding her astride above him and servicing her steadily, no matter what she did. Her own movements only served to inflame her senses; he gave no indication of any effect. She could only take the overwhelming pleasure he lavished on her and hope he wouldn't last much longer.

Next time, she vowed, she'd remember not to bait him—unless she wanted to walk funny for days.

He built her desire the same way he had that night in his hotel—with diabolical patience—riding her sweet spot, leading her to the precipice, then drawing her back. Heat and chill alternating between her thighs as he pumped her. Over and over. Slowly. Making it last, damn him.

A lifetime of nerve-jangling arousal.

Until Rory was ready to beg for relief. If it weren't for their public location, she would have, too. She craved the orgasm he dangled just beyond her reach.

If he would just let her grab it . . .

As though he knew how close she was to release, Damon stopped, holding her locked against him, his cock snuggled next to her womb. Not letting her take that last step.

She clamped her hands over her mouth to muffle her scream of desperate hunger. The whistling silence did little to relieve her excruciating need. Her nipples tingled as another tremor shook her. Suppressing her cries only seemed to magnify her passion, the awareness of the risk they ran fueling her excitement.

He hooked a hand around her neck and pulled her close to murmur in her ear. "Long enough for you?" He had the nerve to sound amused when she was next to jumping out of her skin.

"Finish me, damn it."

"Is that any way to talk?"

"Please," Rory forced out through gritted teeth, not using any names. She could barely remember hers—much less his!

His mouth brushed her neck, followed by a wet lick to the base of her shoulder. Then Damon nipped her, sucking strongly.

The sudden sting was all it took.

A tidal wave of blistering rapture crashed through her, relentless and undeniable, the chance of discovery amplifying its power. She buried her face against his neck, silencing her cries of ecstasy on thick broadcloth.

It was just the first of many. She lost track at five.

Her Adonis made good his vow to give her *again, again, again*, spinning out her climax and inundating her with so much pleasure she nearly forgot where they were. He shattered her with an intoxicating ravishment of her senses that went on and on. Tirelessly.

Until she sprawled in his arms, unable to move, too spent by the overwhelming surfeit of orgasms. Only then did he finally come again.

And though her curiosity stirred much later, just as she drifted off to sleep, Rory couldn't muster the energy to ask even one question.

What *had* triggered that wonderful spate of lovemaking?

Chapter Nine

"Is there a doctor on the plane?" The question was delivered by a troubled soprano in Italian, then repeated in Spanish and English, over the plane's speaker system. It was an annoying announcement to wake up to, given how little sleep Rory'd gotten.

She stretched slowly, reluctant to leave the warmth of Damon's embrace, but the cabin lights were on. While there was still no one else to notice, she slid off his lap and fixed her clothes, pulling her skirt down to her knees. Her sheath clenched in complaint, already missing his thick cock.

Braced for knowing looks from the flight attendants, Rory headed for the restrooms. She couldn't believe she'd spent the rest of the night in Damon's arms, still joined with him.

The stickiness between her legs was quickly remedied. As she dabbed her thighs dry, the announcement was repeated, broadcast over the speakers like a ghostly refrain. Not her concern. Straightening her skirt, she ignored it in favor of checking her hair. Not bad, considering how Damon had sunk his fingers into her curls.

On the way back to her seat, Rory had to give way to the purser and a rumpled woman going in the opposite direction through business class and disappearing into the forward cabin.

While she'd been gone, Damon had tucked his cock back into his pants and otherwise eliminated the evidence of their late-night activities, she was pleased to note. All spick-and-span and unrevealing—exactly how she liked things.

For a Fed, he sure knew a lot about maintaining an impeccable facade. No one would suspect they'd indulged in a night of sexual high jinks to look at him.

He turned to her as she reached her place, a brow raised in polite inquiry. The consummate travel companion.

She gave him a careless bob of her head as she sat down, allowing a frowning flight attendant to continue down the aisle. No worries. Everything was fine.

At least with her.

It seemed the flight crew might have disagreed. They didn't bustle as crews normally did in preparation for serving yet another meal. Their mood was grim—worried and out of sorts, but with none of the tension that would suggest a medical emergency.

As Rory finger combed her tousled curls into a semblance of order, she caught fragments of a murmured conversation between some flight attendants huddled in the service bay just behind her and Damon's row.

"*—muerto.*"

"*Celeste descubrió—*"

That raised mental eyebrows. No wonder they were so worked up. A passenger had been found dead in first class. Well, it had nothing to do with her. As she resumed fixing her hair, she turned toward the window to check the weather.

With a soft grunt, Damon flexed his shoulders, a faint smile on his chiseled lips. His motion snagged her attention, showcasing as it did his excellent physique. But it was the smile that stayed with her.

It bothered Rory, though it wasn't until the breakfast service that she realized why. The smile hadn't had the smugness of sexual satisfaction. Coupled with the cold glint in his eyes, it had been more . . . predatory.

It struck her then. Besides having a reputation for seducing women in their dreams, incubi were also known—according to legend, at least—for causing sudden, inexplicable death in sleep. And that was precisely what he'd said he was.

Moreover, Damon had never clarified what his "usual gig" was, when he wasn't chasing down thieves. Would he have said he was a hit man for the government?

Rory studied her companion with fresh eyes and not a little misgiving. To have such a man traipsing through her dreams—how safe could that be?

A twinge of excitement answered that thought. Once again, she was reminded that she didn't steal to be safe. If she'd wanted that, she'd be headlining her own act in Vegas, alongside Uncle Justin.

Remembering the man who had died in first class, she shivered. Damon had entered her dreams again last night, yet there hadn't been any reason for him to do so. She'd already agreed to undertake his commission. Had it been a postscript to some other purpose?

Did he have a hand in that man's death? Or was it merely coincidence? Even she had heard of deep-vein thrombosis, which sometimes struck passengers on long-distance flights. It was a possible explanation, although unlikely in this case since it sounded like the man had been in the sleeping deck, not trapped for straight hours in a cramped seat.

Could he have killed her when he strode through her dreams? An electric tingle shot up Rory's spine, the same thrill of excitement she got when faced with a chancy approach or scaling the side of a high-rise with only a thin harness as anchor. As conscious as she was of her seatmate, that line of thought made for an uncomfortable meal.

"Did you kill him?" Rory murmured as she leaned across Damon to look out the window, ostensibly taking in the view of the Mediterranean far below. The sudden question broke several hours of brooding silence, monosyllabic responses, and churning emotion on her part. It also explained her withdrawal: she'd connected the dots from seduction to death-dealing, which—granted—common mythology recognized lay within the realm of an incubus's powers, to this particular execution.

Wondering how she would react, he answered honestly: "Yes."

"Why?"

"Most recently?" Damon shrugged, not wanting to go into the long list of al-Hazzezi's crimes. "He was responsible for the embassy bombing in Greece last year. The one that killed twenty-five staffers and six Marines on Christmas Day."

She eyed him sidelong, curiosity bringing out the green in her aquamarine eyes. "So you waltzed into his head and killed him, just like that?"

He inhaled deeply, savoring the whiff of her floral shampoo that the constant blast of coolness from the air-conditioning nozzle overhead carried to him. There was something unspeakably intimate about that little discovery, much more so than the physical act they'd shared. His unusual response to such a minor detail made him wonder if he was losing his edge. "Nothing so simple, but essentially, yes."

Unease rippled across her aura, staining it with shadows. "How could you do that?"

Keeping his face blank, Damon shrugged. "The theory is simple, really. You convince the body that it's dying, and it does."

"But to kill . . ."

"It was necessary."

Rory turned away, her rosy cheeks turning pale as her conflicting emotions rasped his mental antennae. "I can't imagine doing that. Killing anyone."

"Oh, is this the point where I'm supposed to snarl that I hate terrorists because they killed my parents?" Damon nearly bit his tongue when he heard himself make the airy disclosure. He waved a hand dismissively while his mind flailed in disarray. "Consider it snarled, if it makes you happy." Long practice kept the old pain from his voice; he hadn't succeeded in his line of work by wearing his heart on his sleeve.

But why had he told her that? What was it about his master thief that made him drop his guard around her?

Luckily, Rory didn't seem at all intimidated. They couldn't afford to scare her off; it would be impossible to find another master thief at this late a date. She gave him a hard look from narrowed eyes turned turquoise, her thoughts unreadable—save for a lack of fear. That alone permitted him a measure of relief. She might not like what he did, but she wasn't about to back out of the job because of it.

Damon gave additional thanks when she didn't pursue the discussion. With his uncharacteristic openness, he just might have spilled his guts, given the right questions.

Of course, Rory had a few secrets of her own, starting with her true hair color. Although he'd been focused on getting off last night, he hadn't missed the soft, wispy red curls at the entrance to her body, so different from the respectable blond muff from before. She hadn't shaved; it was just—apparently—naturally sparse.

The high regard he held for her ratcheted up a few more notches. To have effected such a thorough transformation—and taken even her pubic hair into account—in the little time she'd had at the airport was surely the height of professionalism. It boded well for their work together.

He took an easier breath when she settled back into her seat, a thoughtful inward look darkening her aquamarine eyes.

Despite the death on board the plane, the rest of the flight to Rome and the remainder of their trip were uneventful. By the time they arrived in Macedonia under another set of identities, fatigue wrapped Rory's brain in thick cotton, jet lag setting in after crossing too many time zones too quickly.

But she managed to rouse her mind into a semblance of alertness when Damon's agency made covert contact.

The pickup and transfer had been smooth, professional. Rory hadn't noticed anything special about the taxi Damon flagged down at the Skopje airport. But when they were dropped off at the hotel, they'd had one more piece of luggage than when they'd boarded: a leather briefcase that matched Damon's bags.

She held her silence while they checked into the hotel and got a single room with a king-size bed.

"What's in it?" Rory finally asked, eyeing the briefcase as her curiosity overcame jet lag.

Rather than answer, Damon worked the combination locks and opened the bag with a click. It was stuffed with sheets of paper, which he laid out on the bedspread. A show of trust so she knew he wasn't holding anything back?

"I guess this means the job's still on."

He smiled, clearly understanding her underlying question. "We have teams working to locate it. If they can seize it before Karadzic gets it to his base, all the better. But we're not betting on that happening." He glanced at her as he continued to unload the briefcase. "Don't worry. You keep your up-front money in the unlikely event that you don't have to go in."

She plucked out a computer print that caught her eye. "Satellite pictures, even." She was tempted to whistle. Whoever had assembled this packet had gone over and above to anticipate their needs. The briefcase was a treasure trove of information, some of which might actually be good.

Leafing through the myriad sheets, she extracted a detailed map that looked too clean to be a photocopy. "How accurate are these?" Even the best maps available, commercial or otherwise, weren't a hundred percent reliable. Mapmakers had an irritating habit of incorporating inaccuracies for copyright protection, national security, or some other idiosyncratic reason.

"Very. They're Company generated."

Rory raised a brow at the rock-hard confidence in Damon's voice. It seemed the Fed had a blind spot. "Nice to have resources," she murmured coolly. Still, she committed the map to memory, forcing her foggy brain to process the information. It was better than nothing, and she couldn't risk standing out by resorting to a hard copy once they were on-site.

He snorted. Perhaps he noticed her expression or heard something in her comment, or maybe he sensed her reservations, because he added: "Fuckups do happen. But the Old Man is giving this mission his personal attention."

And that was that, apparently. His boss must have big brass balls for him to have earned that much confidence.

But when Damon laid a satellite image beside the map for comparison, it became obvious that the agency's mapmakers had access to primary sources.

Difficult though it was, Rory had to concede that the Fed might have some basis for his trust.

She studied the satellite image. Like most old towns, it was a warren of small winding streets and dead-end alleys, with no clear divisions as to residential and commercial or industrial zones. The confluence of two rivers, spanned at several points by bridges, cut through the middle, dividing the town roughly into three sections—though more likely, the town had grown up around it. A potential bottleneck. "Where's Karadzic's base?"

"Here." He traced an irregular block in the northeast section with a long, blunt index finger. "The KLA represents most of the organized crime in the area. But don't mistake that for control. They're a mishmash of gangs that are frequently involved in turf wars."

Bending over the image, Rory nodded to herself. There were similarities to the situation in Peć—much of which was familiar from her prep work for the Ipek Crucifix job. She had to caution herself not to make assumptions on that basis.

The section Damon indicated wasn't that different from other areas—except perhaps for a preponderance of cars. Traffic could be a help or a hindrance, depending on the situation. It was also an indicator for places where people might congregate, like markets . . . or gang strongholds, to cite a not-so-random example.

She checked the time stamp on the image. It was a night shot, which possibly meant lots of activity during the time she worked best. *Oh, goody—not.*

"I propose we stay here." Damon pointed to a spot in the lower half of the image in the middle of a knot of tiny buildings. "It's a hostel run by a CIA asset. He's in the business of selling information, so I wouldn't trust him out of arm's reach. But the revolving tenant population should make blending in easier."

Rory smiled at his reasoning. She wouldn't have trusted a CIA contractor anyway, since he wasn't family. Not that Damon was family, but he was a special case; she trusted him to do whatever was necessary to get the job done.

"This might be a problem." She tapped the lone bridge near the hostel. Unlike the northern portions of the river, which had a bridge every other street or so, there was only one for a long stretch in the south that crossed to the northeast. It would limit her options for getting to the target. Unless she went out of her way and crossed in the north, all her routes would have to funnel through that one bridge, making her somewhat predictable.

"Can't be helped. I'd rather not stay any closer to the target. This area"—he swept his hand across the east side—"is held by gangs with ties to Karadzic. Also, our line of retreat is south, to get back to Macedonia. This gives us more options."

Rory considered the image glumly, unable to argue the point. It would make her job so much easier if she didn't have to lug the nuke halfway across town and through the bottleneck of that single bridge. Unfortunately, his logic was unassailable. "Ugh." But better that than to nest among vipers. Not that the hostel was much of an improvement, but at least it wasn't quite the . . . enemy's home grounds.

She crossed her arms, still uncomfortable with thinking in terms of *enemy*. In the past, it was always *the mark* or *the target*, with no hard feelings involved; this was personal.

Obviously taking her grunt for agreement, Damon unfolded another sheet and they bent over it to harvest whatever intelligence they could get together.

They kept at it until she called a halt, her interest no longer sufficient to keep her jet-lagged brain from protesting the information overload. They'd have to go over it again tomorrow, anyway, to make sure they hadn't overlooked anything in their fatigue.

Rory watched Damon thread his way through the crowd milling in the plaza below, off to secure wheels for the next leg of their journey—and probably a final briefing. She didn't mind sitting that one out; she had her own plans for the day. Marveling at how he managed to blend in despite his exceptional good looks, she tracked his broad back until she lost sight of him when a flock of gray pigeons suddenly took to the air in a flurry of wings, blocking her view.

Assured he'd be gone for some time, she turned away from the window and checked her e-mail for anything from Lucas. Big Brother should have something for her by now, and she

probably wouldn't have another chance to find out in private before they left for Kosovo. While she was willing to work with
Damon, she wasn't about to reveal her contacts to him—
possibly exposing her family to government scrutiny—so the secrecy was necessary. Besides, this *was* why Damon's agency was
paying her the big bucks.

The sufficiently cryptic message waiting in her in-box made
her grin.

Kitten,
Your friend upgraded to a 2RK a few months ago. A sweet
setup. Any ideas why? Drop by the Bear when you're in town. We
should catch up.
The Light of Your Life

Trust Lucas to have the latest news. This would certainly
help, so long as she could get to tapping distance. She knew the
system the code referred to, could recite its weaknesses and the
backdoors built into it in her sleep.

Which meant she now knew what additional equipment to
get. And if Big Brother was true to form, the stuff she needed
would be waiting for her at the Bear.

She checked her watch. She should have time for an errand
before Damon got back.

When Damon returned to the hotel, a strange woman was in
their room, bent over a small black rucksack gaping open on the
bed. He tensed in automatic wariness at her presence, cursing
silently, then his mental sense caught up with trained reflex.

Rory.

She'd changed appearances again.

"What do you have there?"

His master thief looked up at him as the door clicked shut, giving him the full impact of her metamorphosis. "Supplies."

Damon struggled to maintain an unruffled demeanor. He had a sneaking suspicion Rory took a positive delight in throwing him for a loop and didn't want to encourage the behavior. But seeing the extreme change in her appearance made his usual icy calm difficult.

Her hair was mahogany brown, straight, and hung past her shoulders, her skin olive. The bridge of her nose was higher, lacking the delicacy of her previous redheaded persona. Almond-shaped, chocolate brown eyes peered at him from deep beneath equally dark, luxuriant lashes. Her chin was narrower, coming to a delicate point under a smaller mouth with thinner lips.

Feature for feature, she was completely different, and none of it explicable by cosmetics—unless she'd gotten eyelash extensions while he was gone. Damon was reminded of the Asian woman he'd followed from the museum and whom he'd lost in a bleached blonde. If it weren't for Rory's aura, he'd have taken her for a different person altogether. The thoroughness of her transformation was uncanny. How was it possible?

It took an effort to wrench his thoughts back to the conversation. "Electronics?" Joining her by the bed, he raised a brow at the jumble of devices in the bag, wondering at her sources. She'd been busy.

Rory abruptly zipped the rucksack shut, the shrill squeal of plastic cutting the air as her equipment rapidly disappeared from sight. "You hired me for my expertise. Change your mind?" Though she didn't face him, wariness radiated from her in prickly waves he couldn't miss.

"I can help."

"I work alone."

"Normally, so do I. But with the stakes this high, can you afford to turn down help?"

"Good point." Moving the rucksack to the floor, Rory finally turned to meet Damon's gaze. "If I need help, I'll keep you in mind. But in the meantime, just leave me to work the way I know best." The unflinching look she gave him said the point wasn't negotiable.

His master thief didn't quite trust him, which was smart of her since he was willing to do whatever it took to complete this mission . . . even if it meant sacrificing her.

CHAPTER TEN

The whine of jet engines on final approach to the airport filled the night, rousing Damon from light sleep. Tomorrow, they would begin the mission in earnest. Automatically, he scanned his surroundings for hostile intent, but sensed nothing more inimical than feminine annoyance from a foot away—a first for him. Although it had been days since he'd agreed to become Rory's lover, they'd never actually shared a bed for sleep before. So far, the experience was proving to be . . . interesting.

"I'm cold." The plaintive statement floated through the darkness. The wide bed squeaked lightly as though for emphasis.

"You don't have to sleep naked," Damon pointed out in what he considered to be a reasonable tone.

Already clad in pants and shirt in readiness for their early morning departure, he was actually on the warm side—enough that he'd thrown off the comforter—and became more so when he remembered how he'd gotten the full impact of his master thief's disguise. In preparing for bed, she'd revealed that her muff now matched her mahogany brown hair, while the skin around her groin was just as olive as the rest. Large, dark nipples completed the package, every part of which seemed completely natural.

"Clothes are too constricting." The mattress rocked under Rory's weight, accompanied by a flare of mischief from her direction. "Besides, there's something kinky about sex when you're still dressed and I'm not."

He rolled his eyes, reluctantly amused by her reasoning. "Come here." Reaching out, he pulled the minx over and tucked her against his side to share his heat. The chilled skin that met his hand was liberally covered with goose bumps, despite the comforter.

"Damn, you *are* cold. Let's warm you up." Damon pressed his face into her cleavage. Since he'd stopped shaving yesterday in preparation for the mission, his action elicited a startled squeal. Nice to know he could surprise her. He followed it up by capturing a tight nipple between his teeth and nibbling.

"Ooooh!" Rory arched her back, her arms winding around his neck in definite welcome. The musky scent of feminine arousal that reached him matched the delight she radiated.

Fuck, she was so responsive, it went to a man's head—both heads.

Reminding himself that they had an early start tomorrow did little to cool him off. Since he couldn't take his time pleasuring both of them, he decided to make it quick. After all, he'd started making love to her to warm her up, not get his rocks off.

He fanned her curls and parted her pussy lips, which were already hot and slick. Her clit was a hard button just waiting to be pressed and diddled. He tweaked it in unison with a nip on the captive bud in his mouth.

Rory jerked and shuddered under him, fresh cream spurting over his hand as she murmured something approving.

Damon drove his fingers into her, gritting his teeth when she clenched around them, tight and ready. He could easily imagine that grip around his cock. He bit back a groan at the thought. *Back to business, Venizélos.* The delight she projected, however, was just as distracting—and flattering to his ego.

Transferring his attention to her other breast, he continued to finger her, fascinated despite himself by the satiny flesh that clung to his hand and the soft mounds pillowing his stubbled cheeks.

And her scent! Sweat and sex and all woman.

She raised her hips, her pelvis rocking to meet his thrusts, her soft cries sure encouragement. Her scent deepened, a spicy aphrodisiac that fogged his thoughts.

It made it difficult to remember he was just supposed to be warming her, not sending them both up in flames. They didn't have the luxury of staying up all night to sate their appetites.

Knowing sexual frustration lay ahead for him, Damon steeled himself to finish her quickly. Sucking more strongly on her nipple, he circled her clit and pulled on it, searching for a fast rhythm that resonated with her arousal. He varied his pacing until a bright flare of delight announced his success.

Rory fisted her hands in his hair, pressing his face against her breasts with a breathless shout of pleasure. She writhed beneath him, her thigh gliding over his length and rubbing his aching hard-on to painful proportions until his pants felt like a strait-jacket.

Desperate now to cut his self-inflicted torture short, he exploited his knowledge, strumming her clit and G-spot to drive her to a hard climax.

Now, while his control held out.

She shuddered in his arms, her voice breaking on a low moan as she convulsed around his fingers, hot cream pouring on his hand. The heady essence of her pleasure made Damon curse their early departure; he wanted more of it and not just on his palm.

"Oh, God, that was wonderful." The satisfied purr in Rory's voice had his cock throbbing in complaint.

Releasing her nipple, he stole a quick lick of his fingers, stifling a moan of his own at her sweet saltiness. The musky scent of her juices smelled so much better up close. He pressed a kiss on the slope of her breast, noting the lack of goose bumps with a masochistic sense of satisfaction. At least his plan worked. "I guess you're warm now."

"Mmm . . . definitely." The minx wriggled against him, hooking an ankle behind his knee.

Gritting his teeth, Damon adjusted himself in his pants, hoping his hard-on would soon subside. As it was, even his toes ached for relief.

Rory snuggled deeper into his embrace, already falling asleep, her contentment a warm glow to his mental sense.

Damon supposed he would eventually adjust to having a regular bedmate. Certainly it had some compensations. He laid his head on her soft breast to take advantage of one such compensation and closed his eyes.

Just before he, too, succumbed to sleep, he realized that none of what he'd licked, nipped, or touched had felt artificial or part of a disguise. Another what-the-fuck moment with his master thief.

Rory woke to find herself wrapped in sleeping male. Since she was toasty warm and had no objection to her situation, she had to wonder why she'd roused when it was still dark outside.

Oh, yeah. Early departure. She had to dress up.

The tackiness of her thighs registered, reminding her that last night's carnal activities had a price. *Make that wash and dress up.*

Just then, Damon's arms flexed, mashing her against hard male muscle.

But not just yet. Right here and now felt too wonderful to leave at the moment. She'd never really slept with a man before, not in the purely slumber sense. The transatlantic flight with Damon didn't count since it hadn't been in a real bed.

Surfeit with contentment, she sighed, suspecting she could develop a liking for it.

Her human blanket rolled to his back with a grunt. "Awake already?" He raised bent arms beside his head and stretched—back arching, chest rising, pectorals flexing, biceps and deltoids bunching—in a mouthwatering display of prime beefcake.

"Unfortunately." Tempted to irresponsibility, Rory stroked the clean line of his torso, marveling that such an exquisite physical specimen could exist. "So how is . . . *someone like you* different from most?" She didn't say *incubus* aloud, since their room wasn't secure, but surely he'd understand her meaning. Her hand came to a natural stop at his groin, which of course she had to explore, discovering he tucked to the right.

"Not that way." Damon chuckled as his cock swelled under her palm.

"Oh?" She trailed a finger up that long, intriguing ridge, remembering how he'd felt in the park, the very first time they'd met. Even though she now knew what he looked like and how he felt inside her, the knowledge didn't diminish his attraction—especially when she also knew he didn't stuff socks in his pants to look bigger.

"Oh," he echoed firmly, his hand clamping down on hers. "We don't have time."

Rory grimaced in agreement. Unfortunately, he was right; they didn't, not if they were to keep to their schedule. A glance at the clock on the nightstand told her they were past her self-imposed wake-up time—and she hadn't factored a morning shower into her personal timetable.

Damon wanted to get an early start, to make catching and losing a tail easier—in case they had one—and to cross into Kosovo during the daytime. Apparently, there were patrols to avoid. Since he was the expert in such international covertures, she hadn't argued with him. His job, after all, was to get her to where she could do hers; far be it for her to throw roadblocks in his way. Starting right now.

Pulling the lousy excuse for a comforter around her, she sat up reluctantly, shivering as soon as her personal bed warmer got out of bed. Suddenly, the short distance to the bathroom with its bare floor looked as inviting as a skating rink.

"Here, let's speed things up." Before Rory could register his intent, he had swooped down, scooped her—sans cover—into his arms, and was carrying her to the shower, his chest heating her side, if not the rest of her. He thoughtfully kept her off the floor until the water had reached a comfortable temperature, or at least didn't feel like ice cubes on her hand.

"Talk about room service! I could get used to this."

Damon set her down on the cold tiles with a sudden clap on her butt. "Get moving."

"Hey!" Glaring at him for that bit of cockiness, Rory rubbed the affronted cheek. "That was uncalled for." In light of their time constraints, she left it at that, proceeding to wash herself. An argument would be pointless, and she took pride in being professional. Since she was the one running late, she decided to overlook the indignity.

Her professionalism, however, had its limits.

She snuck a glance at her Adonis brushing his teeth while she soaped her folds. There was something indescribably intimate about sharing a bathroom with a lover and watching his toilet. Especially when he was fully dressed and she . . . wasn't.

The potential for so much more was almost irresistible, considering Damon's unorthodox and high-handed method of warming her last night.

"What are you up to now?"

Whipping her head around at the question, Rory blinked guiltily at the suspicious expression on her Adonis's face, which made him look definitely like a Fed despite the stubble on his cheeks. "Huh?"

"You're woolgathering." His gaze dropped to her fingers, which had stopped combing through her pubes to circle her clit.

"I am not." Forcing heat into her denial, she quickly rinsed and dried off, silently cursing her wayward body.

"Yes, you were. I could tell." By his adamant tone and the knowing quirk of his lips, Damon had to mean he'd somehow sensed the carnal trend of her thoughts. Was it an aspect of his incubus skills?

"Were you reading my mind?" Rory demanded as she pulled on a loose beige sweater over her shirt and navy pants, bland clothes to help her blend into the background.

"Not hardly."

She snorted doubtfully. "That's not polite, you know." As she passed him, she poked him playfully to emphasize her point. His hand whipped out to intercept hers, but she managed to graze his side.

At the contact, Damon flinched, a quickly suppressed shiver suggesting that his reaction wasn't due to the near miss.

Rory grinned in delighted discovery. "You're ticklish!"

"I am not." He echoed her denial—a shade defensively, to her critical ear, especially since he twisted away to avoid her trapped hand. It seemed the supercompetent Fed had his share of weaknesses. She tucked that detail in the back of her mind for later, intrigued by the crack in her Adonis's armor.

"If you're done here, time's a-wasting."

"I'm done." Picking up her bag, she followed Damon out of the hotel room, content that the balance of power between them was equal once more.

He led her to an old gray Zastava Yugo, nothing flashy that would draw attention. The boxy two-door sedan was so common, no one would give it a second glance. The interior wasn't anything to write home about, but since it wasn't a luxury car, that was only what Rory'd expected. Unfortunately, very few jobs required her to arrive in a limousine, even though she could afford it.

Damon kept a sharp eye out on the way out of Skopje.

Respecting his need to concentrate, she watched the streets as well, wondering if her gut would warn her of a tail. No one followed them as far as she could tell. That early in the day, all they met on the road were trucks and a handful of cars, just strangers passing in the lamp-lit twilight.

Eventually, they left the sprawling city behind, following the winding road up and around the Vardar River valley. The pastel dawn was a distant memory by the time they reached the foothills of the Šar Planina, the snowcapped mountain range dividing Macedonia and Kosovo.

Rory's first really good view of the peaks made her blink. Her previous trip to Kosovo had been to the western part of the province. She'd flown in, then taken the train. While she'd seen mountains on that trip, they hadn't loomed large in the horizon as did the ones Damon and she were approaching. The thought of getting up close and personal with those rugged slopes, some of which rose more than eight thousand feet high, didn't exactly appeal to her. She shifted in her seat to keep her butt from going numb, feeling the weight of sedentary hours. Luckily, they were just driving through.

Despite the steep, tree-lined mountainsides, picturesque waterfalls and—once they got higher—stunning vistas, the long drive gave her little to occupy her mind. They were taking a smuggler's route across the border and the tension of the unknown was starting to get to her. This was the real start to the job and she had a partner—and lover—about whom she knew next to nothing, save that he could kill in cold blood through dreams and make her body erupt in exquisite pleasure with just his hands and mouth.

With most of their plans in place and her hyperactive imagination beginning to weave worst-case scenarios, she turned to Damon for distraction. "How'd you get into your line of work, anyway?" Twisting around to lean back against the door, she toed off her shoe, pulled her left leg to her chest, resting her bare foot on the seat, and studied his profile.

What was it about him that she found so fascinating? Tall, dark, handsome, he certainly fit Hollywood's bill of a secret agent—though right then with his hair loose and the beginnings of a beard shadowing his jaw, he looked more like a rogue than a Fed—but that wasn't it.

"Did you answer an ad in the classifieds? Attend a casting call?" That didn't seem so far-fetched when she considered how easily he changed personas—and all without her advantages. The man had acting skills to spare. The fact that he placed them in the service of the government was almost admirable.

Damon shot her a sharp glance out of the corner of his eye, then returned his attention to the narrow, winding track. He handled the boxy car with steady competence, avoiding flashy, aggressive maneuvers going up the slopes.

Felix always said you could tell a lot about a man from the way he moved. In that case, Damon was competent and confident— decisive. Since she had to work with someone, Rory was glad it was him.

After a long pause, long enough that she thought he'd decided to ignore her questions, he shrugged. "You might say I was born to it."

The answer didn't tell Rory much, but since he seemed willing to entertain her curiosity, she wasn't about to let the topic slide. "You mean you're the product of some supersecret government experiment?" she asked, tongue firmly in cheek.

He snorted at that, crow's-feet appearing as his eye narrowed and his lips quirked in amusement. A deep dimple flashed in his cheek almost too quick to be seen. Hollywood had missed a great leading man when her Adonis chose to become a Fed. "Hardly that—more a family tradition."

Rory blinked at his answer, taken aback by their common ground. She, too, had followed in her father's footsteps into the family business, although most people wouldn't consider it in that light.

"What about you?"

"The same," she blurted out, still stunned by the similarity of their reasons.

His brow shot up just before his head snapped around in her direction. "Family?"

"Why not?" Rory retorted before her brain finally caught up with her mouth. *Shit. What am I saying?* She bit her lip, horrified by her loose tongue. *Damn it, Rory, why don't you just spill the whole story about lamias and why diScipios live in the shadows?*

"No reason, I suppose. I just didn't—" He broke off and shook his head impatiently. "I wasn't thinking."

"Meaning?"

Damon frowned, obviously unused to being questioned, the hardening of his jaw letting the Fed peek out from behind the rogue. "Meaning exactly that: I wasn't thinking."

Saying nothing, she braced herself against the door as he muscled the Yugo through a sharp curve. Though the rear wheels slid toward the edge, she kept her eyes on him, leaving her silence to speak for her.

"You're a cool one." He sighed. "I just hadn't thought of burglary as a family tradition, that's all." He shot her another of his lightning-quick glances. "Or should I say family *business*?"

It was her turn to shake her head, putting a halt to the conversation. If she wasn't careful, he'd find out everything by the time the job was over.

Chilled by his perspicacity, Rory righted herself in her seat and stared out her window. The scenery passed in a blur of green before her unseeing eyes as her mind raced in thought. With that one slip of her tongue, Damon had come closer to the truth than anyone else who wasn't a diScipio, something her family worked hard to avoid.

And yet . . .

She'd have to decide soon whether she could trust him with her secret. Given how quick he was to pull his gun, it would be unfortunate if he shot her out of ignorance, not to mention her getting injured would put paid to the job. Shapeshifting might work to eliminate bruises, but Rory suspected that bullet wounds were a different case altogether, and she rather preferred not to find out the hard way that she was right. Certainly none of her lamia relatives had mentioned healing major injuries by Changing.

Her heart skipped when she remembered how suddenly that matte black gun could appear in Damon's hand—as though he'd pulled it out of thin air. The threat implicit in its appearance had brought home to her how deadly the commission could be.

At least she'd thought it had . . . until he'd taken out that man on the plane. That was when she'd realized that he could kill her anytime he wanted, just by entering her dreams. Problem was, the danger only made him more attractive.

Aurora diScipio, that's nuts. She had to focus on the job: get the nuke and get out. While Damon Venizélos was fine for a romp, she had to remember he was a Fed. Once he had his bomb, they'd never see each other again.

Tall, snowcapped mountains ringed the low town just across the Šar Planina from Macedonia. They vanished into blue mists in the distance and into fluffy white clouds in the heights. In the valley between, a river bisected what Rory could see of the town, a patchwork of old buildings sprawling on either side of raised stone riverbanks. On the other side of the valley, another river rushed down the slopes of another mountain to mix and mingle its waters with the one she could see, but it was too far away to make out any details. Closer by, red poppies dotted the grassy fields beside the road, startling contrast to all that verdancy.

It would have been charming if she didn't know what lurked behind the picturesque scene. Somewhere in that town, an arms dealer waited to sell a nuke to terrorists.

She turned to her new partner, who'd pulled over by a stand of trees with a commanding view of the town. What was he thinking now that they'd arrived? His clean-cut profile with the black sunglasses hiding his expressive eyes told her little. For her part, she was eager to move on. The job was at hand and she had a commission to fulfill. This stop was an unwelcome delay.

Crouched further down the slope, Damon kept his thoughts to himself. He stayed there for a minute or so, motionless, his dark head bent, wavy locks falling forward to veil his expression.

Perplexed by his inaction, Rory frowned. Was he praying? "What are you doing?"

"Acclimatizing myself to the feel of the town."

After visually gauging their distance to the sprawl of low buildings filling the valley, she blinked. "You can pick up something from all the way here?" Did that mean he could track her across a similar distance?

Damon shook his head, brushing his pants as he stood up. "Nothing specific—just the general flavor of the place, but even that helps."

Rory crossed her arms in front of her, not enjoying the confusion his opaque comments engendered. "Helps what?"

"Me." He cast her a sidelong look before he continued. "It's disorienting, entering a new place cold. The atmosphere, the emotions, can be overwhelming."

"So you're, what, inoculating yourself?"

"You might say that." Despite the dark lenses of his sunglasses, he managed a boyishly rueful smile that did uncanny things to her insides. "But it also lets me concentrate on detecting possible undesirable contact." He pointed to a nearby ridge.

Squinting in the direction he indicated, she made out what looked like a manned checkpoint. After that, she didn't question him the next time he chose to stop.

Entering the town didn't change Rory's impression of age. Sure, there were taller concrete high-rises to the west, but the closer view of stonework and whitewashed facades, of mosques and the slender towers beside them, only reinforced the sense of history—turbulent history at that. Fresh ruins crowning a nearby hill hinted at ongoing tensions roiling under the picturesque surface.

She got out of the car before they reached the hostel, leaving Damon to make the approach alone while she cased the joint. Though she wouldn't have any difficulty disguising herself, she preferred to keep a low profile, and the fewer the people who connected him with a particular woman, the better.

Located in an old section of the town, their proposed base of operations was surrounded by low buildings, none of which looked younger than a century. Rory eyed the moderate slopes of the tiled roofs with approval, noting how they abutted that of the hostel on two sides. That would make access easier.

While her partner was arranging for an outward-facing room, she took the opportunity to study the building that would be their base for the next several days. She hadn't paid much attention to the info on the hostel during their planning sessions, more concerned with the details that directly affected the job. Seeing it now, in three dimensions, she realized it was more of a compound. Rising three stories, it formed a defensible square around a paved courtyard. In a previous life, it might have been a caravansary or the local version of a posting house, since what must have been a stable formed the ground floor of one wing. Today the horses were gone, and boxy cars like their Yugo filled the repurposed stalls.

From what she could see of its exterior, the hostel didn't run to luxury. Faded paint, weathered jambs, single-glazed windows, it probably wouldn't rate even one star in the Michelin Guide. And if there were any security cameras—not necessarily unlikely, given the hostel owner's CIA connection—they were hidden better than most.

Damon exited the building and got their bags from the trunk; apparently he had to leave the Yugo parked on the street. Trailing him back inside, Rory caught up with the Fed at the back stairs.

As she'd expected, their room on the third floor was a sturdy, bare-bones affair, as evidenced by the terra-cotta bricks exposed by broken plaster. The ambience was light-years from a Marriott or a cheerful B&B or even the Y. But since the walls were sound and a thorough check didn't turn up any spy-holes or electronic surveillance, Rory didn't have any complaints.

Still, she wasn't about to take unnecessary chances this early with such an important commission. Stepping into the private bath, she opened the faucet and played her fingers through the running water. The irregular, syncopated splashing echoed in the narrow space. "Is it safe?" she asked in a low tone that wouldn't carry far. Picking up the white bar of soap on the ceramic lavatory, she sniffed it. Detecting only a mild fragrance, she proceeded to wash her hands. Why let the water go to waste?

Damon snorted, turning back from his own examination of the walls, ceiling, floor, and furnishings to watch her, his hands coming to rest on his hips. "We're safe enough, so long as we don't draw suspicion." The answer came in the Oxford-flavored English of Jamil Abdou, his current persona; apparently it wasn't unusual for Middle Eastern men to seek higher education in the UK. He lounged against the jamb, watching her with that steady chestnut brown stare of his that made her arms and nipples prickle with awareness. "You're as bad as I am."

Absurdly delighted by his compliment, Rory gave him a broad smile and went to test the bed. "I'm a professional." It had all the resistance of a down pillow. When she sat down, she sank inches deep in a squeaking, cotton-covered marshmallow that was a struggle to escape—especially while ignoring the smirk on her supposed partner's face. A drawback, but nothing insurmountable.

The too-soft mattress wasn't a problem since she figured Damon would be around to distract her from any discomfort. And if it proved to be more than she could ignore, she could always sleep on top of him.

She probably would, anyway. The bed wasn't that large.

All in all, life was good.

CHAPTER ELEVEN

Damon's stroll through the market nearest the hostel was an exercise in surreality. As easily as that, he'd found three of the targets on his kill list. Two weeks before the auction and they were already here, jostling for position and advantage: some of the most-wanted terrorists in the world walking with bald-faced arrogance in front of UN KFOR troops, so certain of their impunity.

Luckily, the influx of terrorists for the auction was a built-in cover in and of itself, so his presence would be less noteworthy. As Jamil Abdou, a member of the infamous PKU, he was just one more out-of-town tough to the local gangs, not someone muscling in on their action.

It also meant he could start his hunt sooner.

Even as early as that night.

But first, he had to establish his bona fides.

Damon walked up to another terrorist he recognized; the veteran of many a bombing, he was dark and lanky, built like a ferret and just as vicious in a fight—perfect for Damon's purposes. He murmured a name in greeting when he was within earshot. "Ahmad."

Fear and caution sparked in the other man's aura before he turned to present an expressionless face. "Jamil." He matched his pace to Damon's. "It is good you are here."

Despite the words of welcome, Ahmad eyed him guardedly. As he should, even though they'd worked together before; Damon had gone to great lengths to cultivate Abdou's reputation for cold-blooded, no-nonsense results for precisely such a reaction.

Rory gave Damon a few seconds' head start, using the time to adjust her clothes and appearance. Taking inspiration from women she'd seen in their drive into town, she added lines of care, a doughy jawline, and flab on the hips, dulling the color of her face and turning her hair thin and dun drab, until she looked like any Kosovar's tired aunt. Average and not worth a second glance. Perfect.

Then she left the room to perform her own recon. While she had everything Damon's agency could scare up about Karadzic's stronghold, that was no substitute for doing her own prep work. Besides, there was no telling how reliable the info was; after all, it had been provided by a government agency. But even if Lucas or Felix had supplied the data, she'd still have to double-check the details, since deviations tended to crop up when they were least expected. People being people, modifications weren't necessarily documented in a timely manner—or at all—the emphasis on ISO 9000 standards in the corporate world notwithstanding; her brush with ordinary office work had reinforced that lesson.

And there was no time like the present to start.

She headed for a market to listen to gossip and accustom her ears to the dialect, maybe even buy some of that fresh cheese she'd developed a taste for on her previous visit. While she didn't speak Albanian with a local accent, she did so well enough to pass as Kosovar, which meant conversation wasn't a problem, as the Feds had expected.

Just a few minutes on the streets brought home to Rory the wisdom of her guise as a much older woman. No one saw her as a threat, allowing her to eavesdrop at her leisure.

Once across the bridge and in the northeast side, it was even easier to go unnoticed. Most eyes were on the scantily clad women and young girls crowding the sidewalks, calling out offers for sex to passing men. Cars that slowed down were mobbed by women fighting to get in. It got worse the deeper into Karadzic's territory she went. A meat market with the cattle demanding to be bought, sometimes in shrill tones, wrestling with fellow cattle for the honor of being bought.

It made her shudder inside.

Rory had nothing against prostitution. After all, what a woman did with her own body ought to be her choice—if she wanted to exchange sex for money, rather than give it away for free, who was Rory to condemn her? But these were a far cry from the professionals she'd seen in Amsterdam. The desperation in the faces of girls barely into puberty, shivering in crotch-skimming micros, said they weren't in the world's oldest profession by choice. And seeing fresh deliveries of sex slaves, dropped off by the vanload on strings and herded into warehouses just like cattle—the blatancy of their exploitation sickened her.

Yet as much as she hated to witness the abuse, she couldn't look away. In any job, she had to know how to blend in, no matter where she was. Which meant she had to watch and learn, to study the behavior and body language of those she might have to mimic. Who knew what bit of info might prove necessary to fulfill her commission?

When night fell, Rory slipped her disguise and took to the rooftops where she would be less obvious, welcoming the exercise; after the heat in Florida, sixty-two degrees Fahrenheit plus a light breeze was cold.

Part of the reason for her expedition had been to identify the best locations for the relays that would let her into the backdoor of Karadzic's security system; the miniature black boxes needed direct line of sight to get the best signal.

Many of the multistory structures she'd chosen turned out to be whorehouses. Barred windows gave her an appalling view of their dimly lit, dingy interiors. Planting the relays took time—and taught her the folly of looking through the bars. Dirty mattresses on the floors of equally dirty rooms. Barely a curtain for privacy. Obviously customers weren't entertained on the premises. And the fecal stench emanating from one in particular that she'd had to skirt!

Much later that evening, women began to appear, trickling in steadily as though a tide had turned. They had a curfew, Rory realized when a pimp suddenly cursed a small brunette for tardiness and the meager take she surrendered. He proceeded to beat and rape her in punishment, his casual brutality ignored by bored guards.

Steeling herself not to flinch, Rory scaled the adjacent wall, forcing her mind to concentrate on finding fingerholds and toeholds in the uneven brick wall, driving out all else but that. Thankfully, the sounds of flesh hitting flesh faded as she climbed higher.

Finding the right spot to secret the relay became an exercise in willpower. She just wanted to get out of there, but if she placed the black box in the wrong spot, she'd have to return to this hellhole and risk discovery by transferring or replacing it. She couldn't even do it quickly since sudden moves tended to draw attention.

After a nerve-wracking search, while trying to turn a blind eye to the violence in the room below, she found a roof tile large enough to conceal the relay and facing the correct direction. It was with distinct relief that she planted the box and plotted her route to the next location on her list.

Her stomach churning in empathy for the beaten hooker, Rory fled the sight—slowly so as to escape detection—but it was only one of many and she couldn't avoid them all. She suddenly longed to have Damon beside her, his sheer competence a comfort all its own. He might kill people, but he'd never do what she'd seen those men do to a woman.

The memory of the care Damon had shown her during lovemaking, even when she pushed his limits, helped to keep her on her course. As much as she wanted to hightail it back to the hostel, she had a job to do and a commission to fulfill.

But when a squall of rain blew in, she welcomed the excuse to break off. That first beating hadn't been the last punishment she saw, nor the worst. The heartrending sights and sounds were too distracting, interfering with her concentration. She couldn't continue and trust that her nerve would hold out; she might have done something she'd regret before the night was over. Anyway, one night's delay was better than capture.

Rory had another reason for accepting the change in her plan: she craved Damon's arms around her, pleasuring her with all his controlled power—tangible proof that not all men were like the brutes she'd seen in the whorehouses—no matter how needy that made her seem. Her Adonis was the only man she could turn to for that reassurance; she couldn't imagine discussing what she'd seen tonight with her brothers, much less her father—even if she could risk contacting them at this point.

Having avoided the other lodgers at the hostel, Damon slid into the room he shared with Rory, only to find it empty, his master thief apparently still out on recon. Automatically, he stretched out his mental antennae, searching for her distinctive aura, but he couldn't sense her anywhere nearby.

He swore in an undertone, a pang of unfamiliar concern tightening his shoulders. They hadn't discussed what they would do upon arrival, beyond reconnaissance. If Rory was in trouble, he didn't have any idea where to start looking for her. His range while awake was considerably less than in the half-waking state he used when dreamwalking. Too, he'd wanted to start his hunt, get his first kill in that night, but he couldn't do that when she might interrupt him at any time.

When the rain started, Damon moved to the window to watch for her, but the wind blew rain into the room, eventually forcing him to shut the window. Faced with rain-splattered glass, he was left feeling caged and had to pace the simply furnished, lamp-lit room to relieve his disquiet.

Rory was a grown woman, but it was hours past midnight,

and even in the most peaceful of circumstances, he'd never describe their location as safe. It wasn't as if—

Damon had to snort at his rationalization. Okay, so he was worried about her. But surely she was safer at night? She was in her element, sliding through the dark.

It was strange, the responsibility he felt for her, a full-grown woman and expert in her own field. But even though he accepted that she could handle herself, he couldn't dismiss the growing concern he felt at her continued absence. No amount of self-directed ridicule banished the nagging unease.

And that was another thing: the strength of his attachment was worrisome in someone who worked alone. After all, this partnership was a one-shot deal.

The spark of a woman's mind, one whose piquant feel had become intimately familiar to Damon over the past several days, suddenly impinged on his awareness, slowly drawing nearer. Its bright focus was cloudy with dismay and disgust, but there was no mistaking his master thief for anyone else.

His heart leaped in response to her approach, its sudden lightness making him realize the full extent of his misgivings about Rory doing recon without backup. His cock, likewise, stirred, apparently already trained to anticipate her carnal demands. *Down, boy.* Now wasn't the time for that.

The doorknob rattled, then turned, more than enough warning for him to draw his gun and hold it ready by his side, just in case. He couldn't detect any undue interest directed at Rory, but he hadn't lasted as long as he had in his line of work by making assumptions.

The heavy door opened quietly, just enough to allow a middle-aged woman to slip into the room. She closed it behind her, dropping a bag by her feet, and leaned back with a tired sigh. "This is a horrible place." Her honest distaste came through loud and clear, a bitterness in her aura that curdled the tongue and set his teeth on edge, but Damon refused to let that distract him.

There was no reason for the stranger's presence. He hadn't contacted any of the agency's local assets. So who was she and what was she doing here?

About to raise his gun and demand her name, something gave him pause, made him stay his hand. He took stock of the deep-set eyes with their bruised lids, the thin, down-turned mouth, the loose skin along her jaw. Nothing sparked in his memory, only the certainty that he must have met her somewhere before. Yet she had to know who he was; she hadn't evinced any surprise at his presence when she entered the room.

Then it clicked.

Her aura was familiar.

Dumbfounded, Damon stared, his jaw dropping, as he tried to assimilate what his mental sense was telling him. *"Rory?"*

The woman opened faded blue eyes at his whisper, pushed off the door, and trudged toward him. Like stop-motion photography run backward, she shed years with each step. Her irises darkened to sapphire. Thin, ash brown hair beaded with raindrops turned to damp honey gold, while pale lips bloomed cherry red. Deep lines on her face disappeared as her complexion smoothened out and her jawline firmed. Baggy clothes lost shape, hanging on a slimmer figure. A sagging bosom regained perkiness.

He shook his head in astonishment. It had to be magic. He couldn't think of any other explanation for how she did it.

By the time she slid slender arms around his neck, a completely different woman stood in front of him. All in a matter of heartbeats. Nothing remained of the older one who'd entered the room, save for her clothes.

She *was* Rory. There was the familiar aura he'd tracked and grown accustomed to, the brilliance of her mind, the focus, the scintillating spectrum of colors, the dismay and disgust he'd sensed earlier.

Finally accepting the impossible, Damon holstered his gun, shifting his attention to the source of her upset for something he could handle. Despite her facade of calm, her emotions clawed at his mind, raw and hurting, but he couldn't escape them. He had to help her, soothe her somehow. If he didn't, she might not go the distance. But what had overset her ingrained self-possession?

Rory's arms tightened suddenly, her distress spiking. "Help me forget those girls." Tears brimmed in her eyes, threatening to spill over.

Then he understood and his heart turned over in sympathy and remorse. She'd been reconnoitering Karadzic's territory and must have seen the sex slaves walking the streets. Her shock told him much about Rory. In her previous trip to Kosovo, she probably hadn't been exposed to that side of the criminal underworld.

A protective reflex he'd never felt before prompted Damon to take her into his arms, offering her reassurance and support. This was his fault: if it hadn't been for him recruiting her for this mission, she'd have remained happily ignorant of such inhumanity.

"Please?"

Caught up in her urgency and driven to assuage her distress any way he could, Damon gathered Rory up to kiss her, nipping at her lips and forcing her to concentrate on the here and now.

On him and not the horrors she'd seen. There was no room for gentleness. In her current state of mind, to offer gentleness would be doing her no favors.

She responded fervently, welcoming the thrust of his tongue, meeting him stroke for stroke in a carnal duel fueled less by desire than by desperation. Her mouth clung to his as though for breath, the violence of her distress clear in how she tried to sink into him.

That had to change, if he wanted to give Rory at least one night free from the knowledge of the depths of inhumanity that could be visited on women because of their sex.

Damon divested her of her ill-fitting clothes, discovering the slender body beneath. His cock stirred automatically at the sight. Curvaceous but not voluptuous, unlike the platinum blonde who'd walked out of the surf of a Florida beach and overturned all his expectations, but still Rory.

Who needed distraction from the barbarity she'd witnessed.

Holding her attention with his kisses, he carried her to the bed and laid her down, all the while plotting his assault on her senses. As he'd suspected, her nipples were soft, puffy. He thumbed them to stiff peaks, remembering how she'd practically gone up in flames when he played with her breasts.

Rory reared back to gasp, a flicker of pleasure the first true indication of desire from her since she initiated their embrace.

Encouraged by her response, Damon took a nipple between his lips and drew strongly on the sweet bud, rolling and tweaking its partner with his fingers for added stimulus.

She bucked beneath him with a hoarse cry of delight. Her musk suddenly filled the air in definite approval of his efforts. Moaning, she clutched his head closer, her fists tight around his hair.

With the sure knowledge of her willing participation behind him, he set out to drive her wild. He worshipped her breasts, kneading and caressing and sucking, alternating between the soft mounds, and applying his teeth and tongue for variation. No way would she have thought to spare for the horrors in her memory tonight, not if he had anything to say about it.

Her breasts were more sensitive than he'd imagined. Though he used only his mouth and hands, she came suddenly, taking Damon by surprise, her orgasm crashing against his mental sense from out of the blue.

Radiating pleasure and surprise in equal parts, Rory writhed in his arms, lost in her paroxysms of ecstasy. Gasping in delight, she arched beneath him, nearly lifting him off the narrow bed.

It wasn't enough. She'd asked him to help her forget, if only for a little while.

Feeling the tremors of her body begin to subside, he resumed his suction, intent on stretching out her orgasm.

"Oh, God!" Rory twisted, her strong legs locking around his hips as she ground her pelvis against him.

Fighting to ignore the delicious pressure on his aching cock, Damon continued his carnal assault on her nipples. Her breasts had to be getting sore, but he couldn't tell from her impassioned response. The gasps and moans and spikes of renewed desire that replaced her distress more than confirmed the rightness of his decision. He could give her this: a night's respite from evil memory.

Burying his face in her cleavage, he pressed his stubbled jaw into the yielding slopes of her breasts, intent on overwhelming her senses.

She gasped, her back arching. The dark perfume of her arousal filled his head, calling to the primal male in him. Yielding. Ready for the taking.

All he had to do was mount her, his libido whispered. Insidious temptation.

Unable to help himself, Damon probed her pussy, testing her welcome and finding creamy acceptance. He struggled to deny his baser instincts, a battle made more difficult when Rory's legs clamped down on his hand, her flesh hot and slick and tight around his fingers.

"Oh, yes. Please."

Her encouragement didn't help, either. His cock throbbed in demand, wanting in.

Damon hissed, riding out the nerve-jangling surge of aching desire. No, this was for Rory. To take her now, when she was vulnerable, would leave a bad taste in his mouth, no matter what his libido urged. Unlike his initial pursuit, this was no game to press for advantage.

Wrapping his lust in a stranglehold, he strummed his thumb over her swollen folds, adding to his bombardment of stimuli. Brilliant flares of delight rewarded him as his master thief panted with her growing need. Pressing kisses down her torso, he sought her pleasure points with every lick and caress, focusing on her neural centers for maximum sensation.

Rory gave herself over to the pleasure, embracing impetuous delight with reckless vigor. She writhed under him, undulating against his cock with breath-stealing abandon that had him praying for control, rubbing against him with all the flexibility of her supple body.

This time the buildup to her climax was clear, the gathering of her tension so bright he couldn't overlook it. Combing through her fine muff, he bared her clit and tongued the erect nub, lavishing playful licks on the bud.

A choked moan greeted his foray, red sparks of passion

dancing across his mental sense. Immersing himself in her heady perfume, he fed the blaze, suckling on her hard clit and pumping her creaming flesh.

With a harsh cry of relief, Rory came again.

Her ecstasy and relief seared him, her orgasm blinding, its intensity such that Damon could almost feel it. His cock throbbed with need, demanding fulfillment, so swollen he was afraid he'd embarrass himself by spilling in his pants.

He kept at her, drawing out her pleasure, pulling the liquid heat from her in wave after honey-sweet wave until she was too spent even to moan. Then, ignoring his aching hard-on, he released her, leaving her to slide into sleep.

"Damon?" Rory murmured as her eyes fluttered shut.

"Shhh. It's okay. Just rest."

With a sigh, she did.

Clenching his teeth against the justified torment of his balls, he held her in his arms while she slept, gratified that he could bring her such respite. Her peace was a balm on his mental sense, easing the atypical remorse plaguing him.

Only gradually did his hard-on subside, but eventually his mind grew clear enough to marvel at the secret she'd shared. Her trust staggered him.

It all made sense now. The Asian woman, the brash bleached blonde and other versions of blondes, the curly haired redhead, the dusky thief—they'd all been her.

Rory was a shapeshifter. Un-fucking-believable. He'd thought himself open-minded, his imagination made flexible by his incubus abilities, but even he would never have stretched it that far. Small wonder she'd had the agents previously assigned to acquire her chasing their tails. And no wonder she'd smirked when he'd asserted her blondness.

Damon studied her sleeping form, comparing it to her previous incarnations: a darker blonde; wavy, not curly, hair falling past her shoulders; small nipples that made her breasts look larger than average; fair skin but without the redhead's translucence and far from the darkness of the brunette who'd turned the tables on him and rocked his world. It was like making love to completely different women and yet . . . not.

He was reminded of the first time he'd touched her dreams and the multitude of women who'd surrounded him. Which one was her true form?

Did it matter?

After some thought, Damon decided it didn't. His master thief was the same, no matter what form she took—even that middle-aged woman's. Anything that helped them accomplish the mission was a plus.

She snuggled closer to him, wrapping an arm around his waist and twining her legs with his. Such a deep and contented sleep for such a guarded woman.

Because of him.

Damon caressed her slowly, astounded by the change he felt. It wasn't just Rory who was different. *They* were different. By revealing herself to him this way, she'd modified their equation, established an intimate bond he couldn't deny.

Pulling his holster off his belt, he stuck it under his pillow and settled back with his master thief cradled securely in his arms. He could only hope the bond wouldn't prove to be a liability.

Chapter Twelve

Daylight shining on her heavy eyelids tried to drag Rory back to wakefulness, a state of affairs she wanted to avoid for some reason that didn't bear thinking of. The delicious heat protecting her languid body from the cold mountain air made it easier to drift. Her mind felt sluggish, her thoughts refusing to connect, but her muscles had that sweet, wonderfully familiar ache that said she'd had fantastic sex the night before. The steady beat beneath her cheek was a comforting sound that demanded nothing of her.

But the relentless glare eventually proved too irritating to ignore, overcoming her inertia. A blade of sunlight had penetrated the room through a gap between the curtains to assault her eyes. Grunting, she shifted her head from its line of fire.

The sight of her arm, unmarred by wrinkles or other signs

of age, jarred her closer to alertness. Hadn't she Changed to an older woman for the return to the hostel? When had she dropped that guise for this one?

She tried to clench her hand and saw the limb obey. It was definitely hers.

"You alright?" The rumbled query resonated through her limp body, striking deep notes in her responsive core.

Only then did it dawn on Rory that she was virtually plastered to a very cotton-covered male chest—Damon's. She took a deep breath, his male scent overcoming the embarrassment that stirred at the hint of clinginess. "Um, yeah."

How had she ended up in this position?

"Sure?" His hand glided up her back, a soothing gesture that was quite unlike him.

Puzzlement roused at his persistence. Of course she was alright. Why did he think she needed soothing?

Rory rubbed sleep sand from her eyes, rather more than usual . . . unless they were dried tears. She blinked, a heaviness of spirit returning like some half-remembered dream. Had she cried in Damon's arms? She sniffed experimentally; her nose was clear, which, when taken with the relaxation of her body, was a vote against crying, thank goodness.

Spurred by her Adonis's waiting silence, her memory sharpened, recalling pleasure—a rolling orgasm that had wiped away all cares. Just the flashback was enough to warm her cheeks. But why was that any different from—

Almost in tears, she'd begged him for forgetfulness.

Oh.

Slowly, the reason for her meltdown revealed itself, emerging like the image on old-fashioned photo paper immersed in a developer bath.

The memory of the brutality she'd witnessed was now like a dream, the horror held at a distance by the fatigue weighing down her limbs. Sexual hangover had its advantages, it seemed. Obviously, she had Damon to thank for her condition, though the details were hazy.

Toward the end, all she really remembered was one continuous rolling orgasm after another. He'd so overwhelmed her senses that she didn't recall much after that. She must have passed out at some point.

Then a different memory surfaced, one of Changing in Damon's presence, unplanned and unintended. Despite her much-debated concerns, something inside her had instinctively trusted the Fed in the midst of her crisis.

Oh, God. Rory winced, wishing she could start the day over. She couldn't believe she'd revealed her shapeshifting to him just like that—without any forethought or deliberate decision. While she trusted her gut, she preferred logic whenever possible. She buried her face in her unyielding pillow and made a mental note not to mention her slip to her family.

"You sure you're alright?" he repeated. Concern dropped his already deep voice to a lower, core-melting register. He tipped her head up with a gentle finger under her chin, his chestnut brown gaze solicitous. His kiss was slow and searching, clean and sweet, coaxing a response from her she hadn't thought possible, given her sated condition.

Since Rory wanted time to absorb the implications of her slip, she didn't appreciate her body's inopportune arousal. "Yeah, I'm sure."

Opening her eyes reluctantly, she pushed off Damon's chest and pulled the blanket to her chin. The motion made her breasts sting like hell. She hissed, then jerked the blanket down

167

to inspect her body. Her fair skin had an extreme case of beard burn; even her thighs hadn't escaped unscathed. "You marked me!"

He eyed the rash covering her breasts with a distinct lack of concern. "You weren't complaining at the time." The corner of his mouth hitched up in a look of pure male smugness. "I'd say it served its purpose."

Flushing at the reminder of her weakness, Rory glared at him but couldn't work up that much heat against the truth. Her general lack of stickiness suddenly registered. He must have washed her while she was asleep; that he'd been able to do so without rousing her was further proof that he'd earned her trust on a subconscious level. "I hope last night wasn't a problem."

"You were upset."

She faced the window, squinting at the beam of sunshine. "You might say that." It was an understatement, since she barely remembered returning to the hostel.

Damon shifted behind her, his weight making the mattress sway. "I take it you saw the whorehouses."

"They were awful." Rory dug her fingers into the pillow, sheer will driving down the images that tried to rise.

"I'm sorry you had to see that."

As if he had any control over what happened to her. She shook her head impatiently. "You had nothing to do with it."

"Still, you wouldn't have been here if not for me."

Rory turned over to face the Fed. "Why doesn't the UN do anything about it?" She considered herself less idealistic than most, but surely a political construct like the United Nations would have a vested interest in putting down something as blatant as the brutality and exploitation she'd seen last night.

"The UN?" Damon shook his head ruefully, apparently at

her naïveté. "The so-called peacekeepers are some of Karadzic's best customers locally. Human trafficking is big business around here, involving international networks. Besides, the UN's pragmatic. Since the gangs maintain a semblance of order in their territories, they're off-limits."

Stunned by his matter-of-fact summation, Rory made a face of disgust. "Isn't there something *we* can do?" It stuck in the craw to even think of turning a blind eye to that horror.

"Hit them where it hurts." At her look of inquiry, he added: "Their wallets."

She leaned against the headboard, hugging her legs to her chest. "And getting *that* from under them?" she asked, referring to the nuke. Even with daily checks for bugs in the room, they couldn't risk mentioning the objective out loud.

Damon scratched his beard thoughtfully, a habit that had surfaced after a few days of stubble; Rory suspected he preferred being clean shaven. "It'd be a major hit. There's the initial outlay, opportunity cost, and . . . loss of face."

God, just the way he said that—totally dispassionate yet phrasing it in terms she could easily relate to—made her hot! A reaction that made her uncomfortable, given the shift in the balance of power between them.

For some strange reason, Damon picked up a burst of arousal from Rory. He had to wonder what was going on in her head that his answer elicited such a response. He also wanted to ask her what exactly had brought on last night's desolation, but remembered her injunction about wanting to forget. Questioning her about it wouldn't be conducive to forgetfulness.

He shrugged inwardly, then switched to the topic that had

his curiosity on overdrive. "How do you do that?" He twirled his fingers beside his head and down in an encompassing gesture to elaborate on his question. "You know, morph." He still had difficulty accepting what memory told him he'd seen. Incredible as it was, his master thief was a shapeshifter. Even for an incubus, belief took some doing. No wonder his slip of the tongue hadn't fazed her.

She blinked at him, then tightened her hold around her bent legs, wariness slipping over her like a dark green cloak. "I don't know. It's never been studied, and I'm not volunteering to become a lab rat just to find out."

It made sense, although Damon suspected there was more to it than that. "It's not a skill you discovered recently."

Rory gave him a thin smile. "Was yours?"

He acknowledged her *Back off* signal with a nod. "I was fortunate in that I wasn't the first incubus to join the Company."

Now that the attention wasn't on her, she released her legs to lean forward, intense curiosity practically shining from her, banishing all the green from her aura. "You're not?"

Damon found that he wanted to tell her, to discuss that side of him that most people didn't see. "No, I'm not. Luckily, my uncle recognized what I was." Dion Venizélos had been the deputy director of the agency and gotten him into incubus training early to hone his dreamwalking.

She pulled a pillow into her arms, like one of his cousins, when they were younger, snuggling down for a bedtime story. "Your uncle?"

"I was living with him." With the onset of puberty had come the awakening of his mental sense; he'd discovered another incubus in Dion's dreams and turned the tables on the assassin. There'd been no question he'd join the agency after that.

Her face softened. "Your parents really were killed by terrorists?"

So she remembered that? He nodded, keeping his face blank. "They were kidnapped, then murdered, when I was eleven." He looked away to avoid seeing the pity in her deep blue eyes; what he picked up through his mental sense was bad enough. They'd been agents; their deaths had been in the line of duty, though he hadn't known it at the time.

Damon changed the subject, not wanting to dwell on the past. "Did you complete whatever you were doing yesterday?"

He could sense her hackles rising at the question. But she swallowed the *Mind your own business* that had probably been at the tip of her tongue, pursing her lips in irritation instead.

"No, the rain interrupted me." Rory's answer surprised him; he'd half expected her to ignore the question. "In fact, I'd better get moving."

Though she might have said so to avoid further discussion, his master thief rolled out of bed and bounced to her feet, releasing the pillow as though she hadn't taken shelter behind it. Her stride wagged her bare ass provocatively; then she bent over her pack, and his heart nearly stopped.

Pink pussy lips peeked out between her slender thighs, the tender folds spread in invitation, like a vision of heaven.

Damon's cock gave a convulsive twitch, reminding him that he hadn't gotten any last night. Fuck, one would think he'd been celibate for months, instead of just a little over twenty-four hours, the way his brain dropped south at the sight.

Worse, the minx was completely oblivious to his response. She didn't evince even a spark of awareness of his condition, so focused was she on whatever she wanted in her pack.

"Got to go. Work to be done." Radiating determination all at odds with her devil-may-care facade, she squeezed into a minuscule tube dress that ended well short of her knees.

"That's . . ." He blinked, jolted out of his carnal fugue by her choice of attire.

"Nobody really looks at the hookers," Rory explained, plumping a bustline that suddenly threatened to burst her seams, though the rash across her breasts remained, contributing a hefty measure of authenticity to her disguise. She paused before the door, her hands rising to tousle hair that was rapidly turning black and curly.

"What are you doing?" After the lengths she'd taken to hide her shapeshifting ability, Damon was surprised that she now did it in front of him without any hesitation.

She turned an average-pretty face to him, slightly dusky and indistinguishable from dozens of whores in the streets. "Since you're supposed to be alone, I thought it'd be best if the same woman wasn't seen leaving your room every day." She shrugged dismissively, as though her consideration were nothing out of the norm.

And maybe it wasn't, for someone with her background and proven ability—after all, that was why the Old Man had chosen to recruit her for this mission—but it still surprised him that she extended her wary diligence to his end of the bargain.

Just part and parcel of having a partner. Damon had to admire Rory for adjusting so quickly to not working alone. He had better make the same adjustments himself, if their mission was to be successful.

CHAPTER THIRTEEN

All the easy prey—the known quantities—on his kill list were done, leaving Damon the ones with spotty information, such as ibn Turki, the moneyman for a UK-based terror cell and his next target. Damon knew something of the road that had taken the Saudi Arabian to London from the radical Wahhabite madrasah in Riyadh where he'd studied, but not enough for a strike. He needed more.

To succeed in his missions, he had to understand his targets' fears, to apprehend them intimately enough that he could evoke the most dreaded terror in their sleeping minds. So he watched from a distance, stalking his prey, learning the spikes of emotion, the fears and excitement that distinguished the finicky, long-limbed man.

That night, his surveillance led him into the northeast sector, deep in territory affiliated with Karadzic, through dark winding streets to a mean brothel indistinguishable from its neighbors. A not-so-unexpected destination, given the Saudi Arabian's predilection for beating short blondes to death—that much had been in his files.

Shedding his covey of bodyguards outside the three-story building to mingle with the brothel's security, ibn Turki disappeared inside with ill-disguised eagerness. If his purpose was the usual, a hooker would die by his hands before the night was over.

Grateful that the weather provided an excuse for his encompassing cloak, Damon ghosted to the rear of the brothel, tracking his target's murky aura as the Saudi Arabian was led by another man to a second-floor room where a woman waited. The shadowy alley at the back was deserted, which made his job easier; even better, only the upper stories had windows overlooking his position. The view of the building across the alley was blocked by low trees; if he had to, he could hide in their branches.

Obviously an impatient man, it didn't take ibn Turki long to get started. Within minutes of his guide's departure, the woman cried out, a sharp flare of pain to Damon's mental sense. Clearly, the Saudi Arabian was up to his usual tricks. He pitied the hooker who'd drawn the short straw. She wouldn't have a quick death, if his target ran true to form.

Resigned to the drawn-out torture to come, he settled against the thick trunk of his chosen tree. There was nothing he could do for the hooker, except watch . . . and kill her murderer when the time came.

The fury that answered the audible blows was a change from

the usual, but it didn't mean anything to him, since it was coming from the victim, not ibn Turki. The fact didn't expand his knowledge of the target. The dull thuds and cries of pain and anger mixed unpleasantly with the creaking of box springs and the slapping of wet flesh and studied exclamations of passion from the other rooms. A busy night at this brothel. It made him wish he were back at the hostel servicing his master thief instead—or even out breaking someone's neck with his bare hands. Almost anything else would be better than waiting for Death to come visiting.

A sudden crash jolted Damon out of his watchful crouch as the murky aura he was monitoring disappeared. A quick probe told him ibn Turki wasn't dead, only unconscious. Too bad. Because he was just below the window, he saw a woman stick her face out, blond hair catching the meager light. He figured she was the intended victim trying to escape when she grabbed the bars and strained to pry them apart.

The desperation beating against his mental sense had him shedding his cloak before he realized that he'd decided to help her. Backing up for a running start, he leaped up and caught a narrow ledge along the side of the building. Hanging by his fingers, he got his feet under him long enough to lunge up and transfer his grip to a solid bar rough with rust.

Then his brain caught up with the rest of him. *Fucking idiot, are you going to risk blowing your cover for a piece of tail?* Training said he could still salvage the situation. All he had to do was drop down and leave her as she was.

Be damned if I do.

At his appearance, the hooker jerked a damaged hand to her bare breasts, hissing in shock, but didn't cry alarm.

"You're not getting out that way." Damon scrambled up to

stand on the ledge, his hackles rising at the thick, overly sweet stench of fresh blood coming from the room. He didn't waste any more time second-guessing himself. The sooner she was out, the sooner he could be back under cover. Now wasn't the time to browbeat himself for giving in to stupid impulse—and courting discovery.

Setting his feet against the brick wall, he yanked on the bottom rail of the bars until the bolt in the corner that held it in place pulled free of crumbling mortar. The squeal of metal sounded loud over the drumming in his ears, but hopefully the noises of the brothel's other customers drowned it out. He did the same to the other corner, then held the bars away so the woman could slip through the gap.

And still ibn Turki remained unconscious. Damon was tempted to sneak in and complete the job. But that might put the rest of his targets on guard.

While the blonde teetered on the ledge, he hurriedly reversed his ascent, dropping to the hard cobbles of the alley with an involuntary grunt. He straightened immediately and extended his arms, flicking his fingers impatiently when she wavered. They didn't have time for delay.

The woman jumped.

Damon caught her easily, the impact negligible since she didn't weigh much and was totally unencumbered. As soon as her feet touched the ground, she sprang out of his arms, plastering her back to the wall, fearful eyes wide and unblinking in the half-light.

Ready to leave her to her own devices—he didn't need this complication—he sensed a bored spark approaching the corner of the building. With no time to bridge the gap and gather her up, he crouched down, making himself into as small a target as possible and flinging his black cloak around his shoulders and over his head. He didn't draw his gun. A shot would only attract more attention.

Smoke drifted on the wind, acrid with the heaviness of Turkish tobacco, the smoker only a heartbeat behind. A soft scuff announced his arrival a split second later.

Luckily, the woman made an excellent distraction.

Gaping, the guard froze at the sight of the bloodied, naked blonde standing in the shadows, his cigarette falling to the ground. To Damon's surprise, he shut his mouth and spun around, giving her his back, then quickly strode away.

Not questioning his good fortune, Damon stood up and thrust the cloak at the silent woman. "Here. Take it." Even in this area, that much bare skin was cause for comment; she needed its coverage more than he did. When she didn't move, he bundled her into the heavy black cloth, ignoring the smooth skin that brushed his fingers and the flinch she couldn't suppress. None of his business. He couldn't afford the complications. "Go."

She went. Throwing an astonished look over her shoulder, she quickly limped down the alley, skittering like a panicked mouse but with enough presence of mind to duck behind a tree, into another lane and out of sight. In the span of seconds, it was as if she'd never been.

Damon stared after the hooker, wondering at the wisdom of his actions. It was little enough, but he didn't hold out much hope for her chances. Even if she escaped her current pimp, she'd probably continue to pay her way on her back—but a life of whoredom had to be better than death at ibn Turki's hands.

Since she'd had spirit left to fight for survival, he couldn't have stood by and done nothing when it wouldn't—quite—jeopardize his mission. Not when it would have meant facing

Rory with the knowledge that he'd turned a blind eye to that woman's death. Though why he put that much weight on a temporary partner's opinion—and a thief's at that—he didn't know.

The strengthening of ibn Turki's aura cut Damon's internal debate short. Ignoring the raw bite of a sudden gust of wind, he withdrew to a safer distance. Giving the woman his cloak increased the possibility of detection and exposed him slightly more to the elements, but there was no risk of identification. When he'd bought the garment at the market, the shop had been doing land-office business due to the rains and unseasonably cool weather. There was nothing to connect it with him, except DNA. Despite his master thief's abilities, to worry about the latter was pushing the edge of paranoia.

Taking cover behind another tree, he focused his mental sense. It should be interesting to see how his target reacted to the change in circumstances.

Pain and fear flared within the second-floor room, then outrage. After a few minutes, the murkiness moved slowly, in fits and spurts, reversing the route it had taken earlier. The hooker must have clouted ibn Turki a good one; the unsteady progress hinted at a concussion. Tracking it through the brothel, Damon ghosted up an alley to a spot with a view of the building's door, wondering what the Saudi Arabian would do and how he would explain his injury.

Cursing vociferously, the Saudi Arabian shoved someone aside and staggered out the door, blood flowing from a gash on his head. A shout went up from his bodyguards; then they converged on him.

From where he stood, Damon couldn't make out much of the conversation. Anger, chagrin, outrage, all those were clear to his mental sense, but whatever ibn Turki said didn't reach him; however, it must have been effective. There was a concerted rush of brothel thugs to the rear of the building, marked by a furor of resentment, mock indignation—and very real fear.

But ibn Turki wasn't done. Calling up his men, he left the brothel surrounded by a cloud of outrage and bodyguards. Though his gait was unsteady, his direction was unerring. He clearly had a destination in mind.

The Saudi Arabian crossed the mouth of the alley where Damon had taken up station, threatening retribution with typical braggadocio. It seemed that the hooker's single-handed escape had morphed into a deep-seated plot against ibn Turki, with a band of men lying in wait in the brothel to ambush him.

Damon stifled a derisive snort at the self-serving fiction. Naturally, there was no one to gainsay ibn Turki's version of the night's events.

His target staggered on, but he didn't go far. A few blocks later, he accosted the more heavily armed thugs stationed in front of another door. It immediately became obvious that ibn Turki was a valued guest.

The Saudi Arabian was ushered inside with due haste, the fawning reception apparently sufficient to mollify his outrage, since his aura soon shifted to one of calculation. His arrival stirred a hornet's nest, if the number of men who rushed off shortly after was any indication. When ibn Turki emerged hours later, a smile of grim satisfaction thinned his lips, boding ill for someone.

A stocky, swarthy man swaggered beside him, flanked by bodyguards. Damon recognized him from his final briefing: Osum, given name unknown, the gang lord who controlled the surrounding streets. The Saudi Arabian had to be an important customer to merit his personal attention.

Damon drifted closer to study the Kosovar. Someone in the past had battered his nose to painful flatness. Added to a luxuriant mustache and the short bristles on full cheeks, it gave the gang lord a swinish appearance—but not one of a domestic pig. To Damon's mind, Osum seemed more like a wild boar. Feral and dangerous when cornered.

The surrounding buildings discharged more thugs, spewing bunches and clumps until a potential mob filled the street. Dark anticipation hung in the night air, fetid with anger. But even without it, Damon knew something was about to happen.

Heads turned in a wave that started at the edge of the crowd. A subvocal growl rose around a knot of men, flowing on as people stepped aside to let them pass. In the middle, someone was resisting the advance and was dragged forward, in spite of his struggles, to stand before the gang lord.

Damon recognized the captive as the guard from the brothel who'd looked the other way when the hooker escaped. The man hadn't actively helped her, but he hadn't stopped her, either.

Standing on the steps to his building, Osum launched into a diatribe. From the tone of the ranting, much of which was delivered in Albanian dialect, the gang lord blamed the guard for the loss of a whore and his—and thereby the clan's—loss of face with a valued customer, and had decided to make an example of him for his betrayal.

With ibn Turki gloating at the gang lord's side, there was no question as to the fate of the hapless guard: if no one stood up to Osum, he would die.

Damon gritted his teeth against the inevitable. He'd calculated that equation long ago and drawn his conclusion: one man's certain death was as nothing on the scales of duty when weighed against the countless other lives he'd sworn to protect.

If he intervened in this case, he'd risk dying and leaving Rory to complete the mission on her own, essentially abandoning her in the middle of hostile territory. The thought stiffened his resolve.

Osum snorted loudly, setting off a roar of savage laughter from his audience. He shot the captive in the foot, then, while his victim was screaming, shot him again in the knee.

Pain crashed against Damon's mental sense, an explosion of red amidst the fear and anger and sickening pleasure flowing from the crowd. His stomach lurched at the emissions. The pig was inflicting pain simply because he could. He kept his face blank with an effort, his disgust at the unnecessary violence a distraction he couldn't afford. Sure cognizance of where his duty lay clashed with the excruciating pain and gut-wrenching terror the injured man radiated, and was barely sufficient to overcome the urge to interfere.

Damon had stayed too long, exposed himself too much, in his surveillance of ibn Turki. But he couldn't leave without a silent promise: if there was anything he could do to undermine that mad boar without jeopardizing the mission, he would do it.

Stepping out of the shadows into the early grayness that preceded sunrise, he met Osum's gaze, unflinching and determined. Sometimes the most difficult thing in the world to do was nothing. The bitter knowledge that he had to stand by and let the guard die was mitigated only by his vow that his death wouldn't be for nothing.

The wave of cold anger Damon sensed in return told him he'd made an enemy, which was fine by him. He didn't want to be friends. He'd have to step carefully, but even at the risk of exposure the gesture was worth it.

Certain he'd made an impression on the gang lord, Damon withdrew into the darkness. He continued to watch the torture from the shadows, unable to turn away while the man lived, accepting a share of the responsibility for what would follow.

The violence ended abruptly with a shot to the head. Two thugs gathered up the body and took it away, to be buried in a nameless grave like many others before him.

And through it all, ibn Turki had watched with gleeful self-satisfaction. The smug bastard.

If Damon could have taken out his target right at that moment, without risking the mission, he would have done so without any second thoughts. He could only be glad Rory hadn't been around to witness this killing, whatever else she'd seen.

CHAPTER FOURTEEN

On both sides of the river, most of the buildings sat cheek by jowl, their walls built flush to one another. It made crossing to adjacent roofs a walk in the park—or a short climb—with only occasional descents to street level. However, the journey wasn't entirely trouble free.

The cold night air bit at Rory's exposed fingers as she crawled across yet another expanse of weathered brick tiles. Unfortunately, she had to leave them bare to find the nooks and crannies she needed to scale the walls of the town's uneven skyline. Luckily, the rough tiles retained enough heat that her fingers didn't go numb.

She ignored the discomfort, long inured to the realities of her work. Satisfaction sped her steps. Despite the horrors she continued to witness, she'd managed to finish planting the relays—the job interrupted by the storm—and was well on her way to memorizing the best routes to, from, and around Karadzic's stronghold. Not bad for a few nights' work.

Nothing moved in the rooftops. Even the pigeons were bedded down for the night, remaining silent when she passed, noticeable only because of the cloying pungency of their fresh droppings.

In the street below, a pack of dogs scrounged around some bushes slowly taking over the ruins of a bombed-out building. Farther away, a bobbing light illuminated the faces of first one, then another structure. Possibly a roving KFOR patrol.

Rory greeted the sight of the hostel with a sigh of relief, looking forward to getting out of the wind and cuddling up to Damon's furnacelike heat. Confident that no one could see her, she swung off the roof and slipped through the open window. She pushed up her ski mask and pulled it off, releasing her hair from its constraints.

Damon didn't react to her arrival. He didn't even move in bed. She wished it was a testament of his acceptance of her, but the explanation wasn't so heartwarming: he was on another hunt.

It chilled her to admit that, to know that a man she'd taken as a lover could kill so easily. She was safe while Damon needed her, probably even after then; maybe it was foolish of her, or simply because of how they'd met, but she couldn't imagine that he would turn that lethal skill of his on her.

Yet she couldn't countenance his hits. Felix's teaching—that killing in the middle of a job was verboten since it upped the stakes for the cops—was too ingrained in her consciousness to simply disregard.

Rory stared at his sleeping form, clad in shirt and pants,

ready for a quick getaway. He'd brought her more pleasure than she'd had in a while; yet even now he was on a mission, taking out another terrorist in his dreams.

Perhaps it was hypocritical, but the strength of will and ruthlessness necessary to do what he did excited her. However, it wasn't without risk. Damon could die without waking up.

Her foolish heart skipped a beat at the thought.

His chest expanded suddenly, the way it did when he returned to himself. An instant later, his eyes opened, their chestnut brown almost golden, pinning her where she stood. "There you are." As though he'd been searching for her.

The emotions she'd been struggling with choked her into silence. Relief at his safety and anger at his casual disregard for death-dealing twisted inside her, fighting like a pair of clawing, squalling cats. Despite her distaste for what he did, she couldn't bring herself to call it murder, given his targets.

He jerked upright and caught her arm, pulling her down to sit beside him on the bed. "Are you okay?"

"Am I—" Rory sputtered into silence, unable to believe his question.

"What's wrong?" Damon stroked her back, as though trying to soothe her.

"Do you have to do that?" she blurted out in a breathless rush. She was in no position to disapprove but could no longer silence her objections.

His hand stopped, coming to rest on her hip. "Do what?"

"You know." Unable to find the words to explain, Rory flung her free arm wide, encompassing the world outside their room.

Damon's eyes narrowed in comprehension, his gaze drilling into hers. "It's what I do."

"It complicates things."

"Things?"

"I—" Rory shook her head in bafflement, not even sure what she wanted to say, much less how to say it.

"My targets are the same people who're after what we want."

She ground her fingers into suddenly throbbing temples, wishing she hadn't opened her mouth. "I know that."

"Will it be a problem?"

"I don't know."

Needing distance from Rory's sharp agitation, Damon stood up and closed the window. This was how he'd expected her to react when he'd confirmed her suspicions about al-Hazzezi's death, although even now what he was picking up from her wasn't so much fear as . . . confusion.

"It complicates things," she repeated, her conflicted emotions battering his mental antennae.

Indeed. He turned back to his master thief and found her fighting to suppress a shiver. A slight draft reminded him that she'd been out in the cold and was almost certainly chilled.

Reluctantly, he returned to the bed they had to share and gathered Rory into his arms. He couldn't allow this development to adversely affect the mission.

But how to fix it, he had no idea.

Her perspective wasn't something he could change with argument. He was an incubus, and his missions were nonnegotiable. Logically, she understood his objective, but apparently found the means abhorrent.

Would assassination by physical means have been more acceptable?

Damon dismissed the stray thought with a shake of his

head. He was still shocked to awaken to her turmoil, especially just after killing ibn Turki.

Immediate and unquestioning acceptance had probably been too much to ask for, even of someone who stole for a living, but after several days together he'd dropped his guard. Rory's reaction now hurt worse than he'd expected it to—and not just because of her emotions.

Damning himself for a fool, he rubbed her back, unable to resist touching her in the guise of helping her warm up. Despite the agitation she radiated, he couldn't stay away, needed to do something to help her.

Now shivering in earnest, Rory held herself stiffly, not accepting his attentions, but not rejecting them, either. Her stance gave Damon hope that with time she'd resolve her dilemma in his favor.

Decision made, he addressed the one problem he could solve. "Let's get you out of those." Her jumpsuit couldn't be that warm. He worked the stiff zipper down, peeling the tough material off her shoulders and rubbing down the skin he bared with an extra blanket.

Once he had her dry, he bundled her into bed and lay down beside her, struggling to ignore the faint scent of healthy, feminine sweat. Despite the growing pain behind his eyes, his cock responded to her proximity, thickening against his hip with every breath she took.

Rory pressed tentative fingers on his shoulder. "You're not . . . ?"

Resigning himself to a long night, Damon put his arm around her shoulders and drew her to his side, away from the edge. After all, the bed wasn't that big. She'd fall off if she wasn't tucked against him.

He held his breath when she gingerly hitched her leg over his, but luckily she didn't raise it high enough to brush his burgeoning hard-on. "If I took you now, it'd be a grudge fuck. You don't want that."

His master thief didn't say anything after that, though the fist clenched at his waist spasmed.

Damon took her silence for agreement and counted the seconds and minutes until she fell asleep, while his body burned from her softness.

Rory stared at the image on her cell phone's screen, frustrated by the lack of detail for the south section. Until she had that information, she couldn't plan her approach to the fortress Karadzic had made of his base of operations. And she couldn't risk going in blind. That would be suicide, something her family wouldn't appreciate.

The low-powered relays she'd planted carried the signal from Karadzic's system far enough that she could tap it from the relative safety of their room in the hostel. Thanks to Lucas, she had the video feed from the security cameras on her cell phone.

Her jaw ached from clenching her teeth. She'd cracked the security system, and could watch what was going on inside, could slide in anything she wanted, but the building's physical and human defenses were something else altogether. She glared at the telltale gaps in her list. It would take a major diversion to get the data she needed.

Without willing, her gaze flicked to the closed door of silvery oak behind which came intermittent sounds of splashing. What if . . . ?

Shaking her head, Rory dismissed the notion and the image

of her Adonis standing nude under the paltry flow of water afforded by the shower that automatically flashed before her mind's eye. *Out of the question.*

For the past days, their dealings had been strained, ever since she'd voiced her compunction toward his hits. He'd tried hard to act as though nothing had changed between them, but it had. If nothing had changed, her body wouldn't be aching with emptiness, the way it had been since she'd stupidly opened her mouth and inserted foot.

Sure, if she insisted, he'd probably perform, rise to the occasion as the case may be. But that wasn't what she wanted, not unwilling performance. A grudge fuck, as he'd called it, would taint everything that had gone before.

Her gut churned. It wasn't even as if she cared about the terrorists Damon killed. Her problem was just . . .

Words continued to fail her. She couldn't take back what she'd said because she didn't know what she wanted to take back, if anything. She didn't know what was wrong, didn't know what she wanted to happen.

Didn't know how to get into Karadzic's stronghold safely without the info she lacked. Rory scrubbed her hands over her face in disgust. Too much thinking and not enough doing.

If she were making progress in her preparations, she wouldn't be twisted up in French knots about this situation with Damon, might even have figured out how to get back to the way they were before. Preferably without apologizing.

Since she'd hit a dead end, planning-wise, Rory switched screens and opened her e-mail to check the messages in her in-box for anything from Lucas, deliberately ignoring the one from Felix, who was probably demanding she confess her mischief. Easier to ask for forgiveness than for permission. While Big

Brother wouldn't have betrayed her confidence, her father's paternal intuition could be unnervingly accurate at times. Besides, though he was her father and front man, she was an adult and a free agent. She hadn't had to answer to him for years.

The light scent of clean male drifted by her nose.

She looked up to find Damon by her shoulder, a threadbare towel wrapped around his hips, in a good position to read the display. The only man she had to answer to at the moment. She'd been so lost in her thoughts that she hadn't heard the door open.

Sneaky bastard. Of course, she'd have done the same in his shoes. He didn't comment on whatever he'd seen, though, so she let it lie; it was hard for her to get up a good head of steam when she secretly approved of the intent. Besides, she didn't want to stir things up again, just when it seemed they were settling down.

Seeing the look of innocence he kept pasted on his face as he dried his hair with another towel, the notion she had earlier once again niggled at the back of her mind.

The sudden rattle of metal on wood jerked Rory's attention to the table by the bathroom door, where Damon had left his phone before showering. The matte black device vibrated again, jiggering on the hard wood like an epileptic giant beetle.

He picked it up and read something off the screen, his jaw firming with determination as he pressed some keys. His nostrils flared in a predatory expression she'd seen before, whenever he lay down to kill.

Without looking up from his phone, Damon gave her the news. "Karadzic's arriving day after tomorrow with it."

Rory's stomach dropped queasily. In little more than a week, the nuke would be put up for auction. She didn't have time to quibble or find another—more palatable—work-around for her problem.

Taking a deep breath to steel her nerve, she took the bull by the horns. "I have a problem."

That got his immediate attention. "Go."

"There's one side I can't get to, where security detains any idlers." Welcoming an excuse not to meet his narrowed eyes, Rory dropped her gaze to her phone to switch to the screen she was studying earlier. "See?" She tilted the display toward Damon to show him her list as he sat beside her on the bed, his closeness surrounding her in warmth and clean male scent.

"How can I help?"

Rory explained what she needed him to do and the logic behind it, all the while wondering if she was grasping at straws. Or maybe desperate to achieve a détente between them?

Propping his arms behind him, Damon leaned back, deep in thought. His posture made the towel around his hips gape distractingly, the sight prompting a spasm of hunger from her empty womb. Finally, he nodded. "Sure, sounds workable."

"That's . . . great." She fell silent, suddenly filled with misgivings. It was one thing to rely on her Adonis for reassurance; it was something else altogether to work hand in hand when she'd always been a solo act before. It was a deliberate extension of trust to ask for his help in this venture. She hoped it wasn't a mistake.

And that she hadn't suggested it for the wrong reasons.

Steeling himself to run the gauntlet of whores in the street, Damon exited a textile shop deep in the heart of Karadzic's territory. He'd seen as much as he could from that covert without rousing suspicions; it was time to make his move. Rory's instructions had been to meet her at the corner near the abandoned warehouse across from the Turkish bakery.

Nothing had changed since he'd first passed the area to enter the shop. Throngs of whores continued to troll for business, which seemed steady; several cars had driven by and picked up a girl or three from the ones that crowded their doors. A common sight in this part of town.

Just as he cleared the doorway, a Peugeot in camouflage tri-color with KFOR stenciled in white across its door and hood pulled up, one of the many he'd seen driving around town, supposedly maintaining peace. Then, bold as you please, the soldiers aboard made their selections from the whores clamoring for their business as though ordering takeout. It drove away, heavier by three.

Raw emotion beating at his mental antennae, Damon ignored the byplay.

Old and avid eyes turned to him as he approached the rendezvous. Eyes that assessed him quickly and labeled him a potential client. Some in girls young enough to be his daughter—and he'd jumped into the game later than most.

Desperation and greed, fear and despair, all that washed over his mind as scantily clad women flocked to him, clutching at him and rubbing their breasts against him wherever they could. They called out invitations in a medley of sultry voices, offering sexual services in exchange for euros.

Cool determination cut through it all as a pale brunette with dark eyes and big hair sashayed up to him, ruthlessly elbowing her competition out of the way. "You not want them," the brunette declared in broken Slavic-accented English.

She had to be Rory. But a Rory unlike any other he'd seen. She balanced on stilettos as though born in them. And her shapely legs went on forever, an impression heightened by the extreme brevity of her dress.

Damon had to swallow before he could get his throat to work. "I don't have time," he told her, maintaining the Oxford tones of Jamil Abdou with difficulty.

"I get you off fast. Blow, two minutes, sixty euros," she countered, her hands wandering over his body calculated to arouse. Knowing that didn't make her caresses any less effective, as his sudden painful hard-on could attest, especially when it had been days since he'd had any release.

"Sixty for two minutes?" he parroted blankly.

"I very good." Still pretending to negotiate with him, she led him down one side of the warehouse and into a side alley that looked out on the squat three-story building that formed one side of Karadzic's headquarters. Three guards loitered at the end.

Not wasting time, Rory unzipped his pants and knelt at his feet, pulling his eager cock free with a murmur of approval.

Damon shivered at her touch, his balls already clenching and swelling in anticipation of more. Damned if she didn't have him trained.

Barks of cynical laughter rose from further down the alley. Security might be tight, but evidently Rory's assessment of the guards was correct: they saw themselves as worldly men and understood that certain urges had to be satisfied.

Alone, he or Rory would have been detained for interrogation, at the very least. Together, with their intentions obvious, they were safe; provided they didn't take too long, there'd be no problem.

Now, all he had to do was keep his mind on business.

The very next moment, Rory almost wiped his mind clean of everything but sex when she licked his length, her firm grip leaving no doubt that what was coming next wouldn't be a mere semblance of a blow job.

A run of teasing nibbles up his cock lit a bonfire in his balls.

She expected him to conduct a surveillance through *this*?! He'd assumed she intended to put on a show, not the actual thing!

Damon's eyes nearly rolled back as she popped his cock head into her mouth and sucked like there was no tomorrow. Damn, but she had a gift for shaking his control. And he couldn't tell her to slow down—it would have been out of character for the roles they were playing.

"Hurry," Rory muttered around his cock, her aura sparkling with anticipation. Her breath flowing over the damp flesh only made him ache more. The brazen minx. She was enjoying his predicament, too!

Damon let his head fall back, clinging desperately to his control as he shuttered his eyes against the pleasure streaking through him. As he studied the buildings around them, he promised himself he'd get Rory to do it slowly, when they were back in their room and had some privacy. As it was, he was supremely conscious of their exposure, knew there were watchers in the shadows.

A bubble of hilarity lodged beneath his sternum. This would have to be the performance of a lifetime.

He buried his hands in Rory's hair, her chocolate brown curls twining around his fingers. Mortar scraped his back as he jerked his hips to her suction, unable to resist her skillful blandishments.

Four guards on Karadzic's roof. Damon couldn't miss their interest in Rory's impromptu sex show. *None on the neighbors'.* He hissed as she swirled her tongue over his tip, sending delight tripping up his spine in heated spirals. *Two dormers, unbarred, maybe a foot and a half wide.* Molten rapture gathered in his balls and he couldn't stop it. Not if he wanted to stay in character. *Side door, two guards smirking at them.*

Rory milked him, her motion irresistible, drawing his orgasm onward. She took him deeper, down her throat, so tight around his cock head he nearly swore.

Damon barely had the presence of mind not to speak. If he said anything, it would be blunt, four-letter Anglo-Saxon—and would blow his cover straight to hell. No fucking way could he manage any kind of accent except his own.

Fire erupted from his balls, blazed up his spine in a glory of excruciating pleasure. He didn't feel the clumps of mortar digging into his back as his hips jerked, didn't hear the hectoring calls of the whores in the street beyond, didn't see anything save Rory's lips around his cock, sucking him down into rapture.

Their egress had been anticlimactic. The only difficulty Damon had faced was retaining the security details he'd observed in his sex-soaked brain. Trailed by the guards' coarse laughter, they'd left under the pretense of seeking a hotel to continue where they'd left off.

Now, while Rory worked to extract the information she needed from his pleasure-fogged memory, he grappled with the emotions he'd sensed from her in the alley.

No hesitation, no anger or confusion. Nothing but delight in bringing him to climax. That wasn't at all what he'd expected. He suppressed a snort of laughter. Not what he'd expected? Nothing would have prepared him for what she'd done back there. Once again, his master thief had taken him by surprise, going down on him like that in public.

"That's everything?"

Yanking his mind back to business, Damon tried to give her

question the strict attention it deserved and not let his mind dwell on irrelevancies. "Yeah, that's everything."

Nodding absently, Rory pushed a hank of mousy brown hair out of her face. Flipping over the sheet of paper to expose its blank side, she began to sketch. He recognized the layout of Karadzic's base. Then she began filling in the details he'd read off her cell phone and those he'd provided her.

The unerring flow of lines struck a familiar chord in the recesses of his memory. With a bit of nudging, he coaxed it to light: that pretty artist at the park had wielded her pencil with similar confidence. While his master thief's exterior might change, the strengths and skills and quirks of personality that made her Rory remained the same.

It dawned on Damon that that was what he wanted. *She* was what he wanted. But was the difference in what he'd picked up of her emotions at the alley significant . . . or merely a lapse of her memory? Had Rory set aside her objections to his kills or had she just been caught up in the moment, in the risk they were taking?

Or perhaps there hadn't been any difference, simply wishful thinking.

CHAPTER FIFTEEN

Peering through a gap in the curtains, Damon searched the adjacent buildings and the streets below for the source of his disquiet. Someone out there was tripping a mental alarm by radiating the calm patience of a hunter. While Damon wasn't necessarily the target, the indistinguishable source of the emissions made him edgy and impatient for some indication of progress with their main mission.

For distraction, he turned back to the room and the minx who was—as usual—lounging on the bed in her birthday suit. "How's it going? Are you ready yet?"

Sitting up, Rory snagged her cell phone from her rucksack. "Oh, ye of little faith." She snapped it open to reveal a full-function, miniature QWERTY keyboard, which she set on her flat belly. Another click extended a hand-size plastic display that tripled its normal screen size and obscured his view of the tawny brown curls at her groin but not of her perky breasts.

Damon drifted closer to watch as she tapped the keys in rapid sequence with unerring precision and no wasted motion, displaying an unsuspected electronics expertise.

Less than a minute later, a window popped up on the thin screen streaming black-and-white video of a bunch of thugs desultorily playing cards. "I'm in already."

He blinked at the casual assurance in her voice, which was backed up by the steady confidence she radiated. He'd so focused on her disguises and the physical demands of her work that he'd overlooked her other capabilities, having never really thought about the mechanics of breaking and entering. Rather shortsighted of him to underestimate his master thief. He made a mental note not to repeat that mistake.

Rory shot him an indulgent sidelong glance, clearly aware of his surprise despite his attempt to keep it off his face, then pointed to a black box with flashing status indicators on the floor beside her rucksack. "I've been monitoring them for days now." The image changed to show a guarded corridor, then to other views as she switched feeds. "It's how I put together that list."

Watching the video over her shoulder, Damon scratched his itchy beard thoughtfully. Their joint foray into Karadzic's territory had filled in some of the gaps in the checklist she'd shown him, but had it been sufficient? "Have you seen enough? Can you do it?"

She cut the feed and shut her phone. "That's the question, isn't it?" She set the device on the floor and stretched out on the bed, flaunting her nudity as naturally as breathing. Despite her internal conflict over his assassinations, his master thief still insisted on having him as a lover; that gave him hope she would come around.

Recognizing Rory's game for the habitual power play it was, he sat on the floor and pulled out his .45 to occupy his hands, scrounging through his bag for his cleaning kit to hide a grin. While he knew they'd eventually end up in bed, fucking like minks, he refused to succumb that easily to her wiles. As much as his cock stirred at the sight, there was no reason to cut the game short. Anyway, with the frequent rains, it wouldn't hurt to give the pistol another rubdown.

Placing a gray-stained rag beside his weapon, Damon uncapped a small squeeze bottle. Normally, he limited himself to a quick swipe, but this time he seemed intent on a thorough round of cleaning as he applied oil to the tattered flannel cloth.

Rory immediately got a whiff of anise cookies, bringing to mind warm memories of childhood theft—totally inappropriate for her plan to vamp her Adonis. Since she couldn't do anything more until Karadzic arrived with the nuke—and hopefully weakened the current security setup—she wanted to make the most of her sexual arrangement with Damon. "Do you have to do that right now?"

"If you don't take care of your gun, it'll jam just when you need it. So I wipe it down," he replied absently, bending over the gun and setting words to frustrating action.

"Bullets, too?" As soon as the words were out, she bit her tongue, hoping he didn't take it as a suggestion.

"Cartridges. The bullet's just the tip that goes down the barrel." Damon tapped a short length of matte black metal, still not looking at her.

She made a face at the correction, wondering what else she could do without being obvious about her intentions.

"It's just like you checking your climbing ropes for rope wear." He flicked a glance at her, a smile lurking beneath his beard. "Or trying to keep the upper hand by displaying yourself that way."

Finally a response! Unconcerned by her nudity and his astute observation, Rory smiled wickedly. "Distracted?"

Damon gave her a level look as he slowly stroked the rag along the length of the barrel, the exquisite care he took to make sure he got all its nooks and crannies almost loverlike.

Watching him, she had to fight the urge to squirm, her nipples tingling from more than just the cool draft from the window. *Men and their toys.* Although for a phallic symbol, his gun was disproportionately small.

"Tempted to warm your backside."

"In your dreams," Rory retorted before she remembered whom she was talking to.

Chuckling, Damon grinned at her, a raffish expression made all the more intimidating by his unshaven face.

Deciding that silence was the better part of valor, Rory lay back on the bed, pillowing her head on her clasped hands. If he insisted on working, two could play that game. Determined to ignore him, she forced herself to mentally review the guards' rounds she'd studied for weakness.

No matter how she looked at it, she couldn't identify any opening she could exploit: in this case, quantity was a quality all its own. "Security is too tight. If this were one of my usual targets, it would be less of a problem since most places depend on electronics. As it is, there're too many guards."

"So we reduce the guards." He put away his gun and cleaning implements, once more satisfied with his weapon's condition.

Forgetting her pique, Rory raised herself to her elbows to stare at her partner. "I thought the plan was to finesse things? You're planning . . . what? A frontal assault with just the two of us?" She rounded her eyes at him to emphasize the ridiculousness of such an undertaking. The thought of her brandishing a gun like some GI Jane was just laughable.

Damon got to one knee beside the bed and reached out, trailing an anise-scented finger over her breast and coaxing one of her nipples to a peak. "Do I look suicidal?" It was obviously a rhetorical question since he punctuated it with a snort, his mouth twitching in amusement.

Relieved by his response, Rory twisted to her side to consider him. If her movement pressed her breast into his callused palm, that was only an added benefit.

After weeks of not shaving, her Adonis had the beginnings of a respectable beard shadowing his jaw. It made him look less like a Fed and more like the gangsters in town—unless you knew the sharp mind behind the disreputable exterior and the hard body concealed by his rough attire.

Something she knew quite well.

Not that she'd mind a refresher course. She needed to release the tension that impatience had built up while she'd stewed over Karadzic's security; they both might as well enjoy the process.

Rory licked her lips, savoring the familiar desire pooling in her belly as Damon continued to fondle her breast with masterful fingers. Heat flushed her body with readiness, her heart racing in expectation. "No, I wouldn't say that."

"That's good." Laughing softly, he sat down, facing her, his weight making the mattress dip and tilting her into his lap.

With her hands on his thighs and her nose pressed against his groin, she had to laugh, too. "Oh, you didn't actually mean for this to happen, did you?"

His cock twitched and hardened, lengthening into a definite ridge against her cheek. "Serendipity." His male scent strengthened, enfolding her in sensual memories, the tenting of his pants growing more pronounced.

Damon kneaded her shoulders, his hands slicker than usual and still smelling faintly of anise. Cookies and sex. A unique fusion of childhood comfort and erotic invitation that was next to irresistible.

And there was no reason to deny herself.

She leaned forward, caught the tab of his zipper between her teeth, and dragged it down.

He hissed, his hips jerking once before he reestablished that rock-hard control of his. But he also undid the button of the waistband and let his fly gape open.

Smiling to herself, Rory nosed the flaps apart, filling her lungs with his delicious male scent.

His cock emerged from its dark nest, flushed and naked, already thick but getting thicker, the dark vein along its underside pulsing to his heartbeat.

"Well, hello there." She planted a kiss on its velvety head, relishing the singular softness against her lips, one of the few spots on her Adonis's body that could be described in such terms. "Does this mean you're distracted?"

"Minx." Damon gripped her nape, urging her nearer. "If you don't do something, I might go with my first impulse."

Whoops! Knowing she could push him only so far, Rory took the plumlike knob into her mouth to divert him from entertaining thoughts of spanking. The saltiness that met her questing tongue told her he hadn't been as unmoved by her earlier display as he'd pretended, much to her gratification.

She kept the penetration shallow, focusing her laving on his cock head since he was hypersensitive there—not that she could have taken him deeper without Changing her mouth bigger. His thighs tensed under her hands when she traced the flared ridge of his cock, then clamped her lips around him to suck.

Damon groaned, his hands clenching on her hair.

Triumph exploded in Rory's heart in a heady rush of feminine power. There was no mistaking his response, no matter how he might try to hide it. Nothing got to him faster than a vigorous blow job, and after he'd threatened to spank her, she wanted him so hot and desperate his orgasm would obliterate even the shadow of a memory that he'd entertained such a notion.

Problem was, seducing him was a double-edged blade. His excitement spurred her own, making her wet and impatient to be taken. Desire made familiar by weeks of fomentation pooled in her belly. Her labia swelled and spread, the delicate folds slick with cream. Her clit throbbed to her heartbeat, eagerly awaiting the friction from his possession.

She drew on him, remembering how he hadn't held back that time in the alley and wanting the same from him again. But even more than that, she wanted him wild and uncontrolled, pumping her like there was no tomorrow and all they had were these few precious hours.

A harsh gasp told Rory she was getting to Damon, drawing him closer to the edge. Feeling him shudder beneath her lips, the intensity of his desire made something melt inside her, something she couldn't name. She redoubled her sensual efforts, heedless now of the risk.

"Minx." Without warning, he pulled away and flipped her to her back, into the bed's soft depths, covering her in one fluid, predatory motion that reminded her of his lethal nature.

Her heart leaped in anticipation, knowing what would follow. Despite weeks of frequent lovemaking, excitement beyond anything she'd ever felt on her commissions left her breathless. In fact, the inevitability of his possession only fueled her appetite for more.

Damon slid into her in a steady, relentless thrust that brooked no resistance, so thick she was overflowing. Threat and promise rolled into one prize male package.

Wet and aching with need, Rory was more than ready for him. Squirming in the throes of desire, she locked her legs around his hips and drove him deeper, wanting him against the very heart of her.

His cock stretched her sheath all the way in, finding and rubbing her pleasure points, fanning the flames and setting off sensual fireworks made no less powerful for being expected.

They both groaned when he was hilt deep, a simultaneous exclamation of relief at the intimate friction.

The sensation of him inside her—this dangerous man who could kill so easily—seemed to quench an inner hunger Rory hadn't known she'd had and didn't want to face. Ignoring the tumult in her heart, she rolled her hips, swirling him against her delicate inner membranes and glorying in the friction. Letting the resulting conflagration sweep her away.

She didn't want to think, only feel. This was supposed to be a straightforward exchange of pleasure, just part of her payment. Nothing more. Surely that was enough.

Despite her thighs clamped around his waist, he managed to pull out partway, then drive back in. His hands nipped her waist, anchoring her as he started a ruthless pounding that ratcheted the need in her womb to vicious tightness.

Panting, Rory writhed under Damon, clawing the bed and his back as desire grabbed her by the throat and stole her voice. She could only sob in desperation as she strained for release. After all this time, how could she want him so much?

He ground his pelvis against her mound, the pressure jolting her clit and fanning the wildfire inside her.

Still, she needed harder. Faster. More!

Damon bent over her. His lips grazed her neck, glided down the side to nuzzle and suck the base, right where it met her shoulder. The rasp of his beard sent shivers racing down her arms and spine, all the way to her toes, her climax gathering like a hurricane over the horizon.

Rory gulped for air, her bounding heart threatening to leap out of her chest. His scent filled her lungs—musk and that indefinable something that was Damon.

He bit down firmly. Shockingly, the small pain catapulted her over the edge, into rapture.

Her orgasm rolled over her in a tidal wave of pleasure, dragging her under and smashing her into a million shards of pure delight. With a silent scream, she gave herself over to raw ecstasy, barely hearing Damon's growl as he took his own release.

The brutal world outside their room slid away and Rory let it, content to rest in the arms of her Adonis.

"So, what did you have in mind?"

Facedown in yielding cleavage, Damon frowned, not quite registering the languorous question. "Hmmm?" He turned his head reluctantly and was rewarded with the sight of a pink-tipped mountain and endless fields of silken flesh recently explored.

"You mentioned something about reducing the guards," Rory prompted somewhat breathlessly, her pussy feathering his cock once more in another orgasmic aftershock that wafted electric tingles up his spine.

He grunted a curse under his breath. She expected him to talk sense after she'd reduced his brain to mush? Impossible. Surely he didn't have enough blood upstairs to formulate an answer. "Oh, that."

"Yes, that."

Dispersed by ecstasy, Damon's thoughts refused to gel. She had a damned genius for rendering him mindless. All he wanted to do was lie there and enjoy the final quivers of pleasure of her body, and maybe sleep a little.

"Spill," Rory ordered, amusement making her soft breasts quake under his cheeks. "Ve haf vays ov making you talk," she continued in a campy accent, waving her fingers beside his ribs meaningfully.

"No fair."

"You bit me. Fair's fair," she countered, her fingers still held at the ready.

The threat of a tickle attack sharpened his mental focus marvelously. "Divide and conquer. You know, stir things up, so they're spread too thin."

At his answer, she went still, her aura washed clean of playfulness. "How?"

Resigning himself to a discussion, Damon levered his body off his delightful pillow and slid his cock free of distraction. Settling on the bed, he mustered his thoughts. "Basically, by throwing a bone among the dogs. Get them at each others' necks. Sow some distrust. It's happening already, because of the deaths. Maybe give it a shove." Disturbed sleep might not seem like much, but it made people irritable. Which meant that the aggressive men walking the streets would have hair-trigger tempers. It would take very little to create flashover conditions.

"Is there anything I can do?" Rory tilted her head to indicate the black box with its blinking status lights. "That doesn't need me hovering. Everything's up in the air until security's been whittled down."

Inspiration bloomed. The idea took shape immediately, unfolding so smoothly that Damon knew it had been in the back of his mind for some time, just waiting for her invitation. He struggled with himself and an uncharacteristic protectiveness that urged him to keep Rory from further danger. Duty finally forced him to speak. "Can you plant some things for me? It will help stir things up."

"Easily." She leaned over him, her blue eyes bright with enthusiasm. Clearly, she viewed his idea as a challenge, and a change of pace from her usual operation. "When do I start?"

Her pose practically stuffed her breasts in his face, reminding him where he'd left off. "Tonight. But in the meantime, you can get back over here."

Pulling Rory on top of him, Damon slid back inside her, more than willing to be distracted once again. After all, even he couldn't do anything until later, when his targets were asleep.

Chapter Sixteen

The sliver of a crescent moon vanished behind a craggy peak, its meager light casting only a faint halo in the clouds. The wind was gentle, chill, but not the rude slap of previous evenings. With the townsfolk restive, there was just enough bustle in the streets to cover any inadvertent noise. All in all, it was a perfect night for a jaunt across the rooftops.

Rory scaled the wall slowly, the coarse clumps of mortar protruding between its bricks providing sufficient traction for questing fingers and toes. The familiar activity left her mind free to ponder the events of the past days.

The furtive gossip in the markets had whispered of an angel of Death stalking the new-come terrorists. That plus the "gifts" Damon had asked her to plant had tensions running high. Fights had broken out between rival gangs, and random outbreaks of violence were keeping KFOR troops occupied; they'd also had the benefit of forcing Karadzic to lend some of his security to supporters to reinforce their holdings.

It tickled her funny bone to be on the giving end, instead of stealing. In tonight's case, the freebie was schedules and floor plans that would stir a lot of trouble in the wrong hands, for special delivery to one Osum, no first name provided.

Taking them had been simplicity itself. The papers had been exactly where Damon had said they would be, their erstwhile owner dead to the world—literally—with only the body's guards in the adjacent rooms to pose complications. That had been a bizarre experience, breaking into a room with its occupant still there; even at her most daring, she'd never attempted that.

Now, she had to plant them where they would do the most good: the target's office.

Rory didn't know who Osum was and didn't particularly care. The fact that he headed one of the gangs allied with Karadzic was enough for her. Damon apparently intended to use Osum's possession of the schedules and floor plans to sow distrust and dissent among the natives.

Their efforts were already bearing fruit. Their daily review of the video feed from Karadzic's stronghold showed the size of his security detail shrinking in leaps and spurts. The latest riots near the local KFOR headquarters alone reduced his strength by eight men—some due to injuries when the crowds had run wild and damaged a few of Karadzic's own businesses.

The success of Damon's plan was heartening. Besides the improved odds for her job, she liked the fact that he wasn't hidebound by regulations, despite being a Fed.

It struck her that Damon used anonymity to his advantage. Like her, he lived in the shadows and understood its necessity. Again and again, similarities between them continued to emerge, tempting her to believe the differences between them weren't that marked, that the gap between thief and Fed—and a hit man, at that!—was little more than a crack in the pavement.

Foolishness, of course. No matter how she tried to rationalize her attraction to him, it didn't change the fact that she was a lamia who really ought to be keeping her distance from government types.

Still, Rory couldn't silence the inner voice that urged her to plant the documents quickly, so that she could return to the hostel and the strong arms of her Adonis. The memory of his lovemaking warmed her blood, despite the chill mountain air.

She cursed silently when she saw a flickering light coming from the room beside the office that was her target. Someone was working late.

Debating whether she should cut the night short, Rory crept to the window to assess the situation. Her heart sank at the picture that met her eyes.

A guard, to judge by the submachine gun and two-way radio on the table beside him, was watching local porn. She recognized the naked woman on the screen as one of the hookers she'd seen on the streets while casing Karadzic's base. From the cheap furniture visible—familiar from nights spent planting relays—the video was a record of activities in the whorehouse.

Rory made a face behind her ski mask, the exposed tops of her cheeks complaining of the cold air. Waiting through a bad home movie wasn't her idea of a good time. Checking her position for exposure, she hunkered down on the roof tiles, tucking her bare fingers under her arms to keep them warm and limber, resigned to the delay. The office's location at the corner of the top level meant few could see her in the immediate vicinity, but the ledge wasn't that wide and someone farther away could probably make her out if he knew where to look.

Perhaps it was because she knew the woman, if only by face, but a reluctant fascination drew Rory's gaze back to the video. She could only speculate on how the woman had ended up a hooker: kidnapped, duped with promises of a better-paying job, sold off by an uncaring, impoverished family? She couldn't imagine anyone would choose to become a sex slave, subject not only to the lust of strangers but also to ogling by perverts.

The moans from the dimly lit room were coming faster as the guard milked his cock in time to the slurping sounds of the video.

If it weren't for her family, that might have been her fate. Certainly, a life in the shadows didn't encourage one to take an ordinary, nine-to-five job.

Lost in her thoughts, the first punch caught Rory by surprise. The hooker's cry of pain drove home the reality of the violence. Her customer actually seemed to take pleasure in her pain, following it with more blows.

To her disgust, the guard merely grunted at the hooker's mistreatment, almost as though he'd expected it. She scanned the night to make sure no one was creeping up on her and no guard had an angle on her position, grateful for an excuse to escape the abuse.

But a murmur of anticipation drew her attention back to the video just as the man picked up a knife.

No, he couldn't mean to—

Rory flinched as blood spurted. Even at one remove, the violence churned her stomach. Worse, the shithead watching the hooker's murder continued to jerk off, mumbling encouragement as the man on the screen fucked the dying woman.

The radio sputtered to life, scratching out a name. The shithead gave a guilty start, then stuffed his limp cock back into his pants, swatting the monitor off just before he snatched up his submachine gun and radio, and left.

A loud click accompanied the shutting of the light. The darkness didn't help. Rory shivered, still seeing that poor woman's death in her mind's eye, the way her blood had splashed her murderer as he took his pleasure.

How could anyone do that to another human being? Or take extreme pleasure in witnessing that horror?

For some reason, the hooker's death hit close to home. She wasn't even an acquaintance. Rory didn't know her name. But that only made it worse, somehow.

Loud barking recalled Rory to her precarious position. Though the moon had set, there were still guards and KFOR patrols with searchlights that could expose her; even the dark skin she'd adopted for this outing didn't guarantee complete undetectability. She couldn't stay on the ledge forever, nursing her angst.

She had to get the documents planted and return to Damon. Now, more than ever, she wanted his arms around her.

Moving with grim purpose, Rory returned to the window of the office that was her original target. If what she did tonight resulted in that shithead and his boss's deaths, she wouldn't lose any sleep over it. They deserved killing.

Boom! The explosion shook the room, blasting a cloud of plaster dust into the air from the cracked walls.

Reflexively, Damon heaved himself off the sagging mattress, sweeping Rory with him to the floor. He crouched over her, gun in hand, as he sent his mental sense questing for any hint of threat. But he picked up only surprise and annoyance all around, the nearest source being right under him.

When minutes crawled by without any follow-up, he stood up and helped Rory to her feet. "That was close."

"What'd you do that for?" She eyed him with sleepy disgruntlement, naked and gorgeous despite her tousled hair.

"That was a bomb. Somewhere close by, maybe less than three blocks away."

Rory blinked up at him, white showing around green irises. "A bomb?"

Ignoring her question, Damon went to the window to look out, still scanning their surroundings. What he could see of the alley below was empty, the streetlight at one end washing the scene in yellow with dawn more than an hour away.

The night was quiet, as though the world held its breath, waiting for another explosion; even the dogs had been startled into silence. Smoke drifted to his nose, acrid with the stench of burning gasoline. Since the smell could be from an accelerant or perhaps a Molotov cocktail, it didn't tell him much.

His arms prickled with foreboding. In the time since they'd begun their campaign to distract Karadzic's security, there'd been unrest and violence, but this was the closest they'd been to a bombing. And the situation was still heating up.

Rumors were flying like bats at sunset, pitting Kosovar against Kosovar, against Serb, against KFOR. Stirring the pot had been as easy as waking nightmares. It didn't hurt that the rumors held a grain of truth, starting with Osum's murder of a member of his clan.

"Well? Do you see anything?" Rory rose on tiptoes, the upward tracks of her hard nipples along Damon's spine attesting to her movements. Gripping his arms, she propped her chin on his shoulder and peered out.

"Nothing." That was what worried him. There should be something. In a normal world, people would be streaming out of the buildings, rubbernecking and swapping speculation. Even here, members of the gang claiming this sector would normally feel confident enough—territorial enough—to check out the disturbance. Yet no one was about. Had the unrest escalated that much already?

Finally, in the distance, Damon heard the wailing approach of a KFOR unit. And still the street remained deserted. Of course, this time the avoidance could simply be a reflection of local sentiments. But the reasoning didn't reassure him.

Events were getting out of hand. He didn't like it that his master thief was in the thick of things.

Eyeing the bread for sale in the bakery coming up, Rory clumped beside Damon, ostensibly an old woman with her grown-up son. It still felt strange to be studying a mark with a partner. Accepting information and instructions for planting stuff was one thing; that was similar enough to how she operated with Felix that she could overlook it. But for the third time, she was actually providing camouflage while the Fed used his incubus power to observe her potential target. Today, he'd needed an excuse to linger in one of the markets to identify contacts in the target's network. Hence, the fiction of old mother and son, made easier by the forthright friendliness of the vendors.

Technically, it was beyond the scope of the job they'd commissioned her for, but she was taking the long view: anything that undermined the auction was a Good Thing.

She had to admit that working this closely with Damon added a different punch to her enjoyment. It wasn't the usual challenge, but more a sense of . . . fun. She grinned inwardly. It also allowed her to pretend that the Fed was a fellow thief, rather than a government-mandated hit man.

When the bag he carried for her was half-full, Damon signaled that he had what he needed and they could leave. After a final exchange of gossip and pleasantries with the seller, she added to her purchases the cheese freebie she'd been given and moved on.

Having had to eschew the use of the Yugo due to their mother-son fiction, they returned to the hostel on foot, taking a different route back. It was a rare moment of ease. Anonymous behind their mutual disguise, they were free of the leers and sidelong looks directed at whores and their customers. A definite change of pace that Rory savored.

Their desultory conversation was meandering along, touching on nothing of particular import, when Damon's voice trailed off. His hand tightened around her elbow as he stared at something around the corner.

Curious, Rory turned to follow his gaze, then gaped in disbelief, struck dumb by the sight across the street. Someone had trashed a car. Then she realized: that wasn't just any car—it was *their* car, the gray Zastava Yugo they'd driven from Skopje.

More than trashed it, whoever had done the deed had blown it up, shattering the windows of surrounding buildings in the process and leaving scorch marks on the fractured pavement. This was beyond all previous experience. Occasionally, she'd used plastic explosives in the course of a job, but she'd never seen this level of damage before.

Something clicked in her mind: their car had been the target of this morning's bomb. Had Karadzic discovered their purpose? Suddenly, she felt every year of her old woman's guise. They'd been lucky. What if the bomb had gone off while Damon had been driving?

It also meant they were without wheels.

The Fed viewed the scorched metal skeleton—all that was left of the sedan—with seeming equanimity. "Not to worry. There's always Plan B." He murmured the statement so smoothly that Rory had to wonder if he'd expected something like this to happen, maybe even knew who was responsible for stranding them.

"Which is?" She allowed him to steer her away, needing the support of his hand at her elbow as they sidestepped the people going about their business, stoically sweeping up broken glass and other debris.

He hurried her on, walking briskly to put several blocks between them and the wreck. Just another careworn couple trying to survive. They hadn't stopped that long, only enough to seem like rubberneckers and to see that nothing had survived the explosion intact. "A local asset."

"You mean our landlord?"

Damon snorted. "He'd probably sell us out. No, someone else." He didn't volunteer any details and she didn't press him since they were in public. He left her a short while later to return to the hostel on her own.

Damon returned to their room rather too quickly for Rory's peace of mind. He'd shed his earlier disguise—as had she—and resumed his Jamil Abdou persona at some point after he'd left her, but that wasn't what niggled at her gut. The almost imperceptible tightness of his shoulders said that his visit to Someone Else hadn't gone as well as he'd hoped.

"What is it?" Emerging from behind the bathroom door, she narrowed her eyes at him, trying to read his poker face and failing.

"There's a problem." He turned to the window, facing smoke rising in the distance. His stance was easy, concealing whatever tension he felt. "Petrovic's house burned down in yesterday's riots."

The Someone Else he'd mentioned? "And?"

"He's nowhere to be found. I don't know if he's lying low, gone, or dead."

Rory stared at him while she worked through the ramifications of his statement: Plan B was out. "Does that mean we're stuck here?"

"No." Damon shook his head. "It'll just make bailing out that much more difficult, without his support." He shot her a thin smile over his shoulder. "Consider it a challenge."

"Slipping something out from under the noses of gangsters is a challenge," she corrected him drily, spearing her fingers through her long, brown curls. "Traversing three hundred or so miles, cross-country, through unfamiliar terrain and tall mountains, without any support . . . Talk about interesting times." And that was on top of stealing the nuke, which wouldn't exactly be a walk in the park.

"Not necessarily that far," he demurred. "Just to the border."

Rory rolled her eyes at the correction, already wondering where they could steal a car. Hopefully, Damon knew how to hot-wire one; she'd never had to do it, so her knowledge was all theoretical—and rusty in the extreme. Grand theft auto had always been something she avoided, and driving had never been her passion.

One thing was certain: she had no intention of traveling on foot, not when Karadzic's goons would be searching for them.

CHAPTER SEVENTEEN

The clock had run down for the mission. Tonight, they had to steal the nuke—or fail. With the auction set for tomorrow, they had no more time to whittle down Karadzic's security. Brooding over what the night held for them, Damon stared sightlessly at the sparse afternoon traffic below, ignoring the whiff of smoke in the air. So many random variables beyond his control could result in disaster. True, the number of men the arms dealer had on-site was down to what Rory deemed workable, but that was still suboptimal. Worse, his master thief insisted on going in without him for backup—against his every instinct.

A whimper from behind him broke through his reverie. Ignoring the sound of automatic fire at a distance, he returned to the narrow bed.

Rory tossed in her sleep, horror and revulsion radiating from her in equal measure, prickling at Damon's mental sense. Her roiling emotions scraped his mind like jagged shards, leaving rawness.

He bared his teeth against the pain, reminded once again why he preferred to work alone and to keep emotional entanglements at a distance.

But he couldn't ignore his partner's distress. Rory might put on a show of strength while awake, but sleep stripped all masks. Despite her work, she'd been sheltered by her success—or her mysterious contacts—never experiencing the desperation of women forced into prostitution.

Small wonder she was having nightmares. A pang of regret pricked him at the reminder that he was responsible for exposing her to such brutality. And yet she'd continued to brave those horrors after what she'd witnessed that first night. Knowing something of what she must have seen, he had to admire her persistence, which only raised his already high estimation of her. She had heart.

Damon reached over to rouse her, but common sense made him stay his hand. No, they didn't have time for sex. And as sure as his name was Venizélos, that's what would happen if he woke her now. Sex was an excellent outlet for tension, but they needed to be rested for later.

Instead, he carefully took Rory into his arms, immeasurably touched when she snuggled against him with a sigh of relief. When her hands glided over his ribs repeatedly, he had to fight down a shiver, his arms breaking out in goose bumps; she seemed to take some reassurance from the contact, though. Just that little bit had been enough to reduce the horror she radiated. Her trust humbled him.

Taking a deep breath, Damon spiraled down toward sleep and entered her dreams.

That spicy perfume he now associated with Rory immediately surrounded him, once again bringing to mind the harem that had greeted him that first night. But he wasn't interested in that now. Somewhere in this dreamworld his lover struggled for rest.

It was up to him to distract her from the specters that troubled her sleep.

Before he could find her, a cold chill filled the darkness, the change inimical to peace of mind. The dream had changed for the worse.

Damon sent his awareness out, searching for his master thief. Sensing her presence, he reached out to join her.

Abruptly, the darkness took form.

Rory lay in a bed, naked, bound and gagged, but this wasn't one of her sex games. Fear shone in her eyes as her captor crept forward, brandishing a knife.

Dreams were the mind's way of dealing with psychological stresses, so direct interference with her nightmare might not be the wisest course. That knowledge made him hesitate.

But the blade glinted with a macabre light.

What if it wasn't a dream?

Lunging at Rory's assailant, Damon caught the knife as he shot a suggestion to her sleeping mind to banish the threat. The man twisted into shadow, then disappeared, taking with him Damon's fear for her life.

Suddenly free of her bonds, Rory threw herself into his arms. Ignoring her nudity, he stroked her back, forcing down his automatic arousal. Not after that horror show. He didn't want her to associate his lovemaking with rape or murder.

Besides, they both needed to be rested for tonight. Keeping duty at the forefront of his mind, he soothed her into gentle slumber, then withdrew.

On returning to himself, her nightmare continued to trouble Damon. Why had she dreamed of such? In all their time together, he hadn't pegged his master thief as one for such fears. Too, he hadn't seen any signs that she'd been raped since they arrived in Kosovo. She might have been attacked, but he didn't think that was it. Something else was going on with her, though there'd been no change in her professional—and unprofessional—demeanor.

Should he confront her about it?

This was the first time Damon had to face such a situation, never having worked with a partner before. He was entering terra incognita and was loath to raise the issue if she was handling the problem. Rory could be touchy about implied criticism.

In the end he decided to just note the potential for trouble. So long as whatever was going on with her didn't present any difficulties, he didn't have to interfere.

The muscular arms that cradled her flexed gently, pressing her breasts to a broad chest and her belly against hard buttons. One large hand draped across the small of her back to rest on her butt cheek; the other spanned her shoulders, warming her back. The posture felt inexplicably protective. *Damon.*

Rory blinked at the black cotton in front of her nose, sleep still weighing down her limbs. When had her Adonis joined her in bed?

The orangey yellow of streetlights filtered through the curtains. Night had fallen while she slept. It was almost time. This was it. The final phase. Strangely enough, the thought didn't evoke the usual surge of excitement.

She didn't move, for some reason reluctant to end the moment and leave Damon's embrace. It was so pleasant to just lie there and pretend they had nothing more urgent to do than make love again.

Pure insanity, of course.

Don't go imagining things that aren't there, Aurora diScipio. This was supposed to be a straightforward business deal. It wouldn't be wise to get her heart mixed up with her hormones at this late a date.

But what would it hurt to snuggle a little longer? To luxuriate in this little intimacy?

The choice became moot.

Suddenly, Rory realized Damon was awake, though there was no change to his breathing. Temptation stood no chance against professional pride. She didn't want him to think she was goldbricking.

"Time to get up." She slipped out of his arms quickly, escaping to the bathroom before he could do more than grunt, to put off revisiting yesterday's argument until she'd talked some sense into herself. Knowing him, she hadn't heard the last of it. And in her current frame of mind, she'd read all sorts of caring and protectiveness in his insistence.

Pure insanity.

Leaning against the wall, Damon crossed his arms and gave Rory his best level stare. "I really think I should go with you tonight."

"No, you won't, and that's final." Not bothering to meet his gaze, she retracted the prongs of her open grapnel, testing the release mechanism.

He glared at her in frustration. She made him crazy! "You need backup."

"You're my partner on this job, not my babysitter. I don't need you to hold my hand." This time she raised her head to spear him with an obdurate look.

"Not babysitter. Backup," Damon repeated, the unwonted intensity of his concern leaking into his voice.

"Well, you should have thought of that weeks ago," Rory retorted—rather unfairly, to his thinking. Weeks ago, he wouldn't have given her solo jaunt into Karadzic's base a second thought! "I don't have the time to give you a crash course in roof-walking. And, anyway, you have your part to play in this production."

She turned back to her equipment, clearly considering the argument over. "If you want to make yourself useful, keep an eye on what's going on in the fortress." Without looking at him, she jerked her pointed chin at her cell phone, which lay open on the bed with its display running video.

He stared at Rory in disbelief at her cavalier dismissal. Shooed off like some . . . irritating gnat. He sighed inwardly. She might have a point. He was hovering as though she were a newbie off on her first solo mission—which technically it was. But why hire a master thief if he was going to micromanage the operation?

Choking down his concerns, Damon picked up the indicated device and fast-forwarded through hours of video. He ignored the whiff of relief coming from her to concentrate on what he was seeing. "No change. It's still there."

"That's good." She finished checking her equipment and began assembling what she needed for the night. Climbing ropes, night optics, penlight, various lock picks, electronic black boxes, and metal bars of uncertain purpose . . .

His brows rose reflexively when a large gray block emerged from her bag. "C-4?"

"Just in case." Rory slid the explosive—rather more than what seemed reasonable—into a separate pocket of the small, black rucksack she used on her midnight jaunts.

Damon swallowed his objections. Who was he to tell a master thief how to do her job? Stealth might be their best chance at stealing the nuke, but with the auction set for tomorrow, there'd be no second chances. "And if you have to use it?"

"Grab the booty and run like hell." The corner of her mouth quirked.

"I still think you ought to have backup."

Radiating intense concentration leavened by amusement that told him more than anything else that her mind was already on the coming theft, and not on his concerns, Rory didn't pause in her packing. "You'll do me more good setting up an effective distraction."

He couldn't argue with that, though he dearly wanted to.

Rory adjusted the fit of her skin suit, her muscles quivering with built-up tension. This was it. End game. Fighting down the shakes, she put the final touch to her disguise, Changing her skin tone to a darker hue.

Damon's reflection joined hers in the bathroom mirror, his face appearing much lighter in contrast. "Damn, I still can't get over how you do that."

The murmured comment gave Rory a twinge of concern. "Don't like it?"

"I wouldn't say that. What man hasn't dreamed of having a harem at his beck and call?" His chiseled lips curved in a reminiscent smile, the soft light in his eyes easing her heart.

She raised a sardonic brow at his word choice. Probably staying in character but . . . "*Beck and call* being the operative term," she scoffed. "You would know."

He chuckled, the deep, lazy sound barely audible but stirring a lightness in her belly like champagne bubbles fizzing. "Nah, it's definitely *harem*."

Dismissing the idle questions he raised, Rory picked up the backpack at her feet and performed a final check to make sure she had everything she might need. Electronics, burglary tools including plastique, climbing gear, tool belt. She was good to go. Everything else was in her head. "All set. Let's get this show on the road."

Catching her lapels, Damon pulled her close and took her mouth urgently, surprising her with a heated kiss that conveyed a message she wasn't certain he meant to convey. He released her with gratifying reluctance. "Be careful."

She licked her lips, tasting coffee and Damon. How to answer that?

Thankfully, familiar excitement stirred now that the final phase of the job was in motion. The zest was still there. Rory gave him a cocky grin. "Don't be late."

Chapter Eighteen

Rory ran lightly, quickly, along the coping-bricks, the exercise keeping her warm in the cold night air despite a fitful breeze. The nights she'd spent learning the best overhead routes to Karadzic's fortress now paid off, making the rooftops a virtual highway for her.

Normally, she wouldn't risk silhouetting herself against the skyline, but although the fat crescent moon was still up, thick clouds gathering around the mountaintops blocked its light, and soon even that little bit of illumination would be gone. In the interest of time, since she had to be in place to take advantage of Damon's diversion, she ran.

Traversing the darkness at speed didn't bother her. The games she'd played when first Lucas, then Felix, had taken her roof-walking had seen to that. The need to maintain her balance on the rounded tiles was just another game that brought a smile to her face.

An icy blast of air slammed into Rory as she descended a wall, shoving her into coarse bricks and snapping her out of complacency. Grateful for the tough material of her skin suit, she clung to the wall, digging her fingers into its narrow crevices for traction, while she studied the dark sky. The streaming clouds looked like they were moving faster. Possibly a storm brewing.

Damn. Wind was one thing; rain was something else altogether. She didn't need that complication on this night of nights when timing was everything. Patting her tool belt automatically, she checked her watch. There was still more than an hour to go, but she didn't like the look of the weather. Best she got into position.

Conscious of the minutes ticking away, Damon lurked in the shadows of a pub filled with Karadzic's out-of-town guests, nursing a beer. Low, dark, chilly, the atmosphere fit his mood and his thoughts. Timing and the difficulties of synchronization were at the top of his mind as he watched fellow predators wordlessly jostle for dominance. He'd never been in a position to have to coordinate attacks before, and the many random factors that could throw a wrench into the works worried him now that he had Rory to consider.

The arms dealer was supposed to make an appearance tonight, which accounted for the large pool of targets present, here if only to keep track of their competition. Suspicion and aggression were running high—and KFOR distinctly absent. But so far the various terrorists were keeping themselves and their bodyguards in hand.

Their control didn't bode well for Damon's part of the plan. If he didn't get a riot started soon, his master thief would encounter alert security when she went in.

Hardly any streetlight penetrated the shadows where Rory waited, crouched in a back alley a few buildings away from Karadzic's fortress. The gathering storm only contributed to the darkness—its scudding clouds reflected little and obscured the setting moon. Perfect for her purposes.

She checked the time again, then studied the weather, trying to gauge wind speeds. The storm was coming on faster, which meant she'd have to make her move earlier than planned—possibly even before Damon's diversion started.

Rory gritted her teeth, cursing silently. The fitful breeze was strengthening, the sudden gusts forerunners of what promised to be a powerful storm. She could only hope the rain would hold off until she was inside; dripping water on Karadzic's floors wouldn't be conducive to stealth.

A chill ran up her spine as she set off, a shiver of foreboding she really could have done without. Hopefully, it was just her gut's reaction to relying on a partner.

Crouched on all fours, Rory picked her way across a low roof, careful to spread her weight between her hands and feet. The wind helped muffle any noise, though it also made balance on the rough tiles more chancy. But that couldn't be helped and she didn't waste time bemoaning that pesky detail.

Cigarette smoke slashed past her nostrils, shredded by the wind almost before she smelled it. Freezing in position, she eased her IR goggles off her forehead and over her eyes to scrutinize her surroundings, searching for its source. A soft glow on the rooftop of Karadzic's fortress suggested a smoker. As she watched, he was joined by another man who cadged a light.

More heat signatures appeared as she made like a gargoyle: three sentries on ground level; at least five on the top roof four stories higher; someone at a second-story window, which was unexpected; and several warm bodies milling around on the streets. The guards were packing what Damon had said were AK-47s, something she'd never encountered in previous jobs.

The cadger walked on, clearly the roving guard. If he kept to schedule, he'd show up again in another hour.

Though much reduced in number, Karadzic's security were on the ball, as she'd feared. Damon's diversion was supposed to keep the guards' attention down and out and away from the rooftops—but because of the storm, she was nearly an hour early.

After several minutes' observation, Rory continued on, aiming for a dormer gablet and making glacial progress. Oozing like molasses on a cold day. Nothing to catch the eye. Not here.

Matching wits with Karadzic's tight security had blood rushing through her veins so that her perceptions took on a crystalline clarity. Her senses sharpened until she felt as though she could see, hear, taste, smell *everything* if she concentrated hard enough. A familiar state of exaltation she got when cracking a tough system.

This time she had added incentive.

An eternity passed before she reached the meager protection of the dormer, the small ridge barely shielding her from the guards' line of sight.

A sudden gust and a spattering of rain told Rory she'd run out of time. She had to go in now—or risk dripping inside later. The distraction alone of keeping water off her electronics wasn't worth the added safety of waiting.

Tapping the appropriate commands on her cell phone, she initiated the video loop that would blind the exterior cameras to her approach. She smiled behind her ski mask when Karadzic's security reported all-clear. Now, all she had to worry about was the human factor.

Rory crossed to the next roof, now physically on Karadzic's home ground and in full view of his guards. Fifteen feet to the wall of the second story of the fortress. Fortunately, someone looking down from the roof would get light in their eyes. But if anyone took the time to really look, she'd be seen.

She crawled slowly, her chest inches from the rough tiles. Only the bricks existed. The rising wind was nothing. The guards were only a minor irritant, something tracked out of the corners of her eyes.

Luck was on her side, allowing her to cross the open space undetected, until she gained the dubious security of the wall. With her back to the wall, she pulled out her cell phone to double-check the activity on the second floor while she'd been roof-walking. The security video showed no change. No one was in the corridor and—more important—no one had entered the office behind her.

Of course, the situation could change at any time.

Slipping her phone back into her tool belt, Rory jimmied a window open, conscious that the adjacent room was occupied.

Karadzic was something of a technophobe, depending on his reputation and hired guns to secure the premises. His reliance on manpower made entry a breeze since the windows weren't alarmed. However, that didn't mean there weren't more primitive dangers to confound an overconfident thief.

An electronic pass of the empty office and a careful follow-up scan with IR goggles and her own Mark One eyeballs showed that her info had been dead-on: no sensors, not even an infrared tangle field to thread. For all his dealings in high-end weaponry, the arms dealer seemed as little removed from the last century as his fortress. However, she didn't encounter any false floors or trip wires, either.

She went in, then relieved the external cameras of their blindness. No point in risking detection, especially when the weather was shifting.

Crossing to the door, Rory checked the system to make sure the corridor outside was still clear, then triggered a similar loop to blind the first set of a series of interior cameras that covered her route. Surveillance had shown her the general location where Karadzic stashed the nuke: a suite of rooms in the basement. From the second floor, she had to get to the target area unseen. The loop would give her a minute's protection to negotiate the zones of each set, with some overlap between multiple zones to allow for speed or delays.

The door opened silently, thanks to freshly oiled hinges. Soft clicks suggested that the person in the next room was occupied.

No time like the present. She slipped to the dimly lit stairs, fast but silent. Voices drifted to her ears, thin and ghostly, a reminder that men walked the halls even at this late an hour.

Four flights down, voices suddenly filled the stairwell, a heated discussion of the merits of various weapons. Rory leaped for the wall, twisting to brace her hands on the opposite face. Shimmying to the ceiling, she held herself there by the strength of her arms and legs.

The door opened, admitting two guards into the narrow space. Luckily, the conversation held their attention and they didn't notice her wedged between the walls above their heads.

She dropped down after their voices faded into echoing whispers, landing with a soft thud. Hopefully, no one watching the cameras noticed the emergence of those two from a supposedly empty stairwell; the loop would have hidden their entry as well as hers.

All it would take was one man on the ball, and the jig would be up.

With time running down, Rory peeked into the corridor. Clear in both directions. No doors open. She glided out, heading for the target area with her heightened senses filtering for danger.

As expected, the lighting was dim, in keeping with the night, pools of shadow dividing the hall. The high ceiling disappeared in the darkness above the wall-mount lamps. Dry air cycled around her, stale with a hint of yesterday's cigar and warm compared to the storm winds she'd left. Fans throbbed in the distance, the mechanical heart of central air-conditioning.

Nothing else.

Not even her footsteps as she reached the door that was her goal. A single glance identified the simple lock. A thrust of a master key, a love tap, and less than a second later, she was inside and resetting the lock, safe from the security cameras.

It was an armory. The suite of rooms apparently served as storage for inventory in stock, an Aladdin's cave for someone as gun happy as her Fed.

Ingrained wariness and Felix's training prevented Rory from assuming she faced smooth sailing. Each room she searched had to be treated as fresh. Each entry could spell disaster. All it would take was for one person to walk in at the wrong moment and the job was over. It was a challenge she never tired of.

She lost count of the number and types of high-power weapons she found, though Damon probably could have named them all. None of it, however, looked like the nuke.

More than an hour of futile searching later, Rory came face-to-face with a wall where there shouldn't have been one. Having searched the room beyond, she knew its measurements and they didn't account for the wall's presence.

A secret chamber. How quaint.

She played her penlight across its face. Though it looked as solid as the walls of the other rooms, there had to be a way in—unless it was merely an architectural dead end. But her gut told her she was headed in the right direction. None of the walls surrounding the missing space had the look of newer construction.

A sensor scan didn't pick up any electronics; the lock had to be mechanical, then. Rory searched the surrounding area, conscious of time running out. It had already taken her too long to get this far.

Careful scrutiny revealed a hairline crack that encompassed several stones. Logically, the unlocking mechanism would be nearby for convenience and secrecy. As she swept the narrow beam of her penlight along the wall, a dark spot at shoulder height to a middling tall man gleamed, rubbed smooth by use.

After double-checking for traps and decoys, she pressed the stone.

Click.

The crack gaped open; then part of the wall swung aside on silent hinges to reveal a large, steel door of what appeared to be a vault. *Voilà.* Surely Karadzic would stash something as important as a nuke in there.

She studied the door, the combination lock with its two dials and thick handle. Old Soviet technology. Strong but noisy. Quite possibly original installation predating the regime of its current owner. And familiar from her prep work for Peć.

Fishing earbuds from her tool belt, Rory got to work. With her cell phone laid flush to the vault's face, she turned the upper dial, instinct and long training guiding her hand. Amplified by the device's internal microphone, the cascade of rolling tumblers filled her ears, seductive as the rattling dance of the white ball on a roulette wheel. *Place your bets, ladies and gentlemen, before it's too late.*

Karadzic was running late, and Damon didn't have the luxury of waiting longer. Despite the volatile atmosphere, the situation had yet to reach flash point. Though paranoia rode the air, the terrorists jockeying for advantage managed to keep things under control. Conscious of the danger his master thief faced, Damon decided to give the situation a nudge.

A spike of fear bordering on panic helped him locate his next target. Gerhardt Schiesser, a Venezuelan despite his name and Aryan looks, the moneyman of a South American group— and currently out of his depth behind a wall of bodyguards. Stout and white-faced, the object of his interest stood out in the roomful of jackals in more ways than one.

Damon directed his gaze at the nervy man, a stare of intent, unswerving and unblinking.

Like most prey, Schiesser felt it. He turned tense eyes in Damon's direction.

Now certain of his target's attention, Damon leaned back, allowing light from a shaded lamp beside him to briefly play over his features. Then he slid behind Ahmad, returning to the shadows. He had been cultivating the Venezuelan, haunting his dreams, for precisely this moment. He was betting that the rumors flying about an angel of Death would work to his advantage—especially given the nature of his prey.

Schiesser gasped, fear tipping into panic. He grabbed the arm of one of his bodyguards, who drew a pistol. That was all it took to set off a chain reaction of violence.

The pub dissolved into chaos as jackals on hair triggers reacted to an unknown threat with all their pent-up anger. Like a spark on dry tinder, several fights broke out spontaneously as restraint snapped.

Just as Karadzic's aura registered on his mental antennae.

Dame Fortune was working overtime.

As Damon withdrew to the sidelines with the aid of a chair leg to clear his way, he could only hope that the diversion wasn't too late for his master thief.

The last tumbler clicked into place, like drawing that last card to fill an inside straight—as Felix would say. Not inclined toward poker, Rory could only take her father's word for it.

Holding her breath, she pushed the handle down. The door swung back ponderously, its thick armor designed to shrug off high explosives. She stepped inside with due caution, making sure she wouldn't be locked in, before pulling the false wall shut behind her.

The vault was a weird amalgam of a walk-in closet and a locker room. Steel cabinetry lined three sides, rising three-quarters of the height of the stone walls. Unfortunately, the doors didn't have anything as helpful as a sign saying Nuke Stored Here to make her life easier.

Behind the first door on her right was a stack of drawers, none of which looked large enough to hold a suitcase, but unable to rein in her curiosity, Rory had to investigate. Starting with the topmost, she found CD and DVD storage cases, stacks of euros and bearer bonds. She riffled through the bills, her brows rising involuntarily at the results. There had to be over a million euros in just one drawer. Karadzic obviously did very well with guns, drugs, and sex slaves.

But that wasn't why she was here.

Continuing her search, she eventually found a suitcase stashed in one of the other cabinets, alongside what looked like brand-new, factory-fresh explosives. It looked almost exactly as the nuke had been described: outwardly a small, hard-sided suitcase, perhaps a bit more battered, dings and scratches marking the gray plastic, but essentially the same.

She tried not to get her hopes up. It could be a decoy. In her line of work, fakes weren't unheard of.

A thorough examination showed nothing out of place, with no traps or alarms attached. Still wary, Rory gingerly pulled the case out of the cabinet. A glance at her watch told her she was running late, but she couldn't afford to cut corners. There'd be no second chances with this job. If she stole a fake, the nuke would fall into the wrong hands. She tried not to think of what could happen to her family if she made a mistake.

The lock opened to the combination Damon had provided her. Further proof that it was the bomb . . . or, if it was a decoy, that whoever had prepared it was as anal as all get-out.

Maybe someone like her?

Professional respect had Rory using a multitool to raise the lid. She held her breath, alert for tension where none should be.

Still nothing.

Quiescent electronics met her eyes. They filled the case, blank faces labeled with square Cyrillic letters. Another glance at her watch showed over ten minutes had passed since she'd begun her search; she had less than a half hour to get out before the guards did their rounds—which might include a peek into the vault. Still, she performed more checks to confirm it was what it seemed to be.

Finally, Rory sat back, satisfied with its authenticity. Now to get out with the booty.

Something made her pause. She had what she'd come for and time was tight, but . . .

Her eyes darted to the drawers.

Hit them where it hurts: their wallets.

The outrage she couldn't stifle froze her in place. She couldn't leave without doing something about it.

With a moue of disgust at her weakness, Rory pulled the block of plastique from her pack and got to work. She placated the conscience berating her in her father's voice for taking this risk with the job only half-done by telling herself that what she was doing would serve as a distraction as well as lighten her load. Better to get on with it than waste time with indecision.

Every second counted.

Damon ducked a knife a split second before it slashed his neck open. Snapping a punch to his attacker's arm, he buried his other fist in his enemy's throat, cartilage breaking from the force of the blow. He spun away, leaving the idiot to choke to death.

The conflict had devolved into a free-for-all and rioting in the streets. Some storefronts were already broken and burning, looters running off with anything they could carry.

Ahmad had disappeared into the melee, last seen stabbing someone in the back. Good luck to him. If more terrorists were taken out tonight, that was fine with Damon.

Confusion and liberating rage battered his mental sense, an invisible cloud of raw emotion that threatened to sweep him up in the violence. It would be so easy to give in. He struggled for sanity, the adrenaline pumping through him making it more difficult to remember the mission.

Rory.

He had to get to her.

Keeping one eye on the time, Rory strung out the detonation cord, making sure it was tucked out of sight. Based on surveillance, she had less than ten minutes left in her window, then a change of shifts would make it dangerous to use the loop she'd inserted in the system to cover her departure—at least until enough time had lapsed for the new team to have settled in.

Ka-chrik.

She froze, detonator in hand.

The rattle of a doorknob was followed by squeaking hinges and voices. "—do not like it. All this talk about an angel of Death. Feh!"

Rory looked around for their source. Small holes near the ceiling, now visible as ribbons of yellow light, carried the sounds into the vault.

"You cannot deny ibn Turki is dead, and the Basque, and Ivanoff—him in a locked room surrounded by bodyguards."

Heavy heels thudded on the stone floor, punctuating the heated discussion. The men were moving deeper into the suite, coming nearer with each word. "Malek said he saw the angel in the Leather Market, from the corner of his eye, you know."

"Feh. Might as well say a *shtriga* killed them," the first speaker countered mockingly.

She felt her lips tilt up on their own. The local belief in witches that could suck the life force from their sleeping victims did have similarities with Damon's hits.

"Don't joke about that." The voices came to a halt right outside her hiding place.

Adrenaline set Rory's heart racing. Would they enter?

CHAPTER NINETEEN

"Hurry up! Why is that door not open yet?" A new voice boomed farther away, the speaker clearly having just arrived. "We need it now."

Sharp pain recalled Rory to herself, the hard edges of the detonator biting into her fingers. Stashing the nuke back where she found it, she eyed the cabinets, scanning for the fastest—and most discreet—route up. There was enough space above them to hide in, but the steel could creak under her weight; she had no way to test its strength without risking giving herself away. But if they came in, she shouldn't be out in the open.

A clatter of heels suggested the entry of more men than she could evade.

Taking advantage of the noise, she leaped for the vault door, caught one of its massive hinges, and swung onto the nearest cabinet. Metal creaked, the soft shrill lost under the oncoming rush. Decades worth of dust stirred beneath her, making her want to sneeze, even behind her ski mask.

Up there, the sounds from outside came clearer. Feet slowing. Mutters of anger and anxiety. Then the air was filled with the clink of metal and the rattle of hard plastic.

Nothing else.

No alarm.

No exclamations on finding the vault's door unlocked.

What was happening?

"Go, go, go! Quickly!"

They were leaving?

As though in answer to her question, feet pounded stone once more, rushing away.

Rory held her breath. Was the unusual activity in response to Damon's diversion? She tried to remember what weapons had been in the nearby rooms that might jangle like what she was hearing, but couldn't.

Dismissing the question as irrelevant, she switched her cell phone on to count the departures. When the noise stopped, she gingerly descended from her perch, still stifling an urge to sneeze.

Hopefully, no one remained behind. But still Rory waited, just in case, putting the time to good use by finishing her preparations. Now, more than ever, she might need a distraction to make her escape.

Of course, if she'd left when she was supposed to, she wouldn't be in this mess in the first place. Now she was damned late.

When no sounds penetrated the shelter of the vault by the time Rory connected a relay to the last detonator, she figured it was safe enough to egress.

Darkness met her searching eyes when she pushed the false wall open. More darkness in the corridor. Everything looked the same as when she'd entered, despite the earlier tumult.

She walked slowly, taking extra care not to bang the bulky suitcase against anything. The rattle of a doorknob barely gave her time to slip into one of the rooms.

"Hurry, you idiot. The team is about to leave. If you miss the fighting, cousin or not, Alexei will have your head." Light splashed through the doorway; then the corridor resounded with heavy, bounding strides.

Rory swore inwardly, her gut tensing at the delay. Looks like she wasn't the only one running late.

"So I will not miss the fighting, yes?" The huffing response swept past her hiding place without pause, large shadows drawn on the bright floor. "I do not understand why we are being sent. Osum—"

"Osum intends to replace Alexei, it is said. Your cousin does not trust him."

The news brought an involuntary smile to Rory's lips. They'd succeeded in making trouble for that gang lord, after all.

"Pshaw! Him? He does not have the brains."

The laggards hurried out soon after.

To give them a few seconds' head start, Rory pulled out the harness she'd prepared for the nuke and attached it; she'd need both hands free to negotiate the reverse of her original route. She shouldered the suitcase on top of her pack, making sure both were secure. A hard edge dug into her butt. Her pack, slight and with its contents much reduced, didn't provide much padding. In fact, the remaining equipment added pokes and prods that couldn't be accommodated in her tool belt.

A quick check on her cell phone showed that the corridor

outside was clear, the tardy goons out of sight. She triggered the loop to cover her route; it was risky, but she couldn't trust to speed to avoid detection, especially since Damon's diversion had kicked up a hornet's nest of activity.

Easing the armory door shut and locked behind her, Rory adjusted the makeshift shoulder straps. Then, extending her arms and legs out, she scaled the walls by the nearest unlit lamp. Hopefully, the shadows there would hide any scuff marks.

The maneuver left her stretched out between the two walls, wedged in like the keystone of an arch just below the dark ceiling. Perforce, her progress was slower, limited as she was to sidling.

Static crackled, loud and angry, when a door opened. A cacophony of orders suddenly spilled out behind a rangy man, then was just as abruptly cut off when he slammed the door behind him and jogged away.

Ignoring the noise, Rory pushed on crabwise, her muscles starting to protest the unusual position her passage required. *Don't look up. Nothing to see here. Move along.* The nuke shifted on her back, forcing her to stop and, while straining to hold herself up with one hand and two legs, snug down the straps.

Her mental countdown said the loop was still active for this zone. She still had a bit of time.

Activity picked up below her. Another group of guards entered the armory. Some to-ing and fro-ing between rooms. Surely someone monitoring the cameras would notice the discrepancy?

She put it out of her mind. *Face it if and when it happens.*

The draft from a cooling duct chilled the sweat across her cheeks, exposed by her ski mask. It brought with it the smell of dust, which she must have picked up in the vault. Her gut clenched at the slipup—not that she could have done much about it. Hiding had been the right thing to do at the time.

Finally, Rory reached the door to the stairs. But she had to stop there, muscles quivering, until the coast was clear. A strange time to wish Damon were with her, but she found herself doing exactly that and more—fantasizing about a full-body, carnal massage courtesy of her Adonis—while waiting for her chance to get down unobserved.

Despite the increased activity, she attained her entry point without further interruptions.

Raindrops rang on the windowpanes, quick, uninviting pings that sang of strong winds. And Damon was out in it, waiting for her—and if she wasn't mistaken, antsy after her no-show.

Time to get out of here.

Again, she triggered the video loop for the external cameras, hoping to buy time to egress. The nuke on her back made getting out the window an awkward operation, but she managed to squeeze through.

Cold rain pelted her, strong enough to sting. But since that was the only attention she received, Rory was grateful. There were no guards in sight.

A spate of distant gunfire broke through the drumming splatter on the brick tiles, echoing such that she couldn't pinpoint its source. Apparently, Damon's diversion was still ongoing.

She'd crossed to the next building when it happened.

A shout came from above, just as she traversed the peak of the roof. The storm stole the words, carrying nonsense to her ears. Throwing caution to the winds, she burst into a sprint, intent on putting distance between Karadzic's guards and herself.

Big mistake.

As she swerved around a chimney, the nuke on her back

smacked against the flue, knocking her off balance. Her foot slipped on a wet tile, leaving her flailing for a handhold. The edge of the roof tilted toward her. Holding her breath, she kicked off with her other foot, throwing herself to safety.

Rory sprawled on all fours, swearing inwardly at the near disaster. Damn it, she was letting the pressure get to her!

But speed was still of the essence. She had to widen her lead. It would give them less time to respond and make it harder to intercept her.

And if Karadzic's goons opened fire, they'd have a harder time hitting her.

Breaking into a more moderate run, she launched the grapnel at the roof of the next building and ignored the soft thud it made, less interested in stealth now. Once over it, she'd be out of direct line of sight of the guards on the rooftop. Tugging on the line to confirm it was set, she started up the climbing rope, using it to scale one measly story of brick wall.

The bomb was an awkward mass that kept shifting, digging into her butt and driving the odds and ends in her pack into sore muscles, the straps of its harness biting into her shoulders. Its weight pulled her backward, threatening to tip her over onto her head.

On the bright side, if they shot at her, they were more likely to hit the nuke. She had body armor, of a sort. Kind of like a mutant tortoise.

A series of pops went off behind her.

Rory squeezed her eyes shut reflexively. Shards of brick tiles rained down, some bouncing on her unwieldy load. Her heart skipped a beat. *Holy shit, they're shooting at me.* Forget the bright side. Next time, she'd stick with the shadows and stay way out of sight.

Where the fuck is Rory?

Standing in a shadowy alley, buffeted by occasional gusts of cold air and spatters of colder rain, Damon forced himself to maintain his posture of bored menace. He'd packed up their equipment, in preparation for a quick getaway, and gotten to the rendezvous with only minutes to spare. But the agreed-upon time had passed with no thief in sight. Had something happened?

Had she been caught?

He eyed his surroundings, watching the other predators on the street. Most of the windows were closed as people hunkered down to weather the coming storm, both physical and metaphorical. With the sure instincts of battle-weary survivors, the townsfolk knew there was trouble brewing.

It was a risk arranging to meet Rory here on the east side of the river, but he'd refused to wait in the relative safety of the hostel. Leaving her to run that bottleneck of a bridge alone, much less the gauntlet of Karadzic's territory, was too much to ask.

As it was, he was on edge at her tardiness. *Please, let it be nothing more than that.* But it was unlike his master thief to be so late.

More minutes passed with no feminine figure emerging from the darkness.

Worry finally got the better of him.

Damon stretched out mental fingers, searching for Rory's distinctive aura. He found her immediately: moving quickly, flashes of agitation and alarm telling him all wasn't well with her.

Sharp bursts of gunfire reached his ears, unmistakable even through rain and distance: AK-47s on auto.

Were they aimed at Rory or just more of the rioting he'd incited?

Frustration gnawed at his control with jagged teeth. He needed to move, do something, but he couldn't leave to intercept her. This was where she expected him to be. Leaving risked her getting past him and not meeting up.

He scanned the neighborhood with narrowed eyes. There had to be something he could do.

Rory slid around the corner, trying to silence her gasps for breath. Someone had been on her heels ever since her egress. She had cut it too close, and now the deadweight of the nuke was slowing her down, its awkward size making some of her usual routes impossible.

She didn't think Karadzic's goons knew what she'd gotten away with—not yet—but she couldn't count on their remaining ignorant. A woman running around with a suitcase on her back was unusual enough, but one coming from Karadzic's fortress when the nuke went missing? Though she'd kept to the shadows as much as possible, luck only went so far, and she'd pushed hers beyond the limit.

Wishing now that she'd agreed to meet her Fed sooner, she forced herself to keep moving. Unfortunately, his diversion had been a bit too successful. She'd had to detour several times already to avoid pockets of violence, which whittled down her lead on her pursuers.

Rounding another corner, Rory was relieved to spot the bulbous tower that was her landmark for the alley where Damon should be waiting. Just a little farther and she could hand off the unwieldy nuke.

Barking rose a short distance away. Something stirring up the neighborhood dogs. Maybe her pursuers.

She forced herself to run on, her legs feeling like they were tied down with concrete blocks. *Just a little farther.* She repeated it silently, a mantra of hope to give herself strength. *Damon's waiting.*

But the alley was deserted when she got there.

Her heart skipped, shock chilling her body at the impossible scene. *No.*

Had something happened to him during the diversion? Was he hurt? Dead? Dying? She pegged everything on his being here, waiting for her. Hadn't even imagined it could be otherwise.

A hand shot out of the dark, clamped down over her mouth. Another one caught her elbow and pulled.

Horror froze Rory's muscles solid, held her motionless for a heartbeat, then—

"Shhh."

The male scent and the hard body pressed against her side registered.

Damon.

Relief made her weak, a strange reaction since she'd always preferred to work alone. She touched the hand over her mouth, then nodded to let him know she understood.

"This way." The toneless instruction was nearly inaudible. He released her and quickly led the way to a narrow side alley hidden behind a pile of debris. From the smell of half-burnt wood and brick dust, it stood testament to the recent violence.

Rory followed willingly, her ears pricked for sounds of pursuit. They weren't long in coming: a clatter of boot heels on stone approached at a run.

Damon pushed her to her knees into a small niche behind the debris. He hunkered down beside her, his bulk blocking her view of everything except broken bricks—protecting her.

She crouched down, making herself even smaller, under no illusions as to her bulletproof capacity. Still, her heart raced, so loudly the men on her trail should have heard its pounding song of jubilation. *He's here. He's alright.*

The footfalls thudded past their hiding place, then faded into the distance.

"Is that it?" The question was barely audible. He kept to a murmur, not whispering, so the words didn't carry.

"Yeah." Clawing off the straps, Rory surrendered the nuke to him, more than ready to be relieved of its deadweight. She'd thought she was in good shape, but after lugging the suitcase up and down rooftops, her back and butt were sore from the unyielding plastic.

Damon passed her an armful of heavy material in return. "Put that on. It'll change your outline." He stood up and gestured for her to follow him.

The thick, woolen fabric felt like an outsize shawl. Rory complied with his murmured instructions, slinging the garment across her shoulders and around her body in the manner she'd seen it worn in the markets. The shawl hampered her stride, clinging as it did to her legs. She dismissed the hindrance from her mind.

Stealth, not speed, was the priority this time. Their efforts would be all for nothing if they were caught.

At the first opportunity, Damon slung the nuke across his back, over the bags on his shoulders, using the straps attached for the purpose. With Rory obviously spent by her exertions, he wasn't about to add to her load by passing her a bag. It threw his balance off, but doing so left his hands free, in case he needed to fight or shoot.

Using his mental sense, they managed to avoid the search party and various patrols. He kept their pace slower than he preferred, to give Rory a breather. They were inside the net, which gave them some maneuvering room since pursuit would likely be looking ahead, not behind. But there was still that bottleneck to negotiate. "Hopefully, they haven't figured out which way you were going or we might find a welcoming committee on the bridge."

A flare of emotion that felt strangely like guilt radiated from his master thief. It nearly distracted him from a mental spark of hunter red up ahead.

Damon waved her to a halt. Muscles tensing in anticipation, he inched to the corner of a dark, low building, looked over his shoulder to make sure Rory was still behind him, then checked the wide street paralleling the river.

The bridge was swarming with armed thugs, floodlights illuminating the streets leading up to its span. With the circuitous route they'd taken to elude capture, the enemy had had time to put up a roadblock.

Damon turned back to deliver the bad news. "No go. There's a crowd over there."

Rory nibbled on a gloved knuckle, breathing more easily at this point. "If we could just get over the embankment."

"Why?"

"There's a rope under the bridge."

He grinned. She must have placed it for just this sort of contingency. With the brightness cast by the floodlights, the night vision of the force manning the roadblock would be ruined and the shadows made darker. They had a chance.

Despite the situation, satisfaction welled up in his heart at Rory's foresight. Since he had to have a partner, he didn't think he could have had a better one than her. "Any suggestions on where to go over?"

Crouching at the side of the building, she pointed to where the river and the esplanade that paralleled it curved. Beyond the curb of raised stone blocks edging the embankment, some shrubs stuck out where they would screen someone going over the side from watchers on the bridge.

"Good enough." He scanned their surroundings thoughtfully. "Now, we need a distraction."

Strangely, Rory snorted in amusement. "Don't worry about it. I've got that covered." Though Damon shot her a questioning look, she refused to clarify her statement. More of her preplanning? He could understand the rope under the bridge, since she preferred minimal visibility whenever possible, but she'd also expected to need a distraction?

They changed locations, moving to a low wall that was closer to the spot to reduce the distance they had to cross in the open. Out from the protection of the buildings, the wind blew stronger, funneled by the raised riverbanks.

On the bridge, the thugs detailed to the roadblock paced restlessly, too alert for comfort.

Rory reached into her tool belt.

A few seconds later, Damon felt a rumble under his feet. "What was that?"

She muttered something that sounded like "a blow to the pocketbook," then flashed him an abashed look. "Nothing. Just a distraction I put together."

Damon reached out with his mental antennae, searching for a lapse in attention from the bridge. The minutes stretched out while he picked up impatience and unease from the bridge; his master thief, on the other hand, was the soul of coolness, not shifting her weight even once, despite the wait. *There.*

Amidst flashes of surprise, concern, and disconcertment, the roadblock detail spun around toward a man holding up a radio. Whatever she had done seemed to have worked.

He waved her forward. "Come on."

Rory hotfooted it across the street and narrow esplanade, more a windblown wraith than woman with her cape swirling around her. He ran beside her, scanning for spikes of emotion that meant detection.

Nothing.

They took cover behind the bushes, pausing to take stock of their situation. The thugs on the bridge were in an uproar.

"What exactly did you do?" Again, there was that flash of guilt. The fact that she kept looking everywhere except at him suggested to Damon there was more to the tale than a simple distraction. "Rory?"

"I left a surprise for our neighborhood arms dealer."

"What?"

"That"—she gestured with her chin at the suitcase weighing him down—"was in a vault with some funds. You might say Karadzic suffered a major loss."

Damon thought back to the rumble he'd felt. "That blast just now was from that little bit of C-4 you had?" The quake had been rather stronger than what he'd have expected—even if she'd used it all.

Rory sneaked a peek at him, then just as quickly looked away, ostensibly scanning the buildings beyond the river—compounds with closed gates, their tenants minding their own business. "There might have been some other explosives in the vault, too."

No wonder the minx was feeling ill at ease. She'd gone beyond the scope of the mission, and—he realized belatedly— must have risked detection, hell, perhaps even her neck, in doing so. "How much did he lose?"

"I don't know." She shrugged, still not facing him. "Maybe a few million euros."

He stared at her in horrified respect. He was also tempted to tan her ass for taking such a risk, but that would get them nowhere fast. "Fuck. He'll want our heads on a platter after that." He urged her forward, a presentiment of danger making the back of his neck itch. They had to get to the other side of the river before Karadzic put two and two together.

Rory disappeared over the side, so quickly she might not have been there at all. Dropping down to the curb, Damon turned his back to the water to follow. The nuke made him top-heavy, tilting him backward. He cursed silently, unused to feeling ungainly. Hanging by his fingers, he scrambled against the rough stones of the esplanade wall for footing, then dropped down.

There was a grassy bank near where Rory had indicated, loose gravel that had built up at the river bend from countless spring floods. The height of the stone walls cast its base in shadows, which were made darker by the slash of floodlight above their heads.

With rushing water less than a foot away, loud splashing filled his ears. It wasn't the raging river of al-Hazzezi's nightmare, but that didn't make it more inviting—not when it sprung from snowmelt off the mountains ringing the town.

They picked their way over the rounded stones worn treacherously smooth with time. The slightest misstep could spell failure and the nuke falling into terrorist hands. Damon was determined to detonate the bomb rather than risk that.

Garbled snatches of tense conversation, rendered unintelligible by the soughing of the wind, teased their ears as they approached the bridge; however, unhappiness at the duty came through loud and clear to his mental sense.

The space under the span seemed almost pitch-black after the floodlights, and empty. Even after Rory guided his hand to the rope, Damon still couldn't see it. He pulled on it tentatively, following the smooth, braided nylon to where it was attached to the stone footing. Some kind of housing stopped his fingers, probably one of those devices that maintained a set tension level. To his relief, his sight gradually adjusted to the greater darkness.

An arm extended to take the nuke, Rory waved her hand in a *Pass it here* signal, the other holding a cord ready.

Recognizing the wisdom of her suggestion, he divested himself of the nuke. He'd have an easier time crossing over without its bulk throwing off his balance.

Rory looped the short line over the rope and clipped both ends to the handle of the suitcase.

Damon gestured at her to go first. He had to trust that the rope could support them all, but didn't intend to risk stranding her if it gave way under him.

She adjusted her cape, securing it around her shoulders. Taking another, longer line from her rucksack, she clipped it to the nuke, attaching the rest of the coil to her belt. Then, dangling scant feet above the water, she swung from hand to hand along the rope, a darker shadow against the gray stones. As soon as she left the shelter of the footing, her body canted to the right, dragged by the wind.

Damon gritted his teeth, fighting down the tension knotting his shoulders. The gusts were growing stronger with the storm's approach.

Despite his concern, Rory got to the other side without any problem. As soon as she had her feet under her, she began hauling the nuke over.

He started after the swaying suitcase, hoping he didn't have a cold bath in his immediate future. After an initial dip, the rope bore up under his weight. The wind posed less of a difficulty for the same reason, despite the bags swinging from his shoulders. He managed to join Rory with only spray-dampened shoes to show for the unconventional crossing.

But the hardest part was yet to come. They had to get back to street level and within view of the enemy on the bridge.

Behind them, fear and outrage flared.

The stronger emissions helped Damon pinpoint the locations of the thugs maintaining the roadblock. He pointed Rory to the left, away from potential detection. With a bit of luck, the enemy wouldn't be looking in their direction when they emerged from under the bridge. Not that they had much of a choice on where to leave the river; because of the current, there was no convenient gravel bar on this side to aid their escape.

Going up was harder than getting down, but they managed to gain the pavement without drawing notice. It helped that the enemy still expected to intercept them and, thus, were facing the wrong way.

Keeping close to the walls, they headed for a side street, walking normally, fast but not at a run. Nothing furtive that might draw attention. They were almost clear when a sudden gust caught the nuke.

Damon staggered, the hard plastic banging into a gate. Dogs

started barking. Over their clamor, he heard a shout go up from across the bridge. "Fuck." Of all things to give them away.

He shot a glance over his shoulder. The roadblock detail were pointing at them, a few elements already giving chase. "Move. They've seen us."

Not bothering to check his statement, Rory ran for the side street with Damon at her heels.

A roaring of large engines drowned out the dogs. From another street, trucks drove up bearing members of the gang that held the south end of the bridge. Sporting Uzis, AK-47s, and aggression, they intercepted the thugs crossing the bridge.

Finally, something was going their way. Too bad they couldn't borrow a vehicle. But Damon wasn't about to quibble with Dame Fortune.

They turned the corner and kept moving, heading for the edge of town. The roads were deserted. Despite his best efforts, Damon couldn't find a single car to hot-wire. The bombing must have scared the drivers into parking elsewhere, but in the interest of speed, they couldn't backtrack to search.

With wind howling through the trees at the edge of the woods, Rory and Damon escaped into the countryside.

Chapter Twenty

Rory leaned against the low wall that bordered yet another overgrown pasture, glad to get out of the rising squall for even a second. If she never saw another wildflower in her life, it would be too soon. She panted, spent from their mad rush through the night.

Thunder boomed overhead, echoing off the mountains like an overture to hell. The rumble rolled on and on, fading only to be renewed by a fresh lightning strike.

That was another thing. They had to find shelter, and fast. The cold north wind was blowing with a fury, bringing stinging bits of ice that threatened to form hail. She didn't want to be out in it when it reached its height.

The bulky suitcase Damon had set down between them felt

like a lightning rod for bad luck. It would be tempting the Fates to expose the nuke to the increasingly volatile elements.

When Damon indicated he'd seen something he wanted to investigate, Rory couldn't even muster enough curiosity to ask him what it was. She only nodded and pulled the suitcase against her side, where she was sure it wouldn't be overlooked when they continued on their mad flight.

Panting, she was struck by a pang of nostalgia. That was one advantage of most of her jobs: she didn't have to run for her life afterward. None of this dodging-bullets-and-hairy-goons business; just pack up the booty and ship it to Felix. She'd never had to drag the goods along for miles on end while making her escape. True, Damon had done most of the lugging, but she'd had to get it to him first! Now, her calves were killing her and muscles she never knew she had were making themselves known with a vengeance.

Of course, this job had its compensations—and one delicious one, in particular, that she wouldn't exchange for a trillion dollars.

The wind's bite weakened suddenly. She opened her eyes to see Damon crouched beside her, his big body providing a barrier against the elements. The wind had gotten to his ponytail hours earlier, leaving his hair straggled around his shoulders—a far cry from the suave businessman she'd traveled with weeks before; he looked like an ogre out of the fairy tales, what with the mound of stuff he had slung across his back. "I found a place where we can get out of the storm."

"Alleluia." Rory grabbed Damon's shirt to drag him closer. "Tell me it's not across another few pastures?"

He grinned briefly, a flash of white amidst dark beard. "It's just on the other side of these trees." He tilted his head to indicate a thick stand of the aforementioned vegetation, which in the strobe of lightning flashes she could see was swaying wildly before the rising wind.

The trees lined a dirt track that skirted a small field but finally led to a low building with rough stone walls and what looked like the usual tiled roof. Rory forgave Damon his slight understatement about the distance since the cottage seemed deserted—which would be a godsend with the rampaging storm.

"It's empty." Keeping possession of the suitcase, which was on his back once more, Damon nodded at her to take the lead; evidently, he hadn't sensed anyone in the area.

Rory checked the battered door first, a lifetime of caution raising its head, but nothing untoward set off her gut. The weathered panel didn't even have a lock to speak of. Despite creaking hinges, the door eventually swung open after she gave it a hard shove.

Inside was dark—two small shuttered windows kept out all but the cold and the howl of the wind—but nothing moved inside, so it seemed safe enough. She plucked her penlight from her tool belt and switched it on, its narrow, white beam revealing nothing out of the ordinary, not even a wild animal as she'd half expected.

The interior was all of one room. A rough cot took up one corner beside a dinky woodstove, while a crude table sat in another corner. Empty space along one wall might have served as a storage area or a pen for animals. All in all, it looked little more than a shelter for shepherds, long abandoned, centuries of dirt leaving every surface dingy. But after the trek through the storm, its promise of shelter was as welcome as a suite at the Marriott.

Since the cottage was empty, she stood aside to let Damon in, out of the storm.

He edged through the door, the bulky load on his back catching on the low lintel. With what sounded like a muttered imprecation, he backed up and shed the nuke, handing it to her before trying again.

This time he succeeded with only the rasp of cloth against rough wood to mark his passage. While he unburdened himself, Rory ducked outside to check their trail.

Lightning flickered in the clouds, brighter than daylight for a blink of an eye. That instant was enough to see that rain had reduced visibility to the tree line, obscuring the mountains around them. Barely seen branches bent and swayed before the wind, making her glad they'd found the cottage, but nothing else appeared. No lights, no cars, no people. They'd truly lost their pursuers. The relief she felt was enervating.

With the wind resisting her efforts, Rory had to put her shoulder against the door to shut it. A bar appeared in front of her—courtesy of Damon—that fit into brackets on the jamb, locking the door in place.

Her penlight's meager beam only served to emphasize the humbleness of their accommodations. But she counted them lucky to even have it. "It's not much, but it's home."

Damon gave a bark of rusty laughter at her weak quip as he worked the kinks out of his muscles.

Whoever had abandoned the cottage had done so with some haste. Rory found some threadbare shirts on the floor beneath a row of rude pegs, enough to dry with. They left streaks of dust on her skin suit, but beggars couldn't be choosy.

Shivering from the cold, she stripped her top off, leaving it to hang at her waist. As she was about to use the rags on herself, Damon stopped her, looking up from his inspection of the nuke.

"Here, use this." Digging through a bag, he handed her a

shirt that by some miracle had escaped a soaking. It smelled deliciously of him. "Afterward, you can change into something dryer." He held out another bag, a familiar one she'd thought had been left behind in the hostel.

"You mean you've been lugging that along with everything else?" Staring at Damon, Rory wiped off the rain and sweat clinging to her, stripping completely to get dry as quickly as possible. The man was a marvel of endurance to have done that.

He shrugged modestly, downplaying his feat. Setting her bag on the table, he proceeded to copy her actions, putting his muscular body on display with indifferent efficiency that made her want to protest. A show like that was meant to be savored! She'd barely seen anything in the weak light.

Then the enormity of their accomplishment hit her. "Oh, God! We did it!" She grinned up at Damon as exhilaration bloomed. They'd actually gotten away with stealing the nuke!

"We're not out of the woods yet." Despite his cautious words, he grinned back at her, looking equally elated. He swept her into his arms and spun her in the air.

Clinging to his shoulders, Rory threw her head back and laughed, sheer relief bubbling up as giggles. What an adventure, but they'd done it!

"You wonderful woman! That distraction was inspired!" Damon's embrace tightened until she was flush against him, thighs to thighs, belly to belly, chest to breasts. And an unmistakable ridge nestled against her mound.

Reciprocal desire stirred in her core, hot and heavy, a longing to touch and be touched, to claim and be claimed, to stretch and be filled. She inhaled sharply and wrapped her legs around his narrow hips, pulling him closer to where she wanted him. *Oh, yes.*

He caught her lips in an exultant kiss, his hot body vibrating with barely restrained power. Man to her woman. Hard where she was soft.

Rory's fatigue burned away in the heat of his caresses, leaving her flying high on excitement. What a thrill and what a man! All of a sudden she wanted nothing more than to celebrate their success in the most basic way possible.

She raised herself with her legs around his waist, teasing them both with the touch of his blunt cock head nudging her wet slit. "I want you now."

"Whoa." Damon staggered backward. With a bit of fancy footwork, he spun around, sandwiching her against the rough door with her butt on the bar, ending with a sharp thrust of his pelvis that buried his cock deep inside her. He groaned as he settled to the hilt, his cock still swelling. "Damn, you're tight."

"Hurry." She squeezed him with her inner muscles, melting as she urged him to move, to match her touch for touch, need for need.

Then he did—hard and fast, pumping her with all his strength, and she didn't want it any other way. His driving rhythm forced the air from her lungs, a primeval celebration of their success, exhilarating in its pounding beat. The slapping of flesh against wet flesh mingled with grunts and cries of delight, the racing of her heart sounding louder than the thunder outside.

Sinking her fingers into Damon's hair, Rory captured his mouth, claiming him just as thoroughly as he was claiming her. A mutual possession, infinitely thrilling and all the more satisfying for their hard-earned victory.

Passion soared, wild and frenzied. Too explosive to last.

Release came in a searing blast of breathless ecstasy roaring through her veins. Damon followed her soon after, a deep groan escaping him as he spilled inside her, shuddering in her arms. That was all she knew for uncounted time as she lost herself in rapture.

Only gradually did her senses return.

Above them, the rain's drumming on the roof strengthened, the storm letting loose with more thunder. It brought to mind the soundtrack of an old war movie. Since they'd found shelter from the elements, Rory paid it no heed.

The cold tickling her legs and arms and back—in fact, every-where but the parts of her stuck to hot male—was less easy to discount.

Her perch shifted unsteadily, jolting from side to side, mov-ing in spurts and halts. The unpredictable rhythm set off bursts of delight in her fluttering core that were topped by a final sud-den drop of orgastic proportions.

When Rory managed to pry her eyes open, she saw that Da-mon had somehow gotten them to the cot. A man of marvelous coordination, her Adonis. In the meager illumination from her penlight, she watched as he spread over its dingy surface, first, the oversize shawl he'd given her, then a survival blanket he must have taken from his bag. Finally, he lay down with a satisfied groan, looking like a living sculpture of a dissolute satyr.

Separating their bodies reluctantly, Rory settled against his side, pulling the blanket over them. Now that the fury of their passion was spent, her fatigue began to creep back, a reminder of what they'd gone through to get to this point.

Damon stretched, his joints cracking as he exhaled in a sud-den sigh. "Damn, I love it when you do that." A muscular arm curved over her back, pulling her against his side.

Her sensitized nerves stirred at the friction, her heart skip-ping at his choice of words. "Do what?"

"Jump my bones without warning."

Relieved by his explanation, she laughed, allowing the haze of sensual euphoria that had blanketed her senses to enfold her once more. "I'd have thought you'd gotten used to it by now."

The answering grunt Damon gave her sounded distinctly negative, but he didn't expand on it.

Funny. She would have thought the novelty of the experience had worn thin, after all the time they'd spent together; then again, it hadn't for her.

Rory ruffled his chest hair idly, delighting in the featherlight contact. There was something supremely decadent about being wrapped in hot, hard male when the heavens were carrying on like a dissonant orchestra led by a maniacal conductor.

"What are you going to do after we turn in that thing?" After weeks of referring to the nuke only indirectly, not naming it outright had become second nature; even though there no longer was any risk someone would overhear them, she didn't bother trying to break the habit. After all, her commission would soon be completed; then it wouldn't matter one way or another.

Her Adonis sighed softly. "I suppose I'll be given another mission. That's the usual reward for a job well done." The reluctance in his voice implied that he didn't look forward to it . . . or to leaving her?

"More terrorists?" A pang of disappointment pierced her lassitude. Of course he'd be given another mission . . . one that would take him away from her as surely as another woman. How silly of her not to have expected that.

"It's the only game in town these days." Damon caught her wandering hand, his cock stirring against her thigh. "And you? What are you going to do with all those millions?"

"Park it somewhere to earn more millions, probably."

He chuckled, the quaking of his chest bobbling her pleasantly. "That's it?"

"Another job." Rory shrugged, tempted toward indiscretion despite Felix's training. She and her Adonis had been through so much together, it actually felt unnatural to withhold information. "You probably can guess how it goes." To distract him from his line of questioning, she feathered her fingers along his ribs, making him jerk away.

"No, you wouldn't do that to a man while he's down, would you?" he protested—rather unconvincingly, given his hard-on.

Evading his grab, Rory cupped his thick cock with her free hand. "Oh, is that what you call it?" She traced his erect member with teasing fingers. "It doesn't feel down to me." Stroking its swelling length, she was once again struck by his size. "Nuh-uh, that doesn't feel down at all."

"Minx." Damon wrestled her under him, his legs tangling with hers. "Just ignore it. It will subside. I'm too spent to do you any justice."

Her belly cramped at his refusal. Was this it? The beginning of the end, now that she'd stolen the nuke?

It shouldn't have mattered. Though Damon was a fantastic lover and a tolerable partner, Rory had proposed their arrangement knowing it would be temporary. *He's a Fed and you're a diScipio with everything that heritage means.* But the thought of their affair ending so soon still hurt.

"What is it?" He raised himself on an elbow to look down at her, her penlight casting his deep-set eyes in shadow.

She cursed his incubus power that made him so attuned to her emotions. "Nothing, just hungry." And she was, she realized. Now that she was paying attention to her stomach, it felt like a bloody hole had been gouged to her spine.

"You wouldn't happen to have some food in there, would you?" Rory pointed her chin at his bulging bag leaning on the nuke. All she'd had was a day-old piece of *burek*, but the meat pie probably hadn't survived their trek intact.

Though Damon gave her a long look, he didn't call her on her diversionary tactic. "Actually, I do." Sitting up, he tucked the blanket around her. A hard loaf of bread was laid on her lap, on top of the blanket, and was soon joined by sausages, which he cut up, and a round of cheese.

The last item surprised Rory since it was one she liked and he was indifferent to. Its presence had to be deliberate since she knew there had been other cheeses available in the market nearest the hostel. Perhaps she was reading too much into it, but it warmed her heart.

Aurora diScipio, make up your mind! Is he ending it early or does he care? All this second-guessing Damon was giving her mental whiplash, and she didn't like her atypical indecision.

Shoving her confusion to the back of her mind, she tore a hunk from the loaf, then balanced bits of cheese on top. "How much did you bring?"

"Enough for a few days, if we ration it out." He set a plastic bottle of water between them.

About to take a bite, Rory froze in midmotion. "Should we?"

Taking a healthy mouthful of his own hunk of bread, Damon shook his head. "Best keep our strength up," he added, after swallowing. "Once we're across the border, we can buy food and call for pickup." His logic made sense, since they would make better speed that way; even on foot, it was only two days at most to Macedonia, though she didn't look forward to the hike.

Her stomach growled at the scent of food unfairly withheld, sounding louder than a distant roll of thunder. Cheeks hot, she bit into the bread, the simple meal tasting better than an eight-course dinner with her favorite dishes at the Four Seasons. Whoever had said that hunger was the best condiment was right; certainly it distracted her from her thoughts.

Damon, on the other hand, ate with his usual efficiency, the look on his face distant, his mind obviously elsewhere. For once, he lounged naked, an indication of his distraction, since he usually preferred to be dressed, in case he had to move quickly. Unfortunately, his nudity provided evidence of the veracity of his earlier statement—ignored, his hard-on had subsided—to her great disappointment. "Did you say you blew up over three million euros of Karadzic's holdings?"

Chasing crumbs on the blanket, Rory blinked, taken unawares by his question. He was back to that?

Still abashed at the risk she'd taken with her commission, she bobbed her chin. Personal feelings had no place in her line of work, as she well knew from Felix's training, but she couldn't let Damon's comment pass without defending herself. "He deserved it."

Surprisingly, the Fed whistled, one brow raised in a look of admiration. Then the light in his eyes changed to one of calculation. "That might be a mortal blow for his organization."

She blinked, his reaction reminding her again of their dissimilar backgrounds. Even Lucas, who was notorious among her brothers for encouraging her escapades, would have been bawling her out by now. "That was the idea."

"Why'd you do it? I mean, not to be ungrateful for the timely distraction, but that wasn't part of the plan."

Rory shivered, suddenly intensely aware of her nudity. Moving away from Damon, she found a dry set of clothes—the baggy ones she used with her older woman guise—at the bottom of her bag and put it on, grateful for the additional protection. They couldn't risk using the stove for fear of attracting attention, yet now that the fever of passion was spent and her stomach placated, she didn't feel comfortable relying only on his heat to counter the cold.

He gazed at her patiently, once they were both dressed, clearly waiting for an answer. He even returned to the cot, deliberately adopting a nonaggressive stance by lying down.

Sitting at his hip, she hugged her legs to her chest and wrapped the thin blanket around her shoulders, wondering where to start. Considering she'd nearly gotten them caught, he deserved to know why she'd taken such a risk. "It's crazy."

"What is?"

Rory screwed her eyes shut, breathing deeply to hold back the flood of emotion that suddenly welled up, threatening to spill over. With her back to him, she poured out the story of the murdered hooker whose name she didn't even know. All told, it still didn't make sense to her why that death in particular had hit her so strongly.

Damon pulled her into his arms, enfolding her in male heat, regardless of her resistance. He brushed his fingers across her cheek. Only then did she realize some tears had leaked out, despite her efforts.

"I know how you feel." He didn't say anything more, seeming to understand that words wouldn't help. He only rocked her, offering the comfort of his strong body and the steady beat of his heart beneath her ear. He didn't judge her, returning undemanding silence for her temporary weakness.

Somehow, that was enough.

She took a deep breath, feeling the constriction around her lungs release its grip. This close to him, the familiar scent of sex and healthy male overwhelmed the musty odor of moss riding the chill air, bringing to mind laughter and excitement and—inexplicably—a soul-deep sense of profound rightness.

It was a scent Rory could never grow tired of.

And yet, the job would soon be over. How could she bear to give Damon up?

CHAPTER TWENTY-ONE

Sudden, pointed attention, a straining effort flaring gold woke Damon from a light doze. Rory's body was taut, her breath held for some reason. Extending his mental antennae, he opened his eyes to the dimly lit cabin, but saw and sensed nothing to explain her tension. "What is it?"

"Listen."

A harsh sound broke the monotonous whistling of the wind through the eaves: the intermittent full-throated roar of a stuck vehicle being muscled out by brute force and sheer stubbornness. From the deep throb, it had a large displacement engine; therefore, not a Yugo or a Lada, definitely not a car. Maybe a truck. Despite the volume, it was still some distance away, since Damon didn't pick up any emissions, other than Rory's.

His master thief levered herself up, pushing on his chest with her forearms, her head tilted in a listening posture.

The engine throttled down and steadily grew louder, closer. *Company coming.* With the cabin probably the only building for miles, the likelihood that the vehicle was headed there was high. And, chances were, whoever it was wasn't on their side.

If they were caught inside, they'd be trapped.

Jerking upright, Damon pushed Rory off him and twisted around for his gun. Springing to her feet, she scrambled for her penlight. Together they swept up all traces of their presence. He stuffed the survival blanket in his bag, the most revealing item of all, next to the nuke.

Unbarring the door, he turned to Rory and gestured her to stay back while he investigated the noise. Whatever vehicle had caused it was still too far for him to detect any emotions.

The contrary woman shook her head and picked up the nuke, sliding out the door behind him.

He hauled back on his protests, knowing they didn't have time for argument.

Rory motioned toward the eaves of the cabin, lifting the suitcase meaningfully. He caught on immediately and went inside to get their packs. Rejoining her, he got down on one knee to give her a leg up. She stepped on his proffered thigh, then shifted to his shoulders, balancing herself with easy grace. He passed her the bomb, then carefully stood up while anchoring her with his hands around her ankles.

Using the cape he'd given her, it was the work of seconds for his master thief to stash the nuke and their packs high in the shadows in such a way that no one would readily notice it—a testament to her larcenous skills. When she was done, he released his grip, allowing her to drop lightly to the ground.

They moved away, covering their tracks to further conceal its hiding place. Then, against Damon's protective instincts, they separated to find their own coverts. It made sense, however, since the area didn't offer much. Two people together would have more difficulty avoiding discovery.

Damon found a dinky culvert, half-hidden by fallen leaves. It channeled a racing brook under the road but looked like it had space enough for one person. He turned to tell Rory to take it since she'd fit into it more easily, but she'd disappeared from view, her aura somewhere in the field behind the cabin.

He squeezed himself into the canal, sinking into water colder than a witch's tit and smelling of rotting vegetation. It seeped into his clothes, raw and chilling. After this mission, he fully intended to soak his bones in sunshine and not come up for air until he was well-done. Maybe he could talk his master thief into joining him.

The minor weight of his .45 was a reassuring presence in the small of his back. That and the extra magazines might give him an edge against whoever was coming.

A slight adjustment to the leaves shielding his covert and he was as ready as he could be. His position gave him a worm's-eye view of the track that led to the cabin; hopefully it was narrow enough to escape discovery.

Minutes passed with only vague pinpricks of light from between the trees, but a truck finally emerged, its long bed filled with several armed men. Damon's shoulders tightened. Against so many, there was little chance of picking them off one by one. His and Rory's best bet lay in going undetected.

The emissions that reached him confirmed his worst fears. They were alert and feeling mean, searching for the slightest excuse for violence.

Even before the truck came to a stop, Damon knew who would get out: Osum. The gang lord's aura scraped at his mental antennae, all smoldering anger and rank with bitterness.

The truck passed out of view. It pulled up short of the cabin to judge from the emissions beating at him, the roaring engine falling silent. The wary sparks spread out, any noise they made drowned out by the thunder and driving rain.

Eventually, three thugs came into sight by the cabin and two disappeared inside. They quickly emerged, gesturing futility.

Osum bulled past them and entered. Green suspicion flared just before the large Kosovar came out, his thick body stiff with aggression. "This place stinks of fornication. Search the area! Whoever were here could not have gone far."

Fuck. Damon's heart skipped when the bellowed order reached him. Their chances of escaping just dropped.

The thugs sprang to obey. Fourteen sparks of wariness spread out through the lightning-strobed night. A few followed the track; the rest took the cabin as a starting point and fanned out, kicking and prodding the slightest rise that could possibly conceal a person.

Those walking the dirt road didn't go far. After one sank knee deep in marshy grass, they contented themselves with sweeping their flashlights along the track, loath to get any wetter than they already were. Transforming heavy rain into glistening curtains, the bright beams crept over the bowed tufts of grass, exposing each to careful scrutiny. They inched closer to the culvert, in between flashes of lightning. At any other time, such thoroughness would have been admirable, but not when Damon was the prey.

Sudden pain followed by furious chagrin warned Damon that something had gone wrong with Rory. A faint shout of discovery went up.

The beams stopped, short of the culvert. Then the searchers withdrew, retreating to the cabin. Fifteen sparks converged on Osum, one flaring with hostility.

Damon's heart stopped as two of the thugs dragged forward a slender, unmistakably feminine figure. She looked so fragile cowering before the stocky gang lord.

"What do we have here?" Osum tipped her chin up.

A savage growl rose from the gang lord's thugs at the face revealed, and they drifted closer, a predatory motion that made the hairs on Damon's arms stand on end.

Rory had transformed her features to exotic beauty, doe-eyed and fine boned. All budding, virginal delicacy made all the more tempting by the way her wet clothes clung to her body. The frightened expression on her face would have moved a stone statue to pity.

Damon had to admire her instincts for self-preservation. With most other sex slavers, an exceptionally gorgeous woman could be sold to special markets and was therefore more valuable. That alone might have given her a better chance at survival.

Osum, however, was a different proposition altogether. Since he had no qualms about selling women for snuff sex, Rory's gambit would not necessarily help. And from the gang lord's disregard of his men's response to their captive, her looks might actually have increased her danger.

Despite their situation, Damon didn't pick up anything from her stronger than apprehension, a core of cool determination suggesting she was already plotting her escape.

Taking his cue from her, he counted off the opposition. The truck had carried fifteen men. Two held Rory captive. Another two stood by the door to the cabin. Three flanked Osum, leaving seven straggling in from the fields. Too many to pick off, if they remained in visual contact of each other, and too spread out to eliminate in one strike.

But if he had to take anyone out, it would be the gang lord as the leader. Damon wouldn't shed any tears over the necessity.

"Where is your companion?" Osum's growl was nearly lost in the storm.

Rory's lips moved, though Damon didn't catch what she said. Her answer or the blank look she gave Osum earned her a slap. She must have rolled with the blow since she didn't radiate that much pain, but Damon felt it like a pile driver to the groin.

The gang lord grabbed her by the hair, yanked her head back, and leaned down in a show of dominance. Then he flung her away and spun around to glare into the night. "Coward, if you do not come out, I will give this woman to my men to rape. She will die slowly. You can watch." The raw determination Osum radiated underscored the fury in his voice.

The gang lord would do it, too. He already sold women to be killed; what was one more?

Duty demanded Damon remain where he was. One of them had to survive to take the nuke to safety. With his master thief captured, that left him.

His heart rejected the argument. Even if Osum killed Rory, there was no guarantee the Kosovar would leave. More likely, he would order another search. Abandoning her to the gang lord's tender mercies wouldn't further Damon's mission—at least that's what he told himself.

Another slap cracked out, louder in a momentary lull between thunderclaps and gusts. Rory reeled in the grip of her captors, radiating more pain than before, though she still didn't make a sound.

Torn in opposite directions, Damon dug his nails into his

palms, fighting to make the right decision. But he couldn't live with himself if his master thief died for his sake. She hadn't signed up for that.

He couldn't sacrifice Rory.

Faced with no other choice, he slipped out of the culvert, tugging the loose tail of his shirt to ensure it hid his .45. Using the rain and storm to muffle his movements, he waded through the drowned grass, trying for a better position.

One thing was certain: Osum wouldn't kill him out of hand. With luck, Damon could take out enough of them for Rory to escape, maybe even enough that she could complete their mission.

The gang lord cocked an arm back, massive fist raised in threat. This blow would be no slap she could shrug off.

"Don't."

"Who is there?" Osum demanded, wariness flaring.

Damon stood up, his empty hands hanging at his sides.

The thugs reared back, surprise a violent flare of yellow erupting in their auras. Their Uzis came up, a few covering Damon, the others turning to face the storm-swept night, as they clustered closer together, drawing confidence from the reminder of their superior numbers—but not without a double lash of doubt and fear at his sudden appearance in their midst. As Damon had intended. If he could come out of nowhere, who knew what else was out there? He'd use every advantage he could get.

"You!" The large Kosovar's heavy features twisted with rage. "Always you, lurking in the shadows, watching, watching, watching. Now, here?"

No one made a move toward Damon, depending on their firepower to control him. Good. He'd hoped Abdou's reputation would keep him free to act. If they'd tried to tie him up, he'd have had to attack immediately.

"Where is it?" Osum demanded, sudden hope warring with suspicion. "You have to have it. There is no other reason for you to be out here."

"Where's what?" Damon temporized, calculating the distance to Rory and the odds of taking on fifteen men by himself. He had ammo to spare, if he didn't waste his shots. Another plus for his side was the fact that most of the fifteen weren't facing his direction; like good little soldiers, they were trying to cover all the approaches, in case of an ambush. Too bad he was it. On the minus side, his wet shirt would hamper his draw. Too, a .45 was no match for an Uzi in most cases, and he couldn't assume his enemies wouldn't react quickly to his attack.

Osum's black eyes narrowed to furious slits, making the gang lord look even more like a mean-tempered wild boar than he normally did. "Do not play stupid. You know precisely what I mean." He drew a large pistol from his belt, handling it with unthinking competence. "The bomb. It is why you came here, yes? Do not take me for a fool, Abdou. I know all about you."

So his cover had held. The knowledge was little comfort to Damon. It didn't look like Osum feared retaliation by the PKU. Why would he when the only witnesses around were his own thugs?

Still, perhaps the fiction would give him and Rory a chance. It was better than nothing.

Damon twisted his lips in a sneer of condescension. "You really think I'd keep it with me?"

Uncertainty flickered in the gang lord like the lightning above them. If he knew so much about Jamil Abdou, he'd also know that Abdou had been seen in Ahmad's company. Damon could have handed off the nuke to Ahmad.

Osum made a dismissive gesture, desperation smothering his doubts. "If I return with the bomb, Alexei Karadzic will know I am still to be trusted."

"More like he'll believe you stole it in the first place." Damon snorted deliberately to fan the gang lord's uncertainty. He edged toward Rory; the thugs might hesitate to fire if he were in the middle of the pack, for fear of hitting another of their number. "I heard you had plans."

"I am loyal to Alexei," Osum blustered; then he stiffened, his small eyes rounding in a flash of comprehension. "All this is your doing!" The gang lord brandished his pistol at Damon, his finger on the trigger. "I ought to kill you right now."

Fuck. He hadn't said anything that wasn't common talk. How had the Kosovar made the connection?

Fear slammed into Damon like a sledgehammer. Rory's. Until then she hadn't reacted much to the threats. But now fear exploded, bright to his mental sense and just as warming. If he didn't do something soon, she might. He could feel her steeling herself to act.

Osum swore at length. He descended into dialect, his guttural delivery making Damon glad he understood only a word in five. But by the admiring looks the thugs threw their leader, the gang lord was either bad-mouthing Damon's ancestry or making bloodcurdling threats.

Damon ignored the rant, more interested in the positions of Osum's thugs. The way they were drifting closer still, drawn by the gang lord's posturing, was good—clumped together they'd make easier targets.

Eventually, the Kosovar ran down, panting from his excesses.

"Where is the bomb? If you do not tell . . ." The pistol came up—aimed at Rory—murderous rage backing its threat.

And Damon was still too far away to block the shot.

Not her!

"*NO!*" He threw himself in front of his thief, reaching for his hidden .45. But he was moving too slowly. Oh so slowly.

Osum flinched at Damon's shout, then corrected his aim.

Prak!

CHAPTER TWENTY-TWO

The gunshot cut through the sounds of Nature's fury. The howling wind, the drumming rain, the boom of thunder were nothing to the explosion reverberating in Rory's ears. Damon flinched, a grunt of pain escaping him as he lunged at the leader, the look on his face set and fey.

More shots rang out in quick succession, louder and deeper than the first. Her captors jerked at the sounds, their grips loosening, but she paid little heed to their reaction. What absorbed her attention and chilled her heart was the Fed's reckless, headlong attack. Then he crashed into the thugs, bowling them off their feet.

"DAMON!"

Rage exploded in her heart. Fanned by horror and fear for

Damon, it flooded her veins with dreadful power. Fangs sprouted in her mouth as she Changed into the worst nightmare she could imagine. Breaking the hold of her captors, she slashed at the nearest throat with long, razor-sharp talons. Hot blood spurted into her face, blinding her for a moment.

She screamed wordlessly, the taste of copper filling her mouth, mingling with cold rain. Skin and muscle parted under her claws to shrieks of terror. She lashed out at everyone within reach, instinct demanding she protect her lover. They'd *shot* him! She couldn't forgive that.

Damon struggled in the mud, wrestling, punching, and kicking, as more thugs piled in. Still alive, but for how much longer?

She fought to get to him, to even the odds. To save him, somehow.

Gunshots rang out anew, the cracks and booms driving her fury to greater heights.

"Rory, run!" Damon shouted, his voice nearly lost in the rolling thunder. "Get away!"

Never! She refused to abandon him.

Lunging into the melee, Rory drove her claws through bulletproof vests and heavy jackets, ripping and rending with impartiality. The effort to cut deeper and harder to greater effect felt like she was tearing her nails out, her fingers throbbing in complaint. Borne on a wave of exaltation by her killing rage, the meaty impact jarring her shoulders barely registered.

She ignored the buffeting wind and the blows of her enemy, more interested in results.

"Damon!" Screaming her lover's name, she laid backs open, snagged an arm between her fangs, and gnashed down.

With a screech of pain, her enemy jerked away, clutching his stump, and caromed into others.

They whipped around to face her as lightning lit up the skies. The nearest yelled in terror and fled into the storm. The ones that remained didn't seem to realize Damon wasn't the danger.

She pounced on their backs, shrieking her rage and bloodlust. "Kill it!" Someone out of arm's reach fired, emptying his gun at her.

The body in her grasp jerked and jittered. Shocked out of her killing frenzy, Rory crouched behind her makeshift shield. Then more shots filled the air, going off so rapidly they sounded like strings of fireworks.

She froze where she knelt, waiting for pain to register. Surely so many bullets couldn't all miss. When nothing came, triumph filled her with a heady bravado. Baring her teeth in a snarl, she screamed defiance at the enemy, daring them to do their worst. She would kill them all!

The nerves of the remaining few broke. Gibbering in panic, they abandoned their truck and dead associates for the night.

"Rory . . ." Damon's breathless bass was so weak she nearly didn't hear him in the heavy downpour.

Panting, she turned in his direction, the gunfire echoing in her ears urging her to slash and destroy.

He was nowhere to be found.

"Down here."

When she looked down, still snarling, her lover blinked, then raised a brow at her, an incongruously mild expression on his face, sprawled as he was beneath several motionless bodies. "Remind me never to make you angry."

Rory gaped, wondering at his lighthearted quip. Something wet flowed down the corner of her mouth. She licked it off and caught a taste of blood. Spitting in disgust, she reached up to swipe her lips clean and felt hard claws against her cheek. Only then did she realize she still wore the demon shape she'd Changed into. Shivering as adrenaline faded, she shifted to something more human.

And remembered what had set her off.

"Are you alright?" Rory stumbled toward Damon, her knees threatening to fold, the gunshot and his flinch playing back in her mind's eye. He'd been hit, damn it.

Mud made getting to him difficult, her shaky legs nearly sliding from under her. Then she had to dig him out from under the pile of corpses, several of which had bullet holes in them. Damon's handiwork?

She almost lost what little she had in her stomach rolling off the last one. Its head flopped in a different direction from the rest of its body, a prolonged flash of lightning showing its neck almost completely blown away. Decapitation by gunfire. It was the leader, the one built like an ox who'd pointed the gun at Damon. She retched blood and acid at the sight, the noxious combination amplifying her nausea, but fear gave her the strength to finish clearing the pile to get at her Adonis.

Thunder crashed as she knelt by his side, vaguely grateful that the rain washed the air clean of the smells of death.

"You idiot. What did you think you were doing, jumping in front of a gun like that?" She searched Damon's body frantically for his injuries, worried even further by the way he just lay there with only his gun hand raised while she ran her hands over him. "The mission isn't over yet. What if you'd been killed?"

"You'd've been okay, so you'd see it through."

The quiet statement of confidence shook Rory to the core and took the wind from out of her sails. Of course she would have seen it through, but he still would have been dead! "Idiot," she repeated with less heat. "I'd prefer not to finish without you."

He gave a pained laugh. "I'll keep that in mind."

"Bastard."

"Careful, I might think you care."

She bit her lower lip against a snarl. The way her heart jittered in her chest, as though afflicted with Saint Vitus's dance, he might be right, too.

There was only one hole—an obscene blind eye high on his chest—so the bullet was still inside him. She sucked in a breath at the sight, then scrambled for a scrap of fabric that wasn't muddy from the fight. Nothing presented itself.

Damon waved her off. "Never mind that. Get the truck before they come back for it." He collected something from the wet ground beside him—empty magazines for the cartridges he'd expended protecting her, she realized.

"Shut up. You're hurt."

Tucking the magazines away, he staggered to his feet, still holding his pistol at the ready. "It's just a scratch." He fumbled in his pockets, then extracted a clean handkerchief and pressed it on the wound. "Get the truck."

Knowing she couldn't sway his determination, Rory was forced to accept his assurances. It would be faster to carry out his instructions than argue with him. She ran to the truck, wondering if she'd have to hot-wire it; she wasn't sure she remembered how, though she suspected Damon did. Luckily, the driver had left the keys in the ignition.

Wrestling with the unfamiliar controls, she drove it to Damon and leaned over to open the passenger-side door. He slung the muddy suitcase inside, followed by their packs, then got in himself. Her beloved idiot hadn't waited for her to retrieve the nuke.

"Go!"

Stifling useless reproach, Rory put the truck in gear and drove off.

At first, the effort of driving a strange vehicle and finding and following the unmarked dirt road took most of her concentration, especially when her muscles started to shake as adrenaline left her system. But after an hour to recover with only grunted directions from Damon, scenes from the fight began to flicker in her mind's eye. The darkness and hypnotic drumming of the rain on the truck's roof left little else to occupy her.

She'd killed!

Rory waited for horror to rise, but nothing came. The memory of gore was what stayed with her, that and the feel of skin and muscle parting under her claws. Nothing more. She didn't remember much of the actual fight, just an all-consuming fury that blotted out everything else.

She was glad she'd killed them. They'd deserved it. At that moment, they'd come to represent all the vileness she'd seen in the past weeks. She didn't regret their deaths. Maybe she would later, but she suspected not. Right then, she felt as though she could do it again, if she had to.

Her reaction—rather, the lack of it—surprised her. So her condemnation of Damon's hits was all intellectual?

"Are you okay?"

The darkness that cocooned them in a world of their own made it easier to share her thoughts. "I killed them."

"Yeah, you did. Some." He patted her thigh. Injured though he was, he still tried to comfort her. "Welcome to the club."

Rory confessed the important part in a whisper. "But I don't regret it."

He didn't react to her statement. Of course, he probably sensed her lack of remorse.

She shook her head at the emotional energy she'd wasted. "I've been an idiot. I'm sorry." She risked a glance at him. "Forgive me?"

Damon gave her a ghost of his usual smile, almost invisible behind his weeks-old beard. "There's nothing to forgive. I just wish your killing them hadn't been necessary."

Rory choked up at the lack of rancor in his answer, her heart flipping over. "That's it? Anyone else would be crowing, 'I told you so.'"

His breathless laugh was cut short by a groan. "Don't worry. I'll make you pay for it once the mission's over."

"Pay how?" Ingrained suspicion pierced the breathless anxiety that stirred at his sound of pain.

"Oh, maybe another blow job or two would do it."

If Damon could joke about that, maybe he wasn't as badly hurt as she thought. Forcing herself to match his levity, she quipped: "That's cheap. One-twenty euros?"

"Okay, make it daily blow jobs for a month," he countered immediately. "And two on Sundays."

Rory snickered at his nonsense, warmed by the thought of more time with her Adonis after the job was done. "You're on."

Though the winds were abating, the rain came down stronger, obscuring the lousy excuse of a road and forcing her to concentrate once more on driving. Damon had rejected calling for pickup since they had transportation, saying they'd make better time by heading straight for Skopje.

The long haul through the tall mountains dividing Kosovo and Macedonia passed in a mind-numbing downpour that drowned out thought, broken only by her Adonis's rumbled directions. He guided her through the darkness, but not without cost. By the time they reached what looked like a highway and he announced that they'd probably already crossed the border into Macedonia, he was slumped in his seat, pale and sweating profusely despite the heater keeping the cabin slightly cool—set deliberately so to keep them both awake.

Dismay had Rory saying the first thing that came to mind. "Why'd you do it? Draw his attention? Jump in the way? He might not've shot me. I mean, why lose good money?"

A weak snort answered her. "Osum would've shot you. I sensed it."

That gave Rory pause. The ox was Osum, the one ultimately responsible for that hooker's death? She found the knowledge that he'd paid with his life strangely comforting, especially when he'd nearly killed her Adonis. "Still, I could have handled him myself."

"I didn't know you could morph like that."

She spared a glance at him. "I'm a lamia. Of course I could Change like that." Only after the words were said did she realize the inanity of her statement: he couldn't have known; she'd never gone into detail about her abilities. She bit her lip, stricken with dismay.

Beside her, Damon sighed, then added under his breath, "I couldn't risk that. Never could I risk that."

Her gut tightened at the soft-spoken words. Though uncertain that she'd heard Damon correctly, she didn't ask him to repeat himself. That way lay conversational waters she wasn't sure she wanted to explore just yet. Luckily for her, he fell silent after that. She didn't press him, content to let the miles pass without comment.

Endless hours later, the road rounded another ridge to reveal a distinctive outline on top of a distant crest, a solitary brightness that shone through the gentler rain. Rory straightened over the wheel, straining to see better, growing certainty making her heart race.

"Damon, look! That has to be the Millennium Cross." While she hadn't seen the landmark lit up before they'd left for Kosovo, it couldn't be anything else, which meant the end was in sight. Skopje—and their contact—should be just at the foot of Mount Vodno.

She sighed in relief, the prospect of handing off responsibility for the nuke giving her renewed strength.

Then she realized her Adonis hadn't responded to her comment. "Damon?!"

He'd passed out, the stain on his shirt almost doubled in size from the last time she'd checked.

Rory stopped in the middle of the empty road, throwing the truck into a skid in her haste. She should have suspected his injury was worse than he'd let on when he hadn't offered to take over driving! She'd been so focused on getting to Skopje that she hadn't given it a second thought.

Acting on a vague memory of a medical drama she'd seen on TV, she tilted his seat back as far as it would go, hoping that lowering the level of his heart really would help slow the bleeding.

It struck her that he wore an undershirt. So stupid of her to have forgotten. Tugging its tail free of his pants, she tore off the clean hem of the garment, and reduced it further by another several inches. His undershirt was ruined anyway, so she might as well put it to better use. Folding one strip into a wad, she pressed it on top of the blood-soaked handkerchief. Using the other strips, she secured the makeshift dressing to his ribs, ending with a tight knot over the wad.

All the while, Damon remained unconscious.

Rory brushed his hair out of his face, shuddering inwardly at the coolness of his skin. "Damon Venizélos, don't you dare die on me."

He didn't answer her, didn't respond even when she pressed a kiss on his pale lips.

She couldn't lose him now!

With a wary glance at the suitcase at his feet, Rory drove on. There wasn't anything else she could do to help him, except get him and the nuke to their contact. She had to trust he'd fight to stay alive.

And pray she'd get him to help in time.

Chapter Twenty-three

Rory reached the outskirts of Skopje, the capital of Macedonia, in no mood to appreciate the gentle dawn washing the sky with color, grateful only that the rain had finally stopped an hour earlier. The illumination of the imposing cross overlooking the city, her beacon of hope through miles of silent driving, faded into obscurity, no longer able to compete with the rising sun.

The directions Damon had given her led to a nondescript compound, a featureless block of gray, concrete wall that was indistinguishable from its neighbors save for a small, black street number. Only the sentry's speedy response to her password assured her she'd found the right place. Almost as though she'd said, "Open Sesame!" the gate cracked open and ponderously swung back on its hinges.

Inside was a different story. Armed guards stood around the courtyard, where they couldn't be seen from the street, weapons held at the ready. Surveillance cameras kept watch, hidden under eaves, obvious only to her trained eyes.

A man approached the car as soon as the gate was closed behind her. His shock of white hair seemed to glow in the early morning light—a strange thing to notice at a time like this, but Rory was punch-drunk from worry and hours of driving.

She ignored him, sliding out from behind the wheel and rounding the hood at a run to get to Damon's side as quickly as she could. She dragged the muddy suitcase out from under his legs, then touched his pale lips. He was cool, his skin gray and clammy, but rapid puffs of air warmed her fingers. Fresh blood made a large splotch of color where it had seeped through the makeshift bandage.

"I'll take that." The stranger reached for the bomb with a nearly tangible air of absolute confidence, apparently accustomed to obedience.

Instinctively, her hand tightened around the handle. It was her only bargaining chip, and Rory wasn't about to give it up just like that. "No, him first."

Pale green eyes narrowed at her opposition. She met them with her version of implacable determination, ready to kick and scream, maybe even claw a man or two, if that was what it would take to get Damon immediate medical attention.

White Hair seemed to realize cooperation would get him what he wanted more quickly than browbeating—or perhaps she just looked that crazed. He called two guards over, rapping out orders in machine-gun fashion.

Rory lurched back, startled by the staccato words delivered almost next to her ear. The nuke's case whacked her shin, the burst of pain drawing tears from her eyes, but at least access to the door was clear.

Running over, the pair shouldered their weapons and eased Damon out of the car. As they laid him on the ground, more people rushed out of the building, dragging a rattling gurney between them over the uneven bricks of the courtyard.

"I'll take that now, so you can rest." The words barely penetrated her daze, so focused was she on her lover's still form. "Smith, here, will show you to your room."

Rory shook her head impatiently. "Damon first."

"You're out on your feet," White Hair pointed out in a low, sympathetic tone that threatened to undermine her resistance.

She was mortally tired, but the fear that her lover would die if she let him out of her sight made her resist the offer. "And he's nearly dead." Stumbling on worn pavers, she hurried after Damon into the building, hard plastic banging against her leg. "This isn't going anywhere until I know he's alright. I want to make sure he's going to be okay, first."

He humored her, had to be humoring her. Rory knew that in her weakened state, she wouldn't have been able to put up much of a fight if he ordered his men to take the bomb from her. Instead, White Hair let her have her way, keeping pace beside her without much of an effort down the featureless corridor.

To her surprise, Damon was rolled straight into surgery. A mass of medical people converged around him, cutting off his shirt and connecting him to a bag of whole blood. Someone brought out a metal tray of surgical instruments. They weren't going to wait to operate on him.

But didn't they have to do pre-op or something? The medical dramas she'd caught on TV seemed to put a lot of stock in X-rays and an alphabet soup of tests; weren't those necessary?

Since diScipios avoided hospitals like the plague, Rory didn't have any firsthand experience to draw on.

She turned wide eyes to White Hair, who dismissed her misgivings with a remarkably cavalier shrug. "He's unconscious anyway. Might as well get the bullet out and patch him up."

With a faint sense of disbelief, Rory watched them clean the wound, revealing torn flesh. Her stomach lurched at the sight. The handle of the nuke bit into her hand as she clung to her self-control, while they dug for the bullet.

Fighting to keep her gorge down, she looked away and caught the reflection of a mad woman on a shiny steel door. She stared for a moment, then realized it was her. Spiky hair, runnels of dried blood across her face, the odd gob of mud and meat clinging to her ruined clothes. No wonder White Hair had humored her; she looked like a demon out of classical myths. He probably thought she'd go postal on him if he didn't agree.

She might have, too.

It was a miracle that Damon could bring himself to speak and joke with her in the truck, after he'd seen her in that demon form she'd Changed into.

A sharp *ping*, then the rattle of metal careening over metal, pulled her attention back to the surgical table. They'd extracted the bullet, now rolling on the tray, and were sewing the wound shut. The rough-and-ready procedure had taken very little time.

Shutting her eyes against an insidious surge of weakness, she tightened her grip on the nuke when her knees threatened to give way. Not yet.

Rory resisted White Hair's suggestions about handing over the nuke until Damon had been installed in a private room. Handover could wait. After all, it wasn't as though there was any chance of losing the bomb at that point.

"Satisfied now?" White Hair asked in a dry tone of near exasperation.

Knees melting in relief, she dropped onto a chair beside Damon's bed, the bomb landing on the floor with a hard thump. She forced her hand to release its handle, her fingers feeling frozen in place from the tight grip she'd kept. "Yes, thank you."

White Hair must have taken the nuke away when he left, but she didn't notice, too focused on watching Damon. Conscious of the fact she'd nearly lost the man she loved.

The realization came to her like the first drops of a gentle shower that grows into a thunderstorm. Somehow, while she wasn't looking, the sneaky bastard had gotten past her defenses and stolen her heart.

Rory bit her lip to hold back a tearful laugh. Stealing from a thief. Wasn't that a scream?

The seamed face of the Old Man with his trademark head of televangelist white wasn't what Damon wanted to see the first thing after rousing from unconsciousness. If he was honest with himself, it didn't even make the tenth on his list.

Radiating a curious mix of concern and pride, his superior frowned down at him, his bushy brows beetling into a squiggly line over his nose. "Congratulations, boy. You did it. Cut things a bit close, but you did it."

That wasn't exactly what he wanted to hear, either, much as it gratified his ego. Sliding his hand out from under his pillow, he pushed himself up on his elbows, earning an annoying pinch on his left arm, where an IV was stuck in, and a stab of pain in his side.

"Careful," the Old Man cautioned, taking the visitor's chair beside Damon's hospital bed. "Your injury's fairly minor, but you lost a lot of blood."

"Whe—" He had to cough to clear his dry throat, his mouth feeling like a casualty of surgery. "Where's Rory?" Damned if talking didn't send a shaft of pain up his side. He ignored it with the ease that came with practice and familiarity.

"Your master thief?" The Old Man extended a tumbler of ice chips, a noncommittal expression on his face.

Damon glowered in answer, saving his breath in case he needed it for more important things, but his superior pretended ignorance until he'd sipped some water and was sucking on the frozen stuff.

"I sent her off to rest."

Crunching ice, Damon swore silently. She could be anywhere by now. The security of the compound wouldn't stop her; it might even pose a challenge she couldn't resist. She didn't need him to help her leave; she had her own connections in the city. And if she'd left . . .

The Old Man narrowed pale green eyes at him. "What?"

Damon levered himself higher on the pillows, into a sitting position. The effort it took left him damnably weak. "Are you sure she's resting?"

"As tired as that woman was, and after she'd spent most of the day hovering at your bedside? Yes."

Rory had hovered at his bedside? Damon couldn't credit it, but his superior wasn't one for inaccuracy. "Really?" There was no helping the hopeful tone of his voice. At this point, the slightest scrap of encouragement was welcome.

"Something you want to tell me?"

Lifting the edge of the curtain surreptitiously, Rory studied the compound's walls, using her IR goggles to locate the hidden guards. Probably because they were trying to keep a low profile, there were no spotlights to eliminate the shadows, only a zigzag tangle of photodetectors invisible to the human eye.

Ignoring the cold draft undercreeping her too-short towel, she plotted alternate routes through the gaps and gauged the risk from a professional standpoint. It would be so easy to slip between them, into the darkness, and just disappear. Maybe use one of the identities Damon's agency had provided or drop by the Bear for new papers and fly out. She wasn't worried about the rest of her fee; Damon wouldn't let them stiff her, and White Hair didn't seem the type to do so, either.

The job was over, her commission fulfilled. Why hang around for painful farewells? He had his life and she had hers. He was a Fed and she was a thief, something that was in her blood.

The goggles snagged in her wet hair as she pulled them off, her attention given to the debate in her head.

Rory could practically hear Felix advising her to cut the ties cleanly and quickly, his ruined tenor rasping over the words. Big Brother Lucas would say the same in his smoother baritone, she was sure.

Yet her heart clenched at the prospect of never seeing Damon again, of having as her last memory of him the sight of him lying pale and unconscious, wounded, helpless when he was normally so powerful and vibrant with life. Her sexy Adonis laid low because he'd protected her.

But what was the alternative?

She made a face as she imagined the reaction of her family to her pursuing a romantic relationship with a Fed. The Fed and the thief? It sounded like something only Hollywood would dream up. Granted, her female cousins would turn pea green once they got a glimpse of the leading man. Her menfolk, on the other hand, would be a tougher proposition, though she was sure they'd eventually see the possible advantages of such a connection.

Of course, that was assuming Damon would want an inveterate thief hanging around. He could have just been joking, keeping up a strong front and all that.

And if he didn't want her to?

Tears suddenly filled her eyes, her thoughts scattering, disconnected as if forced through a head stuffed with cotton. Weariness weighed heavy on her shoulders, like a ton of rocks dragging her down to oblivion, catching up with her now that the crisis was truly over.

Deciding to leave decisions for later, when she was rested, Rory staggered to the bed and fell into it, still wrapped in the damp towel, fast asleep before her head hit the pillow.

Damon was waiting in her dream, naked and ready, just the way she liked him.

"You again?"

"Hey." He took her in his arms, looking solid and fit when she knew better. "About time you got here."

"I just got to bed, silly."

"I've been waiting for you to join me." Damon claimed her lips in a sweet kiss that belied his injury. If he was hurting, it didn't show. In fact, he felt wonderful.

The man of her dreams.

Uncommonly lighthearted, Rory giggled. "You're delirious. You're supposed to be recovering from that bullet wound."

"Hah. I have more important things to do." He kissed her again, sucking and nibbling on her lips like they were candy, taking his time ravishing her mouth, something he rarely did in real life. "Just don't leave without talking to me. Otherwise, I'll haunt you."

She smiled, relishing the feel of him in her arms, even if it wasn't real. "You already do."

"I'm serious. We've lots of things to discuss."

"Okay." Then she pulled his head down to satisfy her longings. At least in dreams, she didn't have to worry that Damon would overexert himself.

Everything else could wait.

He swept her off into a fantasy of sensual delights, tormenting her with possibilities in a way he hadn't had since he'd lured her into his trap with the jade dildo, arousing her with imaginary pleasures—pleasures she'd experienced for herself at his hands.

"Why are you doing this?" Rory demanded as her body burned with pent-up desire.

"To make sure you come to me tomorrow night."

"Why?" she repeated, desperate for release.

"Because I love you."

The words jolted Rory out of her dream, into wakefulness, her womb throbbing and heavy with carnal hunger. *He loves me?* Terror and exultation warred in her heart. Wishful thinking or true contact? She wasn't sure which she preferred.

CHAPTER TWENTY-FOUR

As another night fell, darkness rose and so, too, did Damon's tension. Would Rory come? The hours had crept by, bringing with them a change of his dressings, the removal of his IV and beard, and bland hospital fare that—more than anything else— proved he was in American hands. A call from the Old Man, already en route with the nuke to the States, was the only other thing that broke his self-imposed vigil.

Toward midnight, the curtain fluttered gently, seemingly stirred by the cold night wind. If Damon hadn't been watching for Rory, he'd have missed the shadow behind it, though there was no mistaking the intense focus and trepidation that radiated from that direction. "I must be getting better at catching you or you're that tired." He slid his hand out from under his pillow where he'd tucked his .45.

A soft laugh answered him. "Just playing safe. Didn't want to get shot, what with your hair-trigger reflexes."

His visitor stepped out from behind the panel, a svelte blonde with brown Tatar eyes and a wicked smile—the same form she'd taken after the fight with Osum—and dressed in the black jumpsuit she'd worn when he'd first caught her. Nothing remained of the berserker who'd savaged the gang lord's thugs, or hinted at the wholesome, girl-next-door artist he'd first met, but he knew that deep inside where it mattered, she was Rory.

Relief at her presence had him sinking into his pillows for an instant. She hadn't run and left him to chase her, after all; he'd been half-afraid she'd disappear into the night, choosing to return to her previous lifestyle. Knowing he was probably in for some resistance, he straightened immediately, mustering his arguments while trying to anticipate her objections.

Rory stalked through the intervening space with her habitual feline grace and perched a hip on his bed. "You're looking much improved. I must say, gray just isn't your color. It doesn't do anything for your complexion," the minx remarked lightly, as though they were merely chance-met acquaintances, not lovers.

Damon matched her easy tone, willing to follow her lead, for the moment. "I can't say I liked it myself."

She bent over him, biting her lower lip as she inspected the white bandage on his ribs. Her fingers barely touched the gauze; the extreme care she took not to put pressure on his injury actually hurt him more. "Not bad. I guess you'll live. You really ought to be more careful."

He figured he wouldn't get a better opening to segue into the topic he wanted to discuss. "Maybe if I had someone to watch my back . . ."

Moving away, Rory raised her brows at him, a ghost of a smile quirking the corners of her mouth. "And a nice back it is, too. Well worth watching." She drifted to the side table, then the curtains and the rest of the room, picking things up and setting them down at random.

Her aimless meandering, in complete contrast with the tight attention he sensed and her usual straightforward manner, made Damon wish he weren't bedridden and could hold her in place to listen to his proposition. "Sit down, damn it. I want to look at you."

She spun to face him on a spurt of surprise. "What?"

"You've checked me out. Now it's my turn."

"Why?"

He glared at her in exasperation, wondering if Rory was deliberately acting dense. "I only have the Old Man's say-so that you're okay. I want to make sure for myself."

Still, she hesitated, which didn't do his heart any good. "Old man? White Hair?"

Damon snorted at the nickname she'd given his superior. "Yeah, that would be him. Now come here." He extended his arms imperiously, since demands seemed to cut through the nonsense.

Rory flowed into his embrace as though she belonged there— which she did. At the contact, something inside him began to relax, relieved by the tactile evidence of her presence. Tucking his head against her neck, he breathed in the scent of soap, cold air, and Rory. She seemed hale enough, smiling indulgently when he ran his hands over her, and he didn't pick up any indications of pain. But that didn't stop him from checking. She felt too good in his arms to give up without a fight.

"You feel sound," Damon said, just to fill the silence, suddenly uncertain. He studied her flawless face, wondering how his master thief would receive his next suggestion.

"I wasn't the one hurt; you were," Rory responded tartly.

"Yeah, well, I've spoken with the Old Man. He was quite complimentary about our results." He paused to inject just the right amount of levity into his voice, so that she wouldn't reject his proposition out of hand.

"As he should be." The minx tilted her head, her slanted brown eyes widening in inquiry and mock innocence.

"He seems to think we make a great team."

"We did work well together," she agreed lightly, after a split second's hesitation. He'd surprised her, though it showed only in a quick blink. "I rather enjoyed it."

"How do you feel about making it more permanent?"

Rory's fulgent shock was almost palpable, her pupils dilating as she stilled in his arms. "You want us to continue working together."

"We've been doing so for weeks. What's so strange about that?" Damon countered, pushing his advantage while he had her off balance. Apparently, she hadn't expected him to propose a more permanent partnership. Had she thought he'd cut her loose and wave good-bye without trying for more? "It won't pay as well as your current gig, but you'll definitely be challenged."

"Me, a Fed?"

"You can be an asset, if that would make you feel better." He watched her expression shift from outright bewilderment, to bemusement, to speculation, the changes coming rapidly as might be expected in someone as canny as she. "You'd be one, too." The amusement that bubbled up behind her amazement took him aback, though.

Rory's gaze turned distant, her thoughts apparently veering off on a tangent. "Wouldn't that be something," she murmured under her breath. "They'd have kittens."

They? Damon didn't pursue the non sequitur, not wanting to derail the discussion. Besides, if his master thief agreed to the partnership, he was sure he'd find out who she meant . . . eventually. He hadn't forgotten that he'd still to learn her real name, despite weeks of working together.

His fingers dug into the bed as her silence stretched out. Finally, he couldn't bear the suspense any longer. "Well?"

"After all that's happened, I'm not sure I could go back to my old life." Rory shrugged, as if her decision was of no great significance. "I think I'd be bored." The minx peered at him from behind lowered lashes. "And maybe lonely, now that I've gotten used to working with a partner."

Yes! Exultation rushed through Damon, accompanied by a dizzying rush of relief. *YES!* He had her now. His heart danced, swooping wildly on wings of joy.

Laughing, he pulled her into his arms for a long kiss of celebration, ignoring the spike of pain in his side. She was his! And if she had any ideas of losing him, once he was recovered, she'd find out differently.

That was the last conscious thought he had for some time as he lost himself in her sweet taste and the lingering caresses of her mouth and tongue, her avid response communicating better than words could that she, too, welcomed the development.

But inevitably Rory drew away, thoroughly kissed and tousled. "Don't you ever do that again," she ordered him in a fierce whisper, her eyes blazing with suppressed emotion, clearly referring to his selfish attempt at gallantry. Her remembered terror flooded into him, the heartfelt relief that followed heady in its potency. She'd feared for him, though she'd probably never tell him.

"I can't promise anything." Damon met her gaze steadily, wondering if that would be a deal breaker. He couldn't stint in his efforts; too much caution could mean the difference between success and failure in his missions. Besides, he couldn't have lived with himself if she'd died from his inaction.

Rory pondered that in silence, her thoughts unreadable, then slid from his embrace and off the bed. Just as his heart skipped in apprehension, she said: "Maybe you just need some incentive to take better care of yourself." With a secretive little smile, she went to the door to lock it and jammed the visitor's chair under the knob, efficiently securing their privacy.

He grinned in anticipation, his pulse kicking up when she turned back to him, her tight nipples poking at her top. He could think of only one reason she would want guaranteed seclusion. When she climbed back on the bed, he was sure of it.

Her excitement teased his senses as she settled by his feet, calling to mind past pleasures. She pulled down the tab of her zipper, its quiet hum loud in the silence that had settled between them. The dark fabric of her jumpsuit parted, revealing pale, smooth skin.

Damon leaned back on his pillows, his heart pounding in his chest. "It'd have to be the right incentive."

She eased out of the top, watching him with mock-serious eyes as she revealed perky, bare breasts just begging to be fondled, hard-tipped from the cold air. The minx had to know what she was doing to him when she arched her back, giving him an even better view of the high mounds. "Withholding judgment?"

He smiled, enjoying the thrum of arousal centered on his

cock. "Waiting to be convinced." Now that he knew he had her, he was willing to play her game.

Rory shimmied the jumpsuit down her hips and off her legs to drop the garment to the floor. "Better?" She rose to her knees to display the minuscule bikini that remained.

Damon frowned in pretend disappointment. "That's all?"

"Impatient, aren't you?" She skinned off that last bit slowly, drawing out the final unveiling to titillating effect.

The pale, trimmed muff she revealed surprised him; she'd always gone natural before. "Ummm . . ."

"Still need convincing?" Rory pouted thoughtfully. "Maybe you want bigger?" She plumped her breasts together and somehow turned voluptuous, the mounds suddenly overflowing her hands and looking pillowy, her hips markedly curvier. "Smaller?" Her bosom adjusted until she barely filled her cupped palms. "Darker?" Her skin and hair followed suit, losing creaminess to become golden, then mahogany, then a beautiful ebony.

"Or maybe you prefer redheads?" This time the change was jarring, from blue black to milk white flesh and copper curls. "Well?"

"You want me to choose?" He shook his head, stifling the helpless laughter that bubbled up his throat. "I can't. I like them all. You could be all green and I'd still find you sexy."

His confession elicited a look of speculation, but the minx morphed back to the initial blonde with Tatar eyes who'd entered his room.

Damon stretched out his arms. "Come here. I want to make love to you." That was stating the obvious, what with his cock tenting the sheet. He needed to touch her. How could it be otherwise after that bewitching show and her naked body less than a foot away?

"You've lost a lot of blood and just had surgery," Rory protested, rearing back. "You have to rest."

He stared at her in disbelief. She'd put on that show without any intention of putting out? "It's just a scratch."

"I watched them dig the bullet out. That wasn't 'just a scratch.'"

"It was whole, wasn't it? It didn't tumble around inside?"

Rory nodded hesitantly. "I guess."

"It was lodged in muscle, nothing important. It was the blood loss that took me down."

"All the more reason we shouldn't be doing that," she insisted, her face set in stubborn lines. "They had to put I don't know how many bags of blood into you."

Damon grinned ruefully. "If that were a problem, I'd've passed out when I got this hard-on."

When she still kept him at arm's length, he played his trump card. "It'll be worse, if you make me chase you." He looked her in the eye to emphasize his sincerity, not letting his gaze drop to ogle the fine pair of breasts pouting at him under an overlay of goose bumps. "I'm fine. I need you more." He placed his hand over her mouth to forestall the argument he could sense rising. "I want you around me, melting over me, coming with everything you have."

Rory muttered something against his fingers that sounded suspiciously like "domineering bastard," but Damon ignored it because he also sensed her resolve wavering.

She pulled his hand away. "On one condition."

"Name it." Reminded of the condition she'd tacked on to their first negotiation that had been the start of his fall, Damon smiled, anticipating victory.

"You don't move."

His jaw dropped. "*What?*"

Her brows gathered in a glower, her full lips set. "I don't want you doing anything that might open your wound."

"But—"

"You don't have to move to have me melt over you." She settled back on her heels, projecting steely determination that was incongruous against her nudity—especially when she crossed her arms under her breasts. "Take it or leave it."

"I'll take you."

Rory drew away.

"Hey!"

"If we're going to do this, me melting over you and you not hurting, I have to speed things up. We can put your imagination through its paces once you're recovered." That said, she cupped her breasts, caressing them, pulling on their tight nipples and circling the rosy areolas. Sweet pleasure radiated from her as her lashes fluttered down, emerging in a low, throaty moan that hit him like a fist in the gut.

Damon groaned—or maybe it was something like "Gah!"— he wasn't sure, just that he'd made a sound. The sight of her playing with herself turned him on faster than anything else he'd ever seen. His cock was suddenly tight to the point of pain. "I can do that."

The minx smiled, her eyes opening to lazy slits. "You'll hurt yourself."

He didn't care. Given how he felt right then, a bomb could go off beside him and it wouldn't register. "Some things are meant to be borne."

"Nope, we're doing this my way." Rory rose to her knees and reached between her thighs. Her slender fingers delved into her creamy pussy in a carnal display guaranteed to torture any red-blooded man. The musky female perfume that wafted to him only underscored the desire and delight his mental sense was picking up from her.

She might be doing it to get herself quickly to the melting point, but her performance also served to incite Damon's libido to rebellion—sure torment when he wasn't in much of a shape to do anything about it. After weeks of frequent lovemaking, he was hardwired to respond to the dark scent of her arousal.

Spiked need coiled in his balls, a savage hunger to have this one woman, Rory, around him, squeezing him, shuddering with unconstrained ecstasy. To know that she was his and have her acknowledge his claim.

Only her.

The image stole his breath. "Oh, you just wait till I'm better."

"I look forward to it." Self-satisfaction tilted the corners of her mouth, gratification in her feminine power, but not triumph. In this game, they would both emerge as winners.

The minx danced before him, an exotic temptress seducing him with her brazen play. That she was doing this to avoid hurting him was even more amazing. The thought made his cock throb even harder, and the hedonic emotions she radiated didn't help.

Finally, Damon couldn't stand the searing ache a second longer. His skin felt like it was stretched taut across his entire body and ready to split. "I need you now."

Dropping to all fours, Rory clawed the blanket off him and crawled up his legs, her hard-tipped breasts prodding his belly, her sleek abdominals gliding over the sensitive head of his twitching cock.

The contrast and her aggressive stance were almost more than he could bear. The hunger she'd whetted threatened to boil up from his balls before she took him into herself.

Digging his fingers into the hapless mattress, Damon fought to hang on to his threadbare control. Just a little longer and she'd be around him, exactly the way he wanted. *Come on, Venizélos, don't go off yet!* Trying to recall his research on probable targets to ramp down his arousal didn't work. Even multiplication tables faded from his mind at the ticklish rasp of Rory's soft mound against his thigh.

He nearly lost it when she slid over him, the crisp curls of her delta rubbing lightly over his cock head. The gentle friction was like gasoline to wildfire. He shivered at its promise. "Hurry." Heaven in the wet clasp of his woman was nearly within reach, tantalizingly close yet oh so far.

Then she slipped over, sheathing him quickly in a hot, creamy embrace that was the last straw.

Raw, unadulterated pleasure erupted from his tight balls, unstoppable as a geyser flood and just as hot. Damon bucked as Rory's tight pussy convulsed around him, unable to hold still, even if his life depended on doing so.

She gasped, arching above him as her cream gushed over him, the silken proof of her pleasure coating his length. He clamped his hands on her hips, anchoring her to him, driving himself deeper as she continued to flutter around him.

Her ecstasy exploded through him in a brilliant starburst of color, scorching his mental sense with its intensity. The paroxysm of delight melded with the carnal storm rampaging in his body, magnifying its power until he couldn't separate what was Rory's and what was his.

Gradually, Damon came back to himself, their climax leaving him spent and barely able to gasp for breath. And feeling better than he'd ever felt before.

Sighing, Rory lay down, twisting around so her weight was off him, clearly still mindful of his injury. "You okay?"

Pulling her against his side into his heat, he smiled at the understatement, savoring the aftershocks as her pussy continued to milk him. "I'm very okay."

He studied her brown eyes with their epicanthic folds, still bemused by her transformations. It was like making love to a different woman each time, yet she was his Rory, deep down where it counted. He supposed he'd eventually become accustomed to having a harem all in one woman.

"So, was that sufficient incentive?" She whispered the question in a husky voice that bid fair to reignite the appetite she'd just slaked. Her breathless delivery inspired a twinge of interest in his limp cock.

"You drive a hard bargain."

"But will you take better care of yourself?" Rory persisted. How she could remember the original conversation was beyond him.

"Well, I can promise to do my best to stay in one piece." Damon pressed a finger to her lips to silence the protest he could sense rising. "Just as I won't ask you not to take too many risks. I know you have to, to do what you do."

She frowned, sucking on her bottom lip, then after a thoughtful pause, nodded. "Fair enough, I guess."

He turned on his unwounded side to sling a leg over hers, not that he could feel any pain; the level of endorphins flooding his veins was probably illegal somewhere. "So we have a partnership?"

"Hmmm . . ." Rory stroked his chest lazily, ruffling the hair on his pectorals. The rhythmic sensation was indescribably soothing, fraught as it was with a certain proprietorial complacence. "You're still a domineering bastard, but you're mine."

"Smile when you say that." Damon planted a quick, hard peck on her soft lips.

"You're mine," she repeated smugly, giving him a toothy grin worthy of a tigress. "Besides, someone has to hang around to pull your nuts out of the fire."

Happiness had Damon's heart leaping when he realized what she'd said—and meant: she loved him and intended to stick around permanently. His master thief wasn't one to relinquish whatever—or whomever—she considered to be hers. He chuckled softly, his relief and amusement rolling up from his belly in easy waves. "Of course." He hadn't realized until then how much he'd wanted that reciprocal claim.

Rory kissed him, a sweet promise conveying everything she didn't say. He answered her with all the hope and joy in his heart, content to float in the aftermath of their lovemaking.

It was a long while before Damon had the presence of mind for anything else, but eventually he remembered another question he'd been meaning to ask. "Are you ever going to tell me your real name?"

For countless heartbeats, she stared meditatively into the darkness surrounding the narrow bed, before turning to meet his gaze. "Are you going to write it down somewhere? Tell someone?"

Suspecting that her hesitation entailed issues other than trust, he shook his head, matching her gravity. "This is as far as it gets." He meant it, too. Unless she voluntarily shared the information with the Old Man, his superior would know her only as Rory—and only in the blond persona she affected.

Still, she narrowed her eyes at him. "This room isn't bugged, is it?"

Damon had to smile at the suspicion in her voice. "It shouldn't be."

Despite his reassurance, Rory pushed up close to breathe into his ear, "Aurora diScipio," with predictable cock-hardening consequences. Then in a normal tone, she added, "And if you call me that anywhere in public or pass it on to anyone, I'll roast your nuts myself." She poked him in the ribs, right where she knew he was ticklish, ruthlessly exploiting his vulnerability.

Flinching away from her finger, he burst into laughter, unable to stop himself despite the pain piercing his orgasm-induced euphoria. She'd do it, too! He hugged her close, resigned to his fate. Rory would never be the quiet little woman, content to wait for him between missions, but he wouldn't want her any other way.

Savoring his lover's cuddlesome form in his arms, Damon smiled, anticipating their work together. She'd keep him on his toes for the rest of their lives. With Rory as his partner, he was in for a hell of a ride . . . one well worth every second of searing emotion.